A
FUNNY
KIND
OF
PARADISE

A
FUNNY
KIND
OF
PARADISE

JO OWENS

RANDOM HOUSE CANADA

PUBLISHED BY RANDOM HOUSE CANADA

www.penguinrandomhouse.ca

Random House Canada and colophon are registered trademarks.

LIBRARY AND ARCHIVES CANADA CATALOGUING IN PUBLICATION

Title: A funny kind of paradise / Jo Owens.
Names: Owens, Jo, 1961– author.
Identifiers: Canadiana (print) 2020026219X | Canadiana (ebook) 20200262246
| ISBN 9780735278820 (softcover) | ISBN 9780735278837 (EPUB)
Classification: LCC PS8629.W4635 F86 2021 | DDC C813/.6—dc23

Text design by Kelly Hill
Cover design by Kelly Hill
Image credits: (woman) © SallyLL / iStock / Getty Images

Printed and bound in Canada

4 6 8 9 7 5 3

Penguin
Random House
RANDOM HOUSE CANADA

THIS BOOK IS FOR:

care aides
health care aides
personal care attendants
personal support workers
carers
nurses' aides
and
care workers
everywhere:
whatever your title,
wherever you work,
you know who you are,
and you know what you do—
thank you.

NOT DEAD YET

Decreased morbidity. That's what most of us think we want. We want to live long, healthy, productive lives until the day we keel over, on the golf course perhaps. Even better, we imagine, to die quietly in our bed one night or float away during a siesta after an especially good meal.

Easy. Painless.

Me, I used to think I'd like to die at a ripe old age, hale and hearty, pausing on my morning walk along Dallas Road to admire the Cascade Mountains in Washington just across from Victoria. The wind coming off the Juan de Fuca Strait filters through the thicket on the bank, blowing that familiar sweet, strong scent past my lips. Salt water and wild roses, I'd think, as I hit the pavement with a fatal aneurysm, and I'd smile while drawing my last breath. A nice way to go.

Some people think they want time to prepare. To say goodbyes, to set their affairs in order. But a minimum of suffering, for sure. And nobody wants to lie there like a vegetable. We don't want it for ourselves, nor for our loved ones. Better to die quickly than to endure a half life. That's what we think.

But I surprised myself.

I just want to live.

Dearest Anna:

I know. One doesn't really talk with someone who is dead. I am aware of that. But I can still talk *to* you. My friend. I still need you. In some ways, you are closer to me than you've ever been, since you are privy to all my uncensored thoughts now. What's left of you is the part that's in me.

So I would like to assure you, Anna, that I am alive and well, though I know you would sigh to see me lying here, unable to speak. Your eyes would flicker to my lunch hanging next to me in a bag on a pole, measured out drip by drop with a kangaroo pump that delivers liquid nutrition through the tube that plunges straight through my skin into my belly. Your face would drop, acknowledging my crooked right arm, my right hand slowly contracting, atrophying, my fingernails growing uselessly on, attached to a dead thing. I know it would grieve you. You would force a smile, make awkward, one-sided conversation, bid me farewell, and walk away upset.

It hurts me to think of you seeing me this way. As it hurt me to watch you suffer as your cancer progressed. But let me reassure you, I am fine. In spite of how things appear.

As I emerged from the fog after I had my stroke and my reality pressed down on me, I was so angry I couldn't even think. But now, a year later, I'm ready to come out of the dunce's corner, like some sullen, grubby, pig-tailed schoolgirl, one knee-high crumpled to the ankle, temper under control but still holding a grudge.

I have time for reflection now in a way I've never had before. Although I complained about being busy all my adult life, I am now beginning to suspect that an element of choice kept me on the verge of overload all the time. We both admired hard workers; we had that in common. But it never occurred to me that working hard might be a way to disengage. For both of us.

I live in a facility, an institution, a so-called extended care hospital. I'm not capable of looking after myself. But I'm not dying. So . . . I won't be checking out anytime soon.

I live on the first floor in the North Wing in the corner room at the end of the hall. And this is important: my window faces east, and the way my bed is positioned, I bear witness to an old chestnut tree. I have watched its leaves change colour and drop, and heard the bare boughs groaning in the squally west-coast winter storms. My heart leapt at the leafing and budding in spring and spread wide like the summer leaves gathering the sun. Now it is fall again, and the leaves have begun to yellow. Although I cannot see the sunrise, I see the glow of it through the branches of my tree on fine days, and I witness the stubborn dark erasure at nighttime when the weather is dull.

This tiny patch of tree and sky, this rectangle is a portal in my universe. This is my home now. I am mute, immobile, tube-fed and on drugs for my pain. This is where I spend out my days.

I just want to live.

My room is a five-bed ward. I survey my domain from my corner. Four other beds, four other souls, four other poor sods stuck here like me: my roommates.

I know the most appallingly intimate things about them. And they about me, those who are still capable of knowing, which does rather narrow it down. We are not as we were, let's put it that way. (But unlike me, you are forgiving. You always were. Even now I am counting on your generous spirit.)

The bed on my left, in the darkest corner, belongs to Janet. Diabetes has made her blind and has taken her legs, amputated just below the knee, a fact that terrifies the new aides until someone teaches them how to position Janet's sling properly to ensure her safe transfer to the wheelchair. Once in a while, she complains about pain in her feet; sometimes she remembers they're gone and sometimes she doesn't. The nurses take her blood sugars, twitter about "spiking" and "dropping," adjust her insulin and tell the aides to push juice or back off. Janet says she doesn't care. Janet hates the food.

Mary has the other bed with a window, but while my head is at the north wall, hers is on the south, so we face each other. Mary is the quintessential little old lady, with her permed hair in stiff white curls, her dentures, and a tissue up the sleeve of her cardigan. She is the darling, everyone's favourite, loved for her smile and her sunny nature. She was still walking with the help of the activity aides when I first came here, but she's on the slow slide, and no one would ever try to transfer her now without the overhead lift. She stiffened up gradually, and she talks a little less every day. We, her roommates, are grateful that she's passed the stage of calling out constantly, "Hey, are you here for me?" thinking that someone was coming to take her home to her mama. Mind you, we do miss some of the more innovative excuses the staff used to try to convince her that her mother wasn't going to be too worried about her whereabouts. "You're so considerate of your mama!" they would coo on a good day. "Your mama knows you're here and she's glad you're safe."

"You're ninety years old and your mama died fifty years ago!" they'd mutter under their breath on their way out the door.

Alice's bed is perpendicular between Mary's and mine, the head at the east-facing window and facing the door. Alice rarely rests. No wonder she's such a scrawny pack of bones, shuffling from bed to bed, night and day, looking for her children or maybe her purse. There's no malice in her, and if there ever was, she's forgotten her spite. She acts like there's something she should have remembered, on the tip of her tongue or tangled in the plaque in her cortex, thoughts like fishes struggling in a net. Poor anxious soul, endlessly tapping and sifting, sorting and folding, a worried expression on her face. Why they have her in the middle bed, open space on both sides, so exposed, I'm sure I don't know. If I had to sleep there, without the comfort of a wall at my back, or a corner to turn my face to when I need to pretend I'm alone, I'd be anxious too. Even with the curtains pulled, Alice's is the worst bed in the room.

Kitty-corner to me is the woman I know only as Nana, and of her, dearest Anna, there is not much left to say. She has reached that stage of living death where she lies completely passive. Perhaps some distant signals reach her or perhaps she has truly gone, leaving nothing but an empty shell. At any rate, if she has a family, I have not seen them yet, and there she lies, day after day, while the nurses shift her from side to side, tucking pillows between her knees to prevent skin rubbing against skin until it reddens and then rots. They raise her ankles so that the weight of her own feet pushing her heels into the bed won't create sores (great blackened holes that must be dressed and never heal, as happened to the poor woman who had Janet's bed before her.) Nana's skin is like tissue paper; a careless fingernail may rip it. One day an aide tried to turn her over by grabbing her wrist, instead of placing a flat hand on her shoulder blade and she left a bruise the shape of her—

Snap! The lights are on, and I'm seeing stars. Molly's voice, the specific tone she uses for training new staff, fills the room.

. . . *just going to follow me, to get the idea of what the rhythm of your day is going to be like. You don't need to help. I'm not interested in training you in nursing skills—if you don't have those by now, you're screwed. My object is to show you how to do a day shift. You need to know what it looks like to take care of six people by yourself, cuz that's what you gotta do. Oh, she's wet, draw the curtain, will you, we're gonna take the top pad off, I don't want her sitting in that.*

Molly is talking about Nana, and now I can hear the sound of the electric bed whirring into the flattened position that allows Molly to move Nana most easily. The blankets flip back with a swish.

Most people are nice here, and they'll set you straight as to who to do first and such, but they have their own workload, you know what I mean.

Okay.

Every now and then you're gonna run into an asshole, that's reality; just tell yourself, "Oh yeah, Auntie Molly told me there'd be days like this," and try not to let the negativity stick, cuz most people here are really good, thank God . . .

Okay, I'm just gonna fold this top pad over, like this, see, and then one quick flip and it's out and she's on her back, got it? Now we can sit her up for breakfast. Give me a lift up the bed, will you, her chin's going to be on her toes. Yup, that's right. Nice body mechanics, Gayla, you got it. There you go,

Nana! Good morning, sweetie! Did you just finish your training, or have you been doing this work before?

I just finished. I did my practicum at Aberhart.

Okay then. Well, the good news is that unlike at Aberhart, you're not expected to get everyone up for breakfast in the dining room at nine here.

Yeah, so I heard. That's why I wanted to work here. It's brutal, that morning rush. Get everyone up, so they can sit there looking at the dining room wall.

Yup, it sucks for the nurses, and it sucks for the patients. I'm telling you when I'm ninety-five, nobody is going to be getting me outta bed at seven fifteen unless I'm drugged to the hilt cuz I'm gonna fight it. All these years of early risin' for the seven a.m. shift—no bloody way I'll be getting up so I can sit on my ass getting pressure sores. Forget it, baby. These people deserve breakfast in bed, I figure.

At Aberhart, by the time breakfast comes, everyone's up and you're so tired you just want to go home.

Too right. Hey, Janet, I'm gonna sit you up for breakfast, here's your napkin. This is Gayla, she's our newbie. Don't bother giving Frannie a napkin, she's a tube-feed, right Fran? Good morning, sweetie!

I wave with my good arm and Molly blows me a kiss before moving on.

First floor gets breakfast first. It comes up from the kitchen at seven forty-five, so you gotta get everyone sitting up, but look, second floor, break-fast comes at eight, so if you're quick you can get a couple of people washed up, and on third floor it comes at eight fifteen. Of course you're starting casual, so you're gonna be working everywhere, all groups. It's a little rough at first, but it's good experience. You learn to be flexible. Sink or swim. You gotta think on your feet, you'll get used to it, don't worry. It's best if you can pace yourself. That way you can treat the residents a little nicer, take the time to do that little extra, eh? After all, most of us went into this job thinking we could spread the love a little, same time as we aim to put bread on the table for those kids, right? You have kids?

Yeah, one. She's five.

Single mom?

Yeah.

You got your daycare lined up? When you're on call, sometimes you don't get much warning. It's so tough at first. Sweetie, sit down. Breakfast is coming. This one's pretty restless, aren't you, honey? Sit down, sweetie. That's right. Here's your napkin. Breakfast is coming. That's it, love. Usually I get her washed up first, she's quick, but we were a little late getting started today, no worries. We'll make it up. Not all these people are in my group, but Michiko, she sits mine up across the hall, and I sit hers up here, saves time, right?

Is she in your group?

Nana? No.

Molly pauses.

I know what you're thinking and you're right. Some of the girls don't like you to touch their resident, but Michiko and I are on the same page. Besides, Nana's mine next month, and I don't want her wet, cuz group change is com—

And that's it. Molly and her charge are out of the room, on to the next task. I can't hear any more, but it doesn't matter because I've heard Molly's training spiel more times than I can count. We, the thirteen residents in the North Wing, are divided into groups of six and seven and assigned to an aide. Molly is about to explain that, like all the regular staff, she and her partner will trade groups on the first of every month. Molly and Michiko have the permanent day shifts in the North Wing. Blaire and Bettina cover their days off, then go down to the East Wing to relieve the two permanent staff there, but their shifts don't line up exactly, so sometimes Molly works with Bettina instead of Michiko, and sometimes Michi works with Blaire. The evening shifts work the same way, but there are only two aides for the whole floor on nights.

I like the system. While it's nice to see a familiar face at my bedside, frankly by the end of the month my aides and I are ready for a change from each other. Of course casuals cover the regular staff for sick days and holidays; they have to fly by the seat of their pants.

Sometimes they're fresh and enthusiastic; sometimes they're so green I'm afraid they're going to drop me.

What can I do? I don't get to choose my nurses.

These girls, these women and sometimes men literally and figuratively touch us in the most intimate way. They come and go like the staff in your diner, Anna. There are the lifers, who always make me think of mine-shaft ponies: solid, dependable beasts of burden, trudging along. Some are hopeless, some cheerfully resigned, some are even passionate about their work, but they just keep working steadfastly on.

Then there are the aides who are passing through. Molly or Michiko or Blaire train them, with varying degrees of cynicism and enthusiasm, because far less than half of new hires will last for long. Molly's good; she's a natural teacher, and she continues to treat every newbie as if she might stay. The work attracts all kinds of people, but it burns them out fast too. Some can't stick it out on call long enough to get their own regular position. Some injure themselves or grow afraid that they will. Some are on their way to bigger, better things; they'll bridge into nursing or work part-time here while going back to school. Some are still searching for what they want to do, but they've got to do *something*.

But no matter what their motivation for choosing this job, everyone starts at the bottom of the casual call list, flying in to work at a moment's notice because who knows when they're going to get around to calling the last person on the list again? And that's the way it is until you move up the list enough to be confident you're going to get sufficient work to pay the rent.

I know what you're thinking, my darling Anna, you're thinking, "Why, Francesca! You've changed! You sound almost compassionate!"

Yes, my dear friend. I've changed. Living here will do that to a girl.

The day that I came here is a bit of a blur. I don't remember having a stroke at all, and even now, I barely remember being at the General

Hospital; Chris tells me I was there for four months. Did they hope I'd get better? Were they waiting for a long-term bed for me? The most frustrating thing about my situation is the loss of my voice and my inability to ask questions. (The loss of my arm comes a close second.) I am almost completely stuck with what people choose to tell me and what I overhear.

My memory of the day I moved here came back to me gradually. The trip in the Medi-Van, the hoist from the stretcher to my new bed ("Ready, set, lift!"). There was a seemingly endless stream of new faces. The occupational therapist had me try to pull myself up using the bar set in the wall in the bathroom, but it was a humiliating failure. My right arm is totally useless and my left, too weak. I should have gone to the gym more, I guess, but it didn't fit well with my sixty-hour work week. The OT told me I'd be a "lift-only transfer" with a "size medium regular sling," in case you wanted to know.

Then the RN checked my skin for rashes and wounds and red patches that might lead to sores. Someone else had a go at putting a numeric figure on the amount of horsepower left in my brain. I could see Chris, looking uncomfortable and sad, talking *sotto voce* to the RN by the door.

I thought, "What's happening to me?" Then suddenly, all the poking and prodding and questions were over and there I was, alone in my corner on my bed for the first time, staring out the window at the September leaves.

"Y'all right, Mom?"

Chris slouched over, his hands deep in his pockets, as if by reaching out or spreading out or opening up, he'd contaminate himself.

I tapped the sleeve of his grey coat and pointed out the window at the chestnut tree. Chris leaned over a bit to have a look.

"At least you've got a view."

I remember the first time we met, Anna. It was shortly after Karl left me; I was having trouble getting my head around that, which wasn't surprising, since he left without warning like a shot from a well-oiled gun, taking everything he wanted in his car and emptying our joint account on his way out of town. He had the decency to call me from somewhere on the Oregon coast that night to say he wouldn't be back and not to look for him. I didn't. I wasn't so much pining for lost love as reeling at how tenuous his commitment to us actually was, how devoid of honour he'd really been. I regretted that I hadn't thrown the grifter onto the street myself.

Fortunately I'd been canny enough to keep a significant amount in a private account; I'd saved well working for Jackson Douglas Accounting before Chris came along. I hadn't planned on getting pregnant with Chris, though, and once that happened, of course they let me go. Grudgingly I have to credit Karl for his help when I started my own business. He had a lot of charm and he knew a lot of people. Most of my original clients came through his influence one way or another. But start-up is always a precarious thing, and there isn't a huge profit margin in small-business accounting. Karl left when he found out I was pregnant again. I think he had hoped I would make a lot more money than I did. What a fool I was.

The woman who was looking after Chris got bronchitis and closed the daycare, so I had him at home. Angelina was heavy in my belly; I felt as swollen and limp as overcooked macaroni. We'd been eating canned soup for days. I couldn't face another night of saltines washed down with tea. I strapped Chris into the stroller and headed downtown, ankles aching but grateful to be breathing fresh air. The sign in your diner window (simply *Anna's*, in cherry neon) called to me like Jesus, and I remember hearing your front door tinkle for the first time as we herded ourselves in. Chris was an angel, he really was, but even an angel at two is a force to contend with, so I ordered french fries from a teenaged waitress in your trademark red-checked apron. When she put them on the table, Chris and I both sighed with relief.

Nothing before or since has ever tasted as good as those lovely golden fries, lightly salted, with their soft white starchy pillows bursting through their crispy skins.

And there you were, with your coffee pot steaming, your bib apron tied around your waist, the eye-catching scar over your upper lip, the reminder of a childhood surgery for cleft palate.

"What a beautiful boy," you said, and I noticed your accent, different from Karl's but certainly Germanic. Chris looked up with those serious, innocent blue eyes, and said, "Thank you."

I watched you fall in love right there. I saw your face melt, the smile soften, the eyes widen. You let your breath go. I didn't know what made Chris's hold on you so strong, at the time, but it was easy to see that he'd stolen your heart.

"Well!" I thought, calm and crafty with my recent infusion of salt and saturated fat. "How can I use this?"

I've never been the type to cozy up to strangers, but some survival instinct must have kicked in, nudging me to behave in a way quite foreign to my nature. From that time on, I made a point of coming to the diner, and gradually, we started to talk.

I wonder what would have happened, Anna, if Rhonda hadn't broken her leg like a stupid donkey. She had her son Michael in the same daycare as Chris. She was such an indecisive, waffling person, not my type at all, but she was always fretting about needing money so I hoped I could tempt her to help me. When Karl left, I asked her if she could keep Chris when I went into labour. It wasn't a great match—Chris didn't like Michael. Rhonda hadn't been able to stop him from biting.

"Bite him back," I told her firmly.

She was shocked.

"Oh, I could *never!*" she said, biting her own lower lip hard and sucking in.

"Couldn't you possibly?" I begged when she phoned to tell me how she fractured her tibia in three places. "He's such an easy child. He's no trouble, really."

"Well . . ." she wavered.

In the background I heard a angry male voice thundering, "Give me that phone!" Then a loud, rough voice in my ear.

"She broke her leg. She can't keep your son. Find someone else!" *Click.*

I'd have laughed if I hadn't been so desperate. I should have realized that when you have kids, cultivating backup babysitting is a total necessity; I'd counted on Karl for that.

"I don't know what I'm going to do," I said grimly as Chris ran his plastic truck around the edge of the high chair at the diner later that evening. He was still a bit too little for crayons and colouring-paper placemats.

"I can take him," you said. "But you will have to let me stay at your place. He'll feel more at home there."

Honestly, I hadn't been fishing and my shock must have been written all over my face.

"What about the diner?"

"I have a good opener right now. Chris will go to daycare, yes? He's there until six?"

"Six at the latest. Five is better."

"Five then. I'll bring him here. Close, feed him and take him home. It will work."

"I'll pay you."

"We will make a deal. You could help me with my taxes, couldn't you?"

"Of course. If that's what you want."

"We had better practise," you said. "He should get used to me. And you must see that you can trust me."

Anna, it never occurred to me not to trust you. I was very surprised when you brought it up.

I wasn't thinking about you, Anna. I was thinking about myself.

So were you, really. It was Chris you loved, right from the start. His blond hair, his blue eyes, just like yours. That thoughtful, steady nature. He could have been your son. It was as though Chris was the exact shape of the hole in your heart. He fit there as perfectly as a lid on a jar.

We can hear the tray trolley being pushed down the hallway. When she's trying to convince her mother to eat, Janet's daughter says we're lucky . . . we have an in-house kitchen where the meals are *prepared*, as opposed to trucked-in premade trays of cardboard airplane food. I've heard people say the food is not bad. Of course I wouldn't know. I don't remember my gastrotube going in, but I do remember choking, the feeling of drowning, of being unable to swallow, and all the meaning and emotion connected to food (memory, comfort, necessity, obligation, a way to show love) collapsing in one great wave of fear, the fear of being unable to catch my breath.

The girls bring the trays in and start feeding the ladies that "need assistance" . . . that is the polite phrase for someone who can't feed herself. Oh, and by the way, those aren't bibs—bibs are for babies. Some of the staff call them "clothing protectors," but it's an awkward phrase. Molly refuses to call them that. She doesn't say "bib" but she won't say "clothing protector." She compromises with "napkin," which I find amusing.

And this is my favourite part of the day; this is when live improv theatre comes into my very own room. I get to listen. Molly, the newbie and Michiko, a young woman with an intimidating dragon tattoo snaking up her arm and bleached blond spiky hair, are twittering like birds.

If you bring a chair right over, you can put Alice right beside you— you might be able to keep her sitting long enough to eat a few bites. Here, look. I hold her hand and that keeps her. If I sit like this, I've still got a hand free for feeding Nana here.

Is that porridge?

Yup.

That's an awful lot of sugar.

Well, they say sweet is the last taste to go.

Really.

Oh yeah. Your taste buds become less sensitive as you age. That's why you get these people just piling on the salt and sugar. They're desperately looking for some flavour.

Hmm. That's probably why you can't get kids to eat Brussels sprouts. Their taste buds are still super sensitive and the flavour is too strong for them.

Ew, you can't get me to eat Brussels sprouts. They're just gross.

No, but you know what I mean. Lots of little kids don't like strong-tasting foods. They like sweet and salty.

Yeah, maybe. Things don't taste the same as you age. No wonder you get these old guys saying "Chicken just doesn't taste like it used to back in the day"!

Chicken doesn't taste like it used to back in the day! It tastes like Styrofoam.

And that's why you're a vegan? How would you know!

The new girl has stirred that whole heaping spoonful of brown sugar into Nana's porridge. I watch her do it and my stomach turns.

I remember making porridge—cheaper than cereal—when the kids were young. Sifting large-flake oatmeal through my fingers into the salty boiling water, throwing in chopped dates or raisins. And scooping it into steaming bowls, with milk and a splash of thick cream. I'd sprinkle a little brown sugar on top, demerara, so that crystals would melt on the hot oatmeal, little bursts of sweetness. Nothing akin to this bland slop, stirred smooth to prevent choking, that the new girl is spooning into Nana's trap. Nana still opens her mouth, a fish in an aquarium, at the touch of the spoon against her lip. That instinct is still there.

Anna, we were two single women without extended family, struggling to make do. We needed each other and our friendship was very practical for a long time. Almost from the beginning, you had the keys to my house. I knew you were decent and reliable. In that way I trusted you, and you trusted me. Although we were both overextended, somehow we were able to help each other. Many times I rolled up my sleeves and washed dishes for you when staff from the diner quit without notice, coming in to heaping sinks after the restaurant was closed, letting Chris play in the booths out front while Angelina slept in her portable playpen. When she woke up, we'd put Chris in there too and he'd play with her. We made a good team, Anna.

Still, it was a long time before we trusted each other enough to show who we really were. You were a deeply private, reserved person. You tossed out nibbles of information like raisins thrown into the batter of a cake, little pieces, never the whole story. The truth is, you didn't like to be asked about your past. Even I, with my lack of tact, instinctively knew that and usually respected it.

I knew you had come to Canada from the Netherlands with your husband and that he was dead. When I asked you how he died, you told me it was a logging accident.

"But he had good insurance, and he forgot to change his beneficiary," you said, standing up. "Thank you, God, I bought this diner. More coffee?"

And you walked away.

You played the local radio station, Ocean 98.5 in the background at the diner. I listened to it too, on occasion, as I had my coffee and got the kids ready for their day. One morning they were giving a gift certificate for a new fancy French restaurant to the twenty-fourth caller. Normally I didn't waste my time on radio promotions; I'd heard people complain on the show about how long they'd been trying to get through while the radio hosts urged them to "keep trying," and I thought to myself that I had better things to do. That day, I dialed in on a whim and won on my first try. In the diner, you heard me on the radio, and called me at home right away with your congratulations. "Anna," I said, "we are going out on the town!"

"Oh," you faltered, "I didn't mean you should take me!"

"Who else should I take?" I retorted.

The cost of the wine pairings that I wanted us to have exceeded the gift certificate but it was well worth it. We both relaxed, thoroughly enjoying the moment, letting our guards down, talking more intimately than we ever had before.

Ang was a pretty good baby for sleeping, but my neighbour's daughter was only in grade nine and it was a school night. I ought to have gone home, but still we lingered. I was reluctant to let the evening end. I bought us both a snifter of good cognac. And another. We clinked glasses, leaned back and sipped, and without warning, you went from pleasantly tipsy to drunk.

You wept as you told me that the last time your husband beat you, he was so violent that you miscarried midterm. "The nurse told me I had a boy," you sobbed. "I lost my son. I knew, even if I could make another baby, we would never be a safe family. So I left him. I would never go back, never!"

"Anna, you are young. You'll meet someone new . . ."

"No! It will happen again. I will end up like my mother, no teeth, no pride . . ."

I called for the bill and a taxi. To tell the truth I was afraid to leave you alone in your apartment in that condition, so I brought you home and paid the babysitter extra with many apologies while you slumped on my couch.

"I like you, Francesca," you said as I threw a blanket over you. "You are a no bullshit person."

That's good, I thought. Someone who likes me for something I like in myself.

You had a terrible hangover in the morning.

"This is why I do not drink spirits," you moaned as you gulped back a handful of tiny pink baby Aspirin with black coffee, the only remedy I had on hand. "Wine is okay, but my family, we cannot handle strong alcohol. I'm so sorry. I know better! Was I terrible? I remember nothing past dessert."

I kept your secret to myself, but after that night, I knew why Chris was so special to you. As the years went by and the children got older, I took advantage of your love shamelessly—I would have stepped on the face of an angel to keep my little family from sinking in the mire that seemed to surround us. But it was a fair exchange, because Chris loved you back. You gave him your heart, your time, and a second home in your diner, and he gave you his loyalty. Of the two of us, he loved you best. Oh yes, he did, and we all knew it—and I didn't mind, I *couldn't* mind, because of Angelina.

Molly comes into our room like the strong wind she is. The newbie (I've forgotten her name) trails behind with an armload of face cloths and towels.

The thing about Alice is, honey, Alice won't wait. You'll want to have her clothes and her pull-ups and every single thing you're going to need for her care because she sure the hell is not going to sit on the toilet and wait for you to go and get something you forgot . . . She's going to get up and go, and if her pants are around her ankles, she'll trip herself, and if she's in the middle of what she should be doing on the toilet, she'll get up anyway as soon as you move away from her, and then you'll be needing a clean pair of pants. So fetch up her stuff and get it all together first.

Molly flings open Alice's locker door and whips out a pair of houndstooth slacks like a martyr of the saints.

I thought I disappeared these! They're too big, they slide right down and one of these days she's gonna break her neck. See, that makes me crazy; we know these pants suck, but you casuals, how would you know, so you get them on her, and they don't work, and then you have to turn around and get another pair, and meanwhile Alice is following you around in her knickers. I'm gonna hide them in the bottom drawer here. Okay, these are good, and yeah, this matches. Grab her lotion from her side table, will you?

Her feet are dry. And there's a necklace in the drawer there. C'mon, sweetie, let's go.

She leads Alice through the door next to my bed into the communal bathroom and sits her on the toilet. Molly washes her there. Sometimes Alice can do her own face and hands with the cloth while Molly puts her pull-ups, pants, socks and shoes on. But sometimes she doesn't know what to do with the washcloth. I can hear Molly's cheerful voice hurrying her along.

Tell her what you're doing, it keeps her from getting startled. I'm gonna wash your back now, honey. Lift your arms, that's it. Darn, I forgot her deodorant, okay, too bad. Over the head now, sweetie. Good girl. Stand up, Alice, hold the bar, I'm going to wash your bottom bits; no, honey, leave the towel there, it'll catch the drip . . . hold the bar, honey. That's right, good. Nice and clean . . . See, Gayla, I always keep gloves in my pocket because once I've got her standing at the bar, I don't want to walk away even to get a glove from the dispenser, because seriously, she won't stay, and it's not safe.

Gayla. Of course. How could I have forgotten?

It must be hard giving her bowel care.

Too right. I've started giving it to her in the afternoon, because we've got a little more time, we're not in such a rush, and I can bring a chair and sit right next to her, keep her on the toilet. I give her the suppository, wait twenty minutes, and then I bring her in and I just stay with her until she goes. Pray it works, because she won't sit, and she won't push.

Does she go on her own?

Mmm, maybe sometimes. It's hard to know because she's all over the place, you know, walking into other people's rooms, or sometimes she'll use the garbage can, that kind of thing. We have to check her before we supp her. You can tell when she's stopped up . . . I mean, first of all there's nothing to her, she's all bones, so when her belly gets distended it really shows, and second, she gets pretty agitated when she hasn't gone for a while. I mean, wouldn't you?

Not so long ago, I would have been scornful of the transformation of the noun "suppository" into a verb (so slangy!), but now I just nod soberly. I look back with nostalgia to those days when I thought of constipation as I did yellow fever or typhoid: something that happens far away to other people. But no, that's wrong, because in the past, I took my bowels for granted, so why would I trouble myself to ever think of anyone else's? In *this* world, however, where limited mobility and a lack of fibre make moving the bowels a feat rather than an unremarkable fact, I get liquid laxative daily in my tube-feed, an extra dose the day before "bowel care," a suppository every four days, and if that doesn't work, I get a Fleet, which, my dear Anna, is the brand name for an enema. It has ruined the expression "fleet of foot" for me forever. But I am lucky. So far I have never required "disimpaction"—and yes, that means exactly what you think it does.

The aides record the products of our bowels in a binder kept for that sole purpose with a religious fervour that I found entertaining until someone messed up my bowel record and I got "missed." I can now infer that if a bowel obstruction is anything like a week of constipation, it must be a very painful way to die, and henceforth I keep my own private calendar on my over-the-bed table to mark with big black Xs.

Things We Don't Want to Know.

Makes me think of Angelina.

We'd come to the diner for waffles before swimming lessons one Saturday morning. It was raining hard and the restaurant was quiet.

Chris and Ang had eaten and were sitting together at one of your booths, and you and I were sitting across from them at another. Chris had his drawings of an imaginary world spread over the table and he was letting Angelina add bits and pieces to both the picture and the story. He was very fair, and so earnest, so serious, explaining like a little professor. Angelina was his opposite, so dark, wisps of hair escaping her braids and floating around her head. Even in a quiet moment, she sparked like tinder. They were so beautiful, my two children. Chris was seven, so Angelina would have been four years old, too small to see sitting down, really. She climbed up on her knees to lean over the table, crayon in hand, her rubber boots dripping muck onto the vinyl seat.

"Angelina, take your boots off the seat, you're making a mess," I said without thinking, hearing my own mama's harsh voice coming out of my mouth as I spoke.

Angelina ignored me.

Chris looked up from his picture and met your eye, a warning, and you set down your coffee cup, unfolded your legs and crossed the aisle. You always moved smoothly, graceful even in the old sweater you'd thrown on over your apron when you sat down with me.

"Here, my *liefje*," you said, slipping Angelina's little boots from her feet and mopping up the dirty meltwater with a paper napkin. Angelina permitted it, relaxed, shifting her weight from knee to knee for you without taking her eyes off what Chris was doing.

"She should learn to do as she's told," I said.

"Did you do as you were told, as a child?" you asked.

I laughed, remembering growing up with Enrica. Mama and I came together like bucks with massive racks of antlers; our clashes left us lurching backwards, until the force of our collisions finally sent me flying across the country as far away from small-town Ontario as I could get. That was how I saw it at the time.

Now, I imagined myself and Mama and my daughter as belonging to a band of fighters. It was the first time I'd thought of conflict as a tradition, one that would carry on into the next generation.

"We are strong women, in my family," I said proudly. "Angelina is just like me."

You looked at me speculatively. "Have you had her hearing checked?"

"There's nothing wrong with her hearing." Dismissive.

In fact, neither Ang nor I had trouble with our hearing. But it takes time to hear what you don't want to hear. And see what you don't want to see.

I have no photograph of this day that we spent together, Anna, and there's no special reason why I should remember it. But I do, and it's become a place I go to in my head when I'm alone and need comfort.

Christian must have been about eight—his hair was just beginning to darken from flaxen to honey—so Angelina would have been about five. We had taken them to the beach with our buckets and shovels, juice boxes and chips, and a Thermos of coffee for us. The kids were making a sandcastle. Chris had strategized—he'd dug a big moat and was keeping Angelina in happy, constructive motion running back and forth to fetch water. This bought him time to do the detail work on his tower. You and I were making desultory conversation about the girls in your diner, my business, your father's prognosis and how unlikely it was that you'd go back home to the Netherlands to visit him before he died.

"Why should I?" you said calmly. "He was a very nasty man." And I laughed.

The sun was warm; the children seemed to brown like buns before our eyes. It was a perfect day. Rare and precious.

Even now, I think of the sound of the ocean lapping the shore, and that cinnamon warmth lulls me to sleep.

But that was when the kids were very small. The older Angelina got, the more uncontrollable she became.

Another memory surfaces, from about the same time.

Ang was doing half days in kindergarten. I picked her up in the van because I wanted to get groceries on the way home. In the store, she ran up the aisles ahead of me, and when I caught up with her, she was eating fistfuls of sugary cereal right out of the box.

"Angelina, you're old enough to know better! We don't buy cereal," I said in frustration. "It's expensive and it's not good for you. Give me that!" I seized the box with one hand and, with the other, I grabbed her arm roughly, twisting her whole body towards me; the sight of the crumbs around her mouth inflamed me and my voice rose. "You ask before you open something, do you hear me? I have to pay for this now."

"That's okay, I can eat it," she sassed.

"You're not funny, Angelina," I said.

"You never buy anything good," she wailed. In a temper, she reached for the cereal and we tussled, spilling little crunchy nubbins everywhere. I held the box aloft and Angelina jumped for it, missed, turned angrily and began swiping boxes off the shelves onto the floor, crying noisily, until in desperation I abandoned my shopping. Leaving Angelina's mess on the ground and securing my daughter by her arm, I dragged her to the till, paid for the half-empty box of cereal and dropped it in the garbage on the way out of the store while Angelina screamed like a tortured cat.

"You've made us late, and *now* what are we going to have for supper?" I yelled, once I had her strapped in the minivan with the doors on child lock.

"I don't care," she screamed. "You're just mean!"

She was impulsive, she was belligerent, she was jealous of any attention I gave to Chris. He was showing me the poster he'd made for a grade five science fair project when Angelina crashed through the door, hollering "Ninety-nine bottles of beer on the wall." It was her favourite song that month.

Seeing Chris and me leaning into each other, Angelina crossed the kitchen in one bound.

"Let *me* see!" she squealed, grapping the poster so roughly that it tore.

"Angelina, for heaven's sake, look what you've done!"

"It's just a stupid old poster," she said, defiant.

"Your brother put a lot of work into that!"

"Your brother put a lot of work into that!"

"Angelina, that's rude. And inconsiderate. Apologize to your brother!"

But Christian was gone, taking his poster with him, while Ang and I raged at each other, oblivious to his disappearance.

Why should I remember in such detail this relatively innocuous thing when there were so many more dramatic disasters? The images come quickly now, indistinctly: Angelina lighting the Christmas tree on fire, Angelina throwing a bowl of tomato soup at the kitchen wall, Angelina swearing at me when she got caught shoplifting in grade four.

I never managed to figure out what was going to set her off. She was so angry. I couldn't control her.

From the start, Angelina had trouble at school. I dreaded report cards and parent-teacher interviews. "Angelina does not follow directions. Angelina has problems concentrating and sitting still. Difficult to engage. Fidgets. Lacks insight into consequences. Disruptive. Angelina is a real troublemaker." As for socialization, while Ang seemed to get along with the other first graders, if there was trouble on the playground, Ang was sure to be at the heart of it. That stupid old bat of a teacher didn't have a good word to say about my daughter, and I wanted to take her teeth out for her with a hockey stick.

Chris was such an easy child. Angelina came as a shock.

You used to close the diner on Sundays in the winter; one bleak afternoon you took Chris shopping for a coat and then for milkshakes. Angelina had been eating sugar with a spoon straight out of the bowl; after telling her three times not to, I punished her by making her stay home with me. By the time you and Chris got back, it felt like Ang and I had been fighting for hours.

"If you'd listened to me . . ." I nagged while I put coffee on.

"Look, Chris, here is the game I was telling you that we played when I was little," you said. Chris started; you winked. You had told him nothing, you were fishing for Angelina. Chris played along.

"We learned English like this," you said, and began a two-person clapping game. "A sailor went to sea, sea, sea . . ." Angelina's attention focused and she watched, wide-eyed.

"Let me try!"

"You play with your mother," you said, and Ang and I began to clap hands together.

Anna, you taught us more and more complicated clapping patterns. We played for a long time that night, laughing as we made mistakes.

Angelina would ask to play until I wished that there was a machine that could do it for me. She loved it. The repetition seemed to calm her down, de-escalate our conflicts.

It wasn't a long-term solution, but it helped for a while.

Now it is my turn to be washed, apparently, because here comes Molly, looking slightly grimmer than she did before, with her Gayla trailing behind. She stoops, grabs my wash basin from the bottom shelf of the side table with her right hand, and gives my shoulder a reassuring squeeze with her left at the same time.

Okay, Frannie here is a straightforward "total care" except for the tube-feed, but I'm gonna show you how to get her up even though she's connected, because we can't touch Calvin until ten thirty; he'll bite my head off.

How do you mean?

Oh, he's one of those obsessive compulsive types, you get that a lot. Even people who weren't OCD before get to be that way in here—they've lost so much control, they get fixated on the little things . . . You're a bit like that, aren't you, Frannie?

At which point, though indignant to be compared in any small way to that arse, Calvin, I am obliged by honesty to nod.

Calvin's got his little routine. Get in there at ten thirty on the dot and follow the cheat sheet on the inside of his locker door, and he's absolutely sweet and easy, but if you're early or late or you don't follow the routine, he bitches and he's nasty and he'll make you put his socks on sixteen times because there's a thread catching on his little toenail, or some such. Two choices, you can go in there like a bulldozer and tell him "This is how it's gonna be," which is good for him from time to time. Or you can follow the routine. Either way, you gotta walk in there with confidence and draw the line, as soon as possible. Say, "Okay, Calvin, I'm willing to try to comb your hair three times, but if that doesn't do it, you're not the only sheep in the heap."

Molly looks over at Gayla, assessing her comprehension, and readjusts her instructions.

Gently tell him, "You aren't the only resident I have to get up today." Okay. Now, Frannie here . . .

Molly doesn't stand still and talk. She's filled the basin and placed it on the side table with the lotion, the soap and my toothbrush in a kidney bowl. While she was lecturing, she opened my locker and held out a loathsome green dress, knowing full well that if I reject the first offer, I'll relent on the second, and I know what kind of a day Molly is having because the second choice is also a dress. I still have some nice clothes, and normally Molly would take the time to put me in them but the one-piece dresses (split down the back, donated to the hospital when someone died and discreetly redistributed by the aides) are the fastest thing to put on and they're polyester, so they last forever. Clearly Molly is behind in her work. I wonder if she'll have time to do my teeth. Teeth are always the first corner to be cut.

Okay, the tube-feed is done, which is good, because she's had a chance to digest for a bit. In a pinch, we can pause the machine to wash her up, but it makes her kinda queasy to roll her back and forth right in the middle of a feed, plus, I can't roll her unless the bed is flat, and there's always a risk she's gonna upchuck and choke. What I'm trying to say is do your best to get in here when the feed is off, and even better if you can give her ten or twenty minutes after it's done. Now I could call the nurse to disconnect the tube, but I'm not gonna take the time to do that.

Can't you just disconnect the tube?

Well, of course I can, but I'm not supposed to, so I'm not gonna. Plus I'll show you how to work around it.

Molly dips the cloth in the water and washes my face, looking over to see if Gayla has the initiative to figure out she should already have a towel in her hand for the *I'll wash, you dry* routine. A little sigh, just a puff of air, escapes Molly's lips as she reaches to the bottom of the bed and tosses Gayla a towel.

Frannie is a classic left-side stroke . . . right-side paralysis, language loss, cautious behaviour. I'm sure you got all that in school. Fun and games, right, Frannie?

She spares a smile for me while she whips off the blankets with one hand, spreads a towel over my body with the other, and while she's down at the end of the bed, she pulls on my socks. Molly doesn't like to waste a movement. The right hand reaches into the water while the left is holding up my arm to get well into the pit.

Some aides like the discreet little wipe with a damp cloth, but Molly likes a sloppy splashy wash that leaves the incontinence pads under me soaking. I never quite feel dry when she washes me. On the other hand, I do feel clean. Little rivers are running over my ribs.

Be super careful cleaning around the gastrotube opening. It looks pretty good today, but sometimes it gets quite red and sore; you can let the LPN know and she'll slap some Polysporin on. There's a package of clean gauze in her drawer here—I wrap one around the opening to keep the plastic off her skin. I change that every day.

Molly dries her hands on the towel quickly before reaching into her pocket and drawing out a pair of gloves. The water runs between my legs, and Gayla barely has a chance to give me a perfunctory dab with the towel before Molly grabs the slider sheet with both hands and gives me a quick tug, flipping me on my side. The institutional towels are rough; propelled by Molly's strong arms, they exfoliate the top layer of skin exquisitely. Heaven.

Okay, now set up so that you only have to roll her once. Flip the pad in half, so the sling doesn't get wet when she rolls back; fold the sling in half and centre it, then scrunch the right half under. Same with the disposable. If you tuck that side under really good, you won't have to roll her; the right side will come through. I'm gonna put a hospital gown on and the dress over that. Now I'm bringing the tube along the side here . . . I'm just gonna let the fabric bunch up a bit, but I'm still gonna tuck that over her hip so you don't have any skin showing when she's up. Okay, Frannie. Come back.

Gayla gives a little tug and over I go, facing Molly. She's got her cloth ready, and this time she's wrung it out.

I want to wash this side, because she was lying on it, and that's where you get that lingering smell of urine, on that offside hip. I know in school they teach you to put that side railing down to protect your back, but if I keep the bar up, Frannie can hold on for me while I pull everything through, there, see. Now I've got her centred on the disposable and the sling. So go ahead and put that gown and dress on her right arm, and I'll give a little pull so we can tuck it properly behind her; that's right. Do up the disposable and Bob's your uncle.

Shouldn't we have put the weak side in first?

Yeah, that's right, good catch, except in this case, the clothes I've chosen have enough room so it doesn't matter.

Meaning I'm wearing a shapeless bag.

Molly is already reaching under my legs, bringing the sling through so that I can hang in the air like a springtime planter basket full of limbs. Molly leaves me on the bed.

There's no room to store her chair in here; we keep it in the sunroom . . .

And she's gone, then she's back with my wheelchair. Molly kicks the brakes on, seizes the controller for the overhead lift from the charger on the wall, and brings the lift down from the ceiling while she crosses the room.

Okay, here's a little trick. If you spread a blanket over the chair, and put the chair pad over the blanket, you can wrap that right around her and one, she's warm, and two, no skin ever shows. So let's hook her up, and away she goes. Now keep your eye on that tube.

And I'm flying through the air, a block on a crane, my gastrotube still connected to the pump. Molly has a grip on the back of the sling and she manoeuvres me into the chair with my bottom smack in the back and my hips square. Ah, thank God. There's nothing worse than being cockeyed in the chair and not being able to do a damn thing about it. Molly's already brushing my hair briskly while Gayla slips a necklace over my head.

As we go by the nursing station, I'm gonna tell the nurse to disconnect her. Then she can come down to the dining room.

She doesn't eat.

No, she doesn't, but she likes to watch the people. Get out of here for a change, right, Frannie?

Molly winks, then rolls her eyes for me, making out that it's just the two of us against the world. Then she's out of here and I'm sitting with my back to the room, looking directly out of the window, hooked up to my silent feeding machine.

Yes, that's right. I am now wearing a polyester dress. And further-more, it's a floral print, dark purple and fuchsia on a black background. My God, I can imagine the expression of disbelief on your face almost as clearly as I can see the quilt on my bed. It makes me laugh.

You know, I cannot think of a time in my life when I didn't believe that the clothes maketh the man. I was brought up that way. I would stop at Papa's dry goods store on the way home from school, and Papa would be in the display window, his dress shirt rolled up to his elbows, wrestling the mannequins into their clothes. "Give me a hand, 'Cesca," he'd say, and while we worked, he'd talk about the fab-rics and what made the ensemble come together as a whole. Mama was always a natty dresser too, of course. Even in the kitchen, she looked ready to step out, with her clip-back earrings and her bouf-fant hair—all she had to do was whip off her apron with one hand and reapply her lipstick with the other, and she was magazine-ad ready. Poor Mama. Always prepared for something to happen, as if Cary Grant might knock on the door, flowers behind his back, and stretch out his hand so she could stretch out hers, kick up her heels and run away into the sunset. Papa and I were such a disappointment to her. I am sure Mama chose Papa thinking he'd take her far, far away from her own strict Mama and convoluted Italian family back in Toronto, which he did, but in Mama's critical eye, he never managed to take her far enough; surburbia was no sunset beach by any stretch.

As far as I was concerned, the store was the finest place in the world, and a great blessing to me because I was always well dressed. At school, what you wore was the first indicator of where you belonged in the pecking order; children are cruel and I was no exception.

You learn how much those childish taunts hurt when they are directed at you, or worse, at your child. Chris was bullied when he was in grade six. My business was doing well at the time, but I had just bought the house. There was no money to spare for kids' clothes that fall and of course Chris was growing fast. He came home from school one day covered in dust, with his jacket torn, and went straight to his room without saying a word.

Angelina was right behind him, slamming the front door open and hurling her book bag across the kitchen floor. "*Mawwm!*"

"I'm right here, Angie, don't yell."

"Mom, you have to buy Christian some new jeans. The kids are calling him 'storm boy' because of his flood pants."

She stood there, defiant, in her faded jeans and boy's T-shirt, looking even more like a hurricane than she usually did. My heart raced. How dare they criticize my son? How dare they cause him pain?

Angelina registered the rising colour in my face—stirring me up always calmed her down. She sauntered over to the sink and began to wash the blood off her knuckles.

"I picked the biggest one and smashed his nose," she said.

"Good for you," I said hotly, before I had the chance to think better of it. To my surprise, my prickly daughter turned and folded into my arms, and we hugged each other fiercely.

When Chris was in middle school, normally he would stop for Angelina at the end of his day and walk her home, but since I was driving them both to dentist appointments across town, I parked the minivan outside of Ang's elementary school to wait for them. We'd had snow, but it was melting fast in the sun, heavy and waterlogged on the ground. I scanned the playground for my children. Partially hidden from view, I watched my daughter.

She was coatless, in a sleeveless terry cloth jumpsuit that stretched to accommodate something large, almost like a camel's hump, on her back. The thing was heavy; Angelina was supporting the weight with both hands behind her, the way a small girl will piggy-back a baby whose short legs won't reach around her hips. A pack of kids were following her; my Miss Smarty Pants daughter was playing to the crowd, enjoying the attention.

I got out of the van and locked it.

As I walked towards Angelina, I could see Chris approaching from the other side of the playground. He was almost jogging, oblivious to the squelching slush his sneakers were kicking up. Ang saw him too; she stopped in her tracks. The parade dispersed, and a tiny girl, much smaller than the other nine-year-olds, began fussing with Angelina's jumpsuit. Even though the neckline and the arm holes had stretched to gaping maws, the thing on her back was still far too big to remove—how *did* she get it in there? The little girl heaved at the lump from the bottom while Angelina wriggled frantically until her big brother stood sternly before her.

Angelina looked up at him, tears welling. He tore his jacket off and gave it to the little girl who held it in front of Angelina like a curtain while Chris unzipped the jumpsuit and peeled back the ruined fabric.

A cannonball of dirty snow fell to the ground, shattering on the cement.

I grabbed Ang's backpack and coat from where she'd dropped them beside the swings. The jumpsuit was soaking. I left it dangling from her waist, roughly pulled her coat over her arms and zipped it up. She sobbed as Chris led her towards the car.

"My back is so cold!"

"Well, of course it is, stupid! What in the name of Saint Mary Mother of Jesus did you do that for?" I asked.

"I just did it."

"You were showing off. It serves you right."

"Leave her be, Mom," said Chris. "You've forgotten what it's like."

"I've forgotten what?"

"School. It's a war zone."

"Don't talk back to me!"

I couldn't understand it. I still don't. Why would anyone injure themselves to entertain a bunch of bratty nine-year-olds?

In the back seat, Angelina rested her little head on Chris's shoulder and he reached across his body with his opposite hand to hold it there.

Molly takes me down to the dining room early, because my place is in the corner, close to the electrical outlet that powers my tube-feed. Once full, the dining room becomes a Tetris grid of wheelchairs strategically organized for maximum occupancy and efficient meal assistance. I can't get out until lunch is over.

But I like my panoramic view of the whole room.

One of the casual aides is bending down to adjust Paul's foot on the pedal of his wheelchair, and Blaire calls her out.

Watch you keep your ponytail out of reach! Blaire's voice is unfriendly.

I haven't had a problem with him, says the casual.

Blaire shrugs. *It's your scalp,* she flings over her shoulder on her way out the door with her hands full of trays.

He bruised Blaire's arm pretty good, offers Michiko.

The casual is dubious. *Could it have been approach? Blaire's kind of . . . um . . . rough.*

Nah. He just has his moods and you can't tell when they're coming. He's unpredictable. You know Bettina? No one could be more gentle than her, right? He took a real good swing at her. I was there. She was lucky, he missed her by a hair.

The girls jump in so fast I can't tell who's saying what.

I heard family said, "No meds."

Yup. No meds. Period. No matter how agitated he gets.

That's not fair.

True that.

They don't care if we get hurt.

It sure doesn't give me that lovin' feeling.

They should take him home, if they think it's so easy to look after him!

Issue football helmets for us!

Suddenly Michiko's voice dominates.

You know what really bites me? He's got dementia and a bad heart, and his quality of life is poor. But the injury I could get if he nails me, that'll last me long after he's dead and gone. I mean, thanks, dude. Thanks for the memories.

Molly gives Nana the last bite of her mush.

Just keep your ponytail well out of reach. For some reason, the guy loves long hair.

After lunch, the girls clear the dining room so that the housekeeper can wash the floor. One by one they wheel us out.

"Do you want to go back to your room, Frannie, or do you want to go to the sunroom?"

In my room, the aides are putting Nana back to bed; she's too old and frail to be up for more than a couple of hours. They'll be taking Alice to the toilet and putting Janet on the commode. They probably won't change Mary, now that she can't pull herself up at the bar. She's wearing disposable briefs, which are supposed to last for a shift— they'll keep her up, let evenings put her back.

I have watched all these things before. From the sunroom, semi-private, I can see my tree, the whole tree, not just a piece of it, and I can see the last of the summer roses. It's a gorgeous autumn day.

I make the "onward troops!" sign with my good hand, and Molly, the driver of my chariot, guesses, "Sunroom?" I nod, and away we go.

I hear our little community purring in the background: the aides putting away personal laundry and passing out nourishments. The housekeeper making her way from room to room. Someone is laughing in one of the residents' rooms—probably Hilda's, she loves to make jokes. Outside, someone is running a leaf blower. Otherwise it's a quiet day. No activities organized to amuse us, no music in the dining room, no games intended to stimulate our brains. I drift, half-asleep in the sun.

Half-asleep, I am still thinking about Angelina in those troubled days.

By the time Ang was in middle school, she mimicked the stereo-types of older, wilder, more rebellious teenage girls in every possible way.

We were sitting in a restaurant, eating Chinese food, Chris, Angelina and I.

(It was an occasion, I think. Or was I simply too tired to cook? No—I remember. It was Chris's first day of high school and I wanted to celebrate.)

"Angelina, please don't slouch."

"You've got something in your teeth."

I excused myself and went to the ladies' to check. In the mirror, the lines on my face jumped out at me but my teeth were fine and my lipstick was perfect.

"It's still there, you'd better look again!" Ang said maliciously, and I realized she had been manipulating me all along.

All the shrimp had disappeared while I was gone and I smiled at Chris, partly to acknowledge his starving adolescent status and partly to show off my teeth. But then I went to take a sip of my wine, and there was only a half an inch left in the bottom of my glass.

Angelina had a satisfied smirk on her face. Chris studied his plate. Celebrate.

By the time she started high school, Ang had stopped talking to me altogether, or she yelled. There was no in-between. Her peers were all-important to her, nothing I said had any value to her. She got a part-time job at a fast-food joint. I thought it would make her responsible, and maybe it did help her learn to control her temper, but her financial independence was another blow to my authority. No threats were powerful enough to make her tell me where she was going or when she'd be coming back, and fear moved into my belly like a snarling, chained beast. More than anything, I worried about Angelina getting into drugs, but when I tried to talk to her she just rolled her eyes. There was no way to connect to my daughter and I thought with longing of the days when we clapped hands together until I thought my eyeballs would fall out from boredom.

I knocked on her door one Friday night with an armful of clean laundry.

"These are yours," I said.

She didn't answer, so I sat down on the end of her bed.

She still had the pink painted child-size dressing table with its valentine-shaped mirror that I'd bought for her at a garage sale when she was the age to swoon for that kind of cotton-candy kitsch. She had to lean down to look in the mirror. She was painting her eyelids with shiny, tropical fish colours.

I searched for a neutral topic.

"Are those jeans new?" I'd been giving the kids a clothing allowance and a free rein in using it for a long time.

"Don't you like them?"

"I was only thinking they look nice on you."

Ang looked at herself critically. "I'm too fat."

I snorted. "Who says so? If you were any thinner, you'd blow away."

She gave herself another once-over in the mirror. I stood up.

"You are beautiful, Angelina. Don't let anyone tell you differently."

I shut the door gently on my way out, feeling triumphant. It's true that we didn't talk about anything important, but it was the most peaceful conversation we'd had in months.

Ang went out with her friends and didn't come back until Saturday afternoon. I was up to my elbows in flour, a full-body apron tied securely around my waist. The sun came through the window low. Angelina slammed through the door in her fancy new jeans, her off-the-shoulder shirt stretched further than it was meant to be, smelling of vomit. She had a new eyebrow piercing. She stood in the doorway, wobbly, but with her chin up.

Our conversation was short but to the point.

"Where the hell have you been?"

"I hate you."

She stalked away, as dignified as a teenager can be with a slight stagger, and I was left with my mouth open; there were motes suspended in the clear sunshine and the taste of raw flour on my tongue.

I went to see a therapist just after that incident; Ang was fifteen. She was still living at home, still pretending to go to school, and the guidance counsellor called me in to talk about her ongoing absences. I remember feeling on the spot: How are things at home? Is there a father figure in Angelina's life? Is there anything we should know about, anything at all? So humiliating. In the end I agreed to "get help." We were supposed to go to the therapist as a family. But although initially Angelina seemed to like the woman, she refused to be in the same room as me and she simply didn't show up for her individual appointments. After two weeks of that, I walked her to her appointment, where she asked for the key to the bathroom and disappeared from there, taking the key with her. I found it in the hydrangea bush about twenty steps down the sidewalk.

Chris just said no, and I was too worn out to fight him, reasoning he wasn't the one I was worried about anyway. I ended up going to see the therapist alone, the captain of my leaky boat, talking to a granola pseudo-hippy in a wrap-around skirt with beaded earrings and crystals hanging in her windows. How was I supposed to take anyone who hangs crystals in her windows seriously? Really, now.

It wasn't so bad. *She* wasn't so bad. If I hadn't been so hostile, it could have been better, I guess, but of course I didn't know that then. Fear and anger. My left and right crutches. That's how I was coming to the table, and I couldn't even imagine peace and power, standing tall on my own. Poor Angelina. She was a hellion, but I didn't make things any easier.

We'd pretty much given up smoking, you and I, by that time. At most we'd share a cigarette after closing if I came by the restaurant late. Sometimes I would still have cravings, and the therapist said that wanting a cigarette was a message from my brain telling me to check my body for tension: my gut muscles tightening, my breathing becoming shorter and faster, my shoulders crowding up to my ears, my neck knotting. "You can't release tension if you don't know it's there," she said.

I don't need those messages now. The stroke has left me "emotionally labile," and the feelings that I've struggled so hard to contain (or at least disguise in shrouds of anger) are naked for all the world to see. I literally lack the muscular strength to suppress them.

But here is the gift. I don't care. I don't care! My right hand is useless, I can't speak and more people have seen my bare ass in the last year than if I was a streaker at the opera, because I need my *diaper* changed, for God's sake. Do you think I care if you see me cry?

I wipe my face with the back of my left hand and smear my fist on my gown. Oh yuck. Polyester and tears. There I go again.

The RN was after her to cut out the salt. Her feet are swollen up like pontoons.
  She says the food here is so bland, and I don't blame her.
  Well, she's downtown in her power wheelchair right now buying chips.

She's got a right to live at risk, I guess.

Okay then, but don't accuse us of not doing anything to help her with those sore feet, that's all I'm saying. There's a direct connection between your sodium intake and that effin edema, so quit yer bitchin'!

I love salt.

Yeah, me too.

The nursing staff changes shift at three o'clock. Fabby, my evening aide, is a fresh-faced young woman. Her partner, Stella, is much older, but the two of them get along fine. Fabby looks up to Stella, and Stella respects Fabby because she's a good worker.

It's funny how the energy changes in the evening. All the administration and housekeeping staff go home and the hospital hums along quietly, with a completely different rhythm from days. It can be very busy, though, depending on who is sundowning. People with dementia get a little bit wackier in the evenings. Did you know that, Anna? I didn't, until I came here.

After shift change, Fabby wakes me up, bouncing into the sunroom to ask if I'd like to go to bed. My bottom is killing me, so I nod yes.

Stella is already doing Nana's evening care behind the curtains.

Why don't you wash her in the chair? she asks, as Fabby hooks me up to the sling and I begin my slow ascent.

I like to do her on the bed, says Fabby, shortly, then laughs. *That doesn't sound good, does it.*

True, but I know what you mean.

Fabby can't resist venting.

Gosh, Stella, Ivy is breaking my heart!

Calling out?

"Don't leave me, don't leave me!" But what can I do?

Shut the door. You're too tender-hearted.

Well, if it was me . . . so sad. Would she do better in a double room?

Actually she was in the five-bed when she admitted, but she drove the other ladies crazy.

So it's not company she needs . . .

No. She wants one on one, one hundred percent of the time.

So pitiful.

Some people will never be satisfied, even when they get dementia.

Well, thank God for group change.

Amen. Are you going to put Mary in?

I think so. Everyone else wants to go down right after supper; I've only got two hands. And I'm sure she's wet, she's been up quite a while.

You can feed her and Nana together. I need to stay in the dining room.

Yeah, okay, that works.

Fabby finishes quickly, reversing the morning routine. Flip—she folds the sling under me, passes a damp cloth over my back, slides in a clean disposable and rolls me back to face her. The sling comes out and Fabby attaches the disposable diaper tabs. She flips my pillow, smoothes back my hair and brings my table tray within reach. She remembers to leave my gastrotube accessible so the nurse doesn't have to dig for it, and she checks to make sure I've got my call bell. She's an efficient worker. I feel safe.

And then the room goes quiet again.

The sun is coming through my window now, setting the dust motes dancing in the air. Alice trip-traps over to my bed, the smallest Billy Goat Gruff looking for greener pastures. It's the click-clack of her shoes that makes me think of that fairy tale, or maybe the fact that she's far too thin for any troll to eat. She picks at my quilt with her bony fingers. The touching used to bother me, but I've adjusted, and as long as she keeps her paws off the things on my over-the-bed table (and I am able to reach far enough with my good hand to defend that), I no longer care how much she harmlessly admires the fabric in my quilt.

Yes, Anna, the quilt you bought for me.

We were sitting in your diner, late, with the lights down and the doors locked, sharing a single cigarette (such a guilty pleasure, smoking inside) and a glass of wine. It was, ahh, that fabulous wind-down at the end of another gruelling day. Once again I was in the middle of some work marathon, but working myself to death certainly felt better than worrying myself to death; at least hard work brought me a sense of accomplishment and a paycheque. Angelina was at the peak of her rebellious maelstrom. If she was out, I fretted myself sick wondering where she was, and if she was home, her stony silence made me feel even worse. It wasn't that I'd stopped worrying—I never stopped worrying—but I'd reached a plateau of novocaine numbness. I knew she was making unhealthy choices . . . God, that sounds so prim! She was drinking and sleeping around with her pack of friends, and I'm pretty sure she was smoking dope. She came home when she needed laundry or makeup or a shower.

"Back home, there was a trades option in high school. I took cooking."

Even that harmless comment was enough to put me on the defensive.

"I talked to the guidance counsellor about that. Angelina didn't even begin to listen, she has no interest!" I cried.

You spread your hands out between us: peace. I took a deep breath.

"You know I named that girl for you, Anna," I said. "I had no one, and you helped me when I needed it the most, like an angel. So I named her for you. But she's not the least bit like you, more's the pity. I swear she's half devil."

"It is an honour, to have someone named for me. Angelina isn't finished yet. You must have faith."

"I don't believe in God. You know that."

"Have faith in Angelina. Leave God out of it."

"Well." Absent-mindedly, I tore the napkin into shreds.

"You've been a sister to me," you said.

I had to think about that. I wasn't sure why you were changing the topic.

"We neither of us have a real sister. So we have made one," you continued.

You took a drag on the cigarette and passed it to me, slid out of the booth and went into the back, while I sat there watching the smoke curl in the half-light. The nicotine and alcohol hitting my nervous system was such a profound relief.

You came back with the quilt. "It's not your style, normally. But I think it is right for you at this time. I found it at the farmer's market," you said, as you smoothed the fabric—a crazy quilt made with the most beautiful velvets, soft and rich as custard. My hands reached out of their own accord, drawn to the colours, the texture of the thing.

"Take it," you said. "Every piece is a prayer."

When the supper trays come down, Fabby does her best to encourage Janet to feed herself, while walking between Nana's and Mary's beds, helping them both—bite for *you*, bite for *you*.

Never eat when you're not hungry. It's one of my life rules.

But your blood sugar is low. You need to eat.

And if I don't?

You will lose consciousness.

And die?

Eventually, yeah.

Did it ever occur to you that there might be a good time to die?

Janet, you're only sixty-seven. You could still have a good life here if you try.

Stella comes in with Alice in tow.

Did she eat?

Not really. The dining room is too distracting for her. I'll give her an Ensure later. Come, Alice.

Stella holds Alice by the hand, and takes Janet's spoon. *Open up, Janet.*

Janet opens. Stella is the law.

Melissa is gaining weight, Fabby says.

Naturally. You see the way she eats.

They put her on a special diet . . .

And she just goes right downtown in her power wheelchair and gets whatever she wants.

Family are always bringing in treats too. It's all she's got left, I guess.

Nonsense. She has more than a lot of people here.

She eats for comfort.

If she gains much more, she will not be able to turn herself. But we're not going to change her. She's been living this way for years. That's how she got here in the first place.

Stella gives Janet a severe look, as if to say, "Same goes for you!" But fortunately Janet can't see.

Open, Janet.

Janet opens her mouth.

Your daughter found work yet? Fabby asks.

No such luck, says Stella in disgust.

I'm sure she's trying.

And I'm sure you'd find something nice to say about the devil himself, my girl.

Another supper is over. Fabby dims the lights on the way out. It may be six fifteen, but for us, another day is almost done.

I got home very late from seeing a client and the house was dark and uninviting. I didn't expect a welcoming committee, but Chris was usually home by seven thirty—was home or had been home, leaving the lights on and crumbs on the kitchen counter.

That night the house was oppressively still, and instead of immediately changing from my good slacks into blue jeans, I poured myself a glass of white wine and lingered in the shadows by the kitchen window, looking out over the backyard. Mired in loneliness, I waited without realizing I was waiting.

It was much later still when Chris finally came home, late enough that supper had been made, grown cold and scraped uneaten into a container to languish in the fridge.

"Where were you? You didn't call."

"Out."

"What kind of an answer is that?" The kid was in grade twelve—he was almost a man. But he still lived under my roof.

Chris opened the fridge and pulled out the milk.

I was about to say, "Get a glass, this isn't a barn," when he spoke into the cold of the refrigerator. "I was following Angelina."

Suddenly I could barely breathe.

"What made you do that?"

Chris turned around to face me.

"I just want to know what she's up to. Make sure she's not getting too crazy with those friends of hers out there. Make sure she's safe. Y'know?"

I could see the worry on his face.

"And was she? Is she?"

"I don't know, Mom. I really don't know. She's partying pretty hard."

"Did you try to talk to her?"

"I can't talk to her when she's drinking like that."

"Where are they getting their booze?"

Chris shrugged. "You can always get booze if you want to badly enough. Don't tell me you didn't do the same when you were a kid, because I'd know you were lying."

"Why didn't you make her come home?"

"I can't make her come home, Mom. I can't make her do anything. I can't watch her all the time either."

"That girl makes me crazy. She makes me crazy, I tell you!" And I threw the mug in my hands against the wall as hard as I could.

Stella comes in at about ten to put Alice to bed. They keep her up late in the hope that when she does lie down, she'll stay. Stella washes her quickly in the bathroom and leads her past my bed, a little old ghost in a long-sleeved white nightgown. The pill nurse walks in just in time with Alice's evening meds and a warm blanket. We've all been checked and changed. Everyone will try to be extra quiet now, hoping Alice will have a good night. When the night staff come on at eleven, they will slide into the room like shadows, placing the night linens on our side tables, ready for the mid-shift wet round, when everyone who needs a disposable change gets one. There are only two aides for fifty patients on nights. They don't want Alice up and wandering, going from room to room, disturbing the other residents.

Stella puts Janet on her side; Janet grumbles. *Why did you wake me? I was dreaming of snow.*

Stella sighs, murmurs, *Go back to sleep.*

Stillness falls, thick like a narcotic haze.

ARE YOU GLAD TO BE ALIVE?

Molly looks much more relaxed without her newbie in tow.

"I'm sorry I didn't put proper clothes on you yesterday, Miss Francesca," she says. "I had a hell of a day. I'm gonna make it up to you. What would you like to wear?"

She opens up my locker and starts pulling out clothes . . . my grey pants and the soft black sweater with pearl beading around the neckline, the navy pants with the tailored shirt in a rich geometric pattern of purple and sky-blue on black. I choose a bright red knit tunic with sleeves that end just below the elbow. Cleverly positioned stitching gives it shape. It's a lovely piece.

I bought it at Carlotta's Boutique on a rainy afternoon in February years ago; it's worn well. I remember because Carlotta had decked out the windows for Valentine's and there were reds and pinks of every shade in the store. Quality consignment clothes. I was there so often that Carlotta got to know me better than my doctor did. She knew my taste and saved things out for me. Once I discovered Carlotta's, I never looked back, not even when my business became successful enough that I could have shopped wherever I wanted.

It wasn't just loyalty, though God knows because of Carlotta, for years I dressed myself in the kind of clothes I otherwise would never have been able to afford . . . not if I wanted to feed the kids. At first I approached second-hand clothing like a shame-faced suburban housewife looking for a hit from a downtown pusher—gracious, what would my father have thought! However, I got so that I appreciated the pleasure of the lucky find (that single piece, in just my size) and the satisfaction was intensified by the price: designer labels at a fraction of the original cost. Carlotta was meticulous in her acquisitions. No one could tell they weren't new, and I certainly would never have revealed that fact.

God, how I loved good clothes. I told myself it was all part of the plan: Dress for Success and Act the Part. The dress code at Jackson Douglas was decidedly rigid back in the days when they employed me, so I'd acquired an excellent selection of business-appropriate clothing during my four years there. And certainly I relied on my wardrobe to create an image of authority I didn't necessarily feel during the early days when I was trying to grow my business. I told myself I would never choose an accountant or a financial planner who had dirty fingernails. How could one infer meticulous attention to detail in a person with a wrinkled shirt? These were my excuses for what felt like extravagance when grocery money was so tight. But I needed the confidence that came from knowing that I was well turned out from the tips of my black leather pumps to my pearl earrings. Perfectly pressed business suits with buttoned up silk shirts were my armour. They were my superhero cape, they made me invincible. And as I became more financially secure, my clothes reflected not only the promise of prosperity but the confirmation of it.

But kids and nice clothes don't mix. That's a fact. I used to shed my client clothes the instant I walked in my front door, before I even flicked on the lights. I kept a kimono hanging in the entranceway so I wouldn't get caught in my bra and panties. Yet between daycare pickup and the time I got home, something always seemed to happen. Baby puke on my silk blouse, Christian's snotty face pressed into my linen dress pants—it was enough to make me wild. Chris learned to wash his hands before running to embrace me, but I swear Angelina dirtied hers on purpose, wicked imp that she was, thinking she was being funny. How I laughed one time when I swept her into my arms, holding her wrist to show her the grubbiness of her little brown paws. "I don't have time to wash my hands," she said, mimicking me. "I'm a very busy woman!" Even Chris smiled, turning his face away, as though to keep his amusement private.

I squeeze my eyes shut as Molly manoeuvres me into my pullover.

Shortly after I came here, my aide was a square-faced young woman with hands smelling of soap and lotion, whom I've never seen since. She was earnest but plodding, and she must have been fairly new or perhaps a little dull because when she tried to put my teal green dress shirt on me, she put my good arm in first, and then of course she couldn't get my bad arm in, and I couldn't help her at all. We wrestled like washerwomen struggling to wring out double sheets by hand, my body wayward and bulky, my aide's homely face glistening with perspiration. Two other aides wandered into the room and, offering to help, they wrestled too. Once the shirt was on, they rolled me back and forth, shimmying my pants up inch by inch one side at a time. In the end, I sat in the chair, queasy and humiliated but decently dressed, centre seams only slightly askew. The girls panted in a semicircle before me.

We have got to get her clothes geried!

Yes, that was a challenge.

Does she have family we could ask?

Just take the scissors and split them!

No, you can get in big trouble like that. We've got to ask the family for permission.

We could phone her son.

Ask her. She knows what she wants.

No for Chrissake, don't do that. If she says no, management will take her side and we'll be screwed. It's got to be done. We'll break our backs here. Call her son and make him say yes.

One of the girls had hurt my rigid arm quite badly, and I could tell that my hair was sticking up in a most undignified way. Watching their faces like a cornered cat, I didn't know what to think. A girl with soft blond hair in a ponytail reached out to place a slender hand on my arm.

"Do you know what we're talking about?" she asked.

I shook my head. The other two aides left the room but the blond girl went to one of the lockers and began quickly selecting an assortment of clothes.

"I'm Lily," she said. Now, with fewer distractions, I had a chance to study her face. It was a valentine, like Angelina's, and the willowy figure was similar too, but where Angelina, fierce or joyful, always had a wildness, Lily's expression was calm and gentle and her eyes were clear-skies-forever blue.

"That was quite a struggle, wasn't it? You don't want to be doing *that* every day."

Inadvertently I touched my sore arm.

"Oh," she said quickly, "did we hurt you? I'm so sorry. But Francesca, that's what I want to talk to you about. It doesn't have to be that hard to get you dressed."

She reached into Mary's closet and pulled out a shirt: a simple, tailored dress shirt with standard cuffs and collar just like the one I was wearing, but in a pale blue paisley pattern.

"From the front, it's just a shirt, but here's our little secret: see how it's split up the back so that we can easily get it around your shoulders to slip that second arm in? Now look at these pants. They're cut so that we can tuck one side under, and then the other, and voila, you're dressed."

She was watching my face for clues. I didn't like it, but I could see what she was getting at; in spite of myself, I nodded my head.

"Now, your knit tops will be fine, Francesca, because the fabric has some give . . . especially if the girls remember to put your bum arm in first . . ." (and here Lily smiled). "But these kinds of things, these tailored shirts . . . Is this your style, Francesca? Is this the kind of thing you prefer to wear? These are very hard to get on and the buttons take a lot of time.

"But if you let me cut a slit up back, about to the shoulder blades—*here*—I can reinforce the top with a bit of seam binding so that it doesn't tear further. Then I can slip your weak arm in, and bring the shirt around your shoulders, and you can help me with your left arm. See? You're dressed!"

She had the blue shirt on, or almost on, right over my other shirt. I could see what she meant. The fabric had no give. Without a slit down the back, my dress shirt was a straitjacket. My chest was tight and I was afraid to breathe. Lily didn't look away.

"That's not all, Francesca," Lily said gently. "We *can* get you into regular slacks, but we have to roll you back and forth to get them up. I know that makes you nauseous. If you need the toilet, you have to go back on the bed and the pants have to come down, and then you have to get up again with the lift to get on the commode. By the time we've done all that, even supposing we answer your bell promptly, you'll have lost the feeling." Again Lily gave me a searing look. "This is a hard truth, I know." She put her soft hand on my arm, as if to steady the blow.

"But if I split the slacks in the back, like I showed you, we can tuck them in around your hips, and from the front, it looks like you have regular clothes on."

I let my face go then; clearly they didn't expect me to walk again, if they wanted to split my pants. My heart caved in; the whole foundation of my life, crumbling into the abyss.

"The thing is," Lily said softly, "it's hard on you, but it's hard on us too. The reality is that one of two things is going to happen. Either the girls won't put those clothes on you, because it's too much work. Or one of them is going to come in and split them with a pair of scissors. Francesca, it's far better to let me take them and alter them properly."

I felt a tear making its way down my cheek and I swiped at it angrily. Lily glided to the side table, taking up the box of Kleenex in one hand and my brush in the other. She set the box in my lap and walked behind me, out of view.

"Let's see what we can do with this hair, Francesca. You look a little wild." I let the tears fall.

"It's not just the clothes, is it?" said Lily, reading my mind. "It's everything, isn't it? Being here, not being home, losing your mobility, not having any privacy . . . It's so hard, isn't it?" Brush, brush, brush.

Lily leaned in and whispered in my ear so privately I almost thought I imagined it. "Hold on, Francesca," she said. "There are angels everywhere. Hold on. You'll be okay."

Surprised, taken aback, my breath burst out.

"So," said Lily. Her normal voice was almost ringing by contrast, and I started. "Let's try a couple of pairs of pants, okay, Francesca? And maybe this shirt and this one. Let's do that much for starters, alright? Once you see how much easier this is, we'll talk about the next step. What do you say? Are you willing to give it a shot?"

Well, I nodded. What else could I do?

That's how I met Lily.

Lily brought my clothes back two days later, impeccably sewn. She was working my group, covering Blaire's holidays, so she washed me up before putting them on.

"Is that your daughter, Francesca?" she asked, moving Angelina's picture as she pushed the over-the-bed table out of the way.

I nodded.

"She's so beautiful. Was she a good child?"

Who would think of asking that? I shook my head, no. Changed my mind and nodded.

Lily sighed. "It happens. I have a six-year-old. Thank God she's in school now. It was so hard when I had to pay for full-time daycare."

She flipped me on my side to wash, and started talking to my back, quietly.

"I thought I was going to be such a great mom, unlike my own mother. But as it turns out, babies aren't dolls, and I'm not sure I do any better as a parent. My mother is a nurse, but she isn't much of a motherly type. She's either working or partying. I used to watch her dressing up to go out. She always wanted to find that one special guy. Instead we had a garden full of them. I guess she's still looking. I used to blame her, but I don't anymore. I want that too. But at least I don't make Sierra part of the search party."

Lily gave a slight shiver.

"Waking up on weekends and there's a big hairy, naked stranger coming out of the bathroom like a Sasquatch. That's an unpleasant experience for a child."

I rolled back and looked into Lily's face; she was far away.

She noticed me looking at her and smiled. "I have a date tonight. I hired a babysitter. I feel guilty leaving Sierra, but I don't want to introduce her until I'm sure this is the one.

"But look at you, Francesca! Isn't this good? You didn't even notice me getting you dressed, did you? And it was easy for me too. Now I'll get you up, and you're all put together. What do you think?"

Her eyes were shining and I felt the full force of her attention and affection, and I couldn't help but smile back at her.

Anna, do you remember Rachel? You were such a capable manager, such a firm and practical boss, but every now and then your heart would get in the way of your common sense and you'd turn around and hire a lost lamb like Rachel. She was such a good waitress. Her hair pulled back and pinned up exposed her face, a hopeful flower. Her apron was always clean, the bow at the back jaunty and cheerful and her figure was light and pleasing, tucking in at the waist. The buttons over her breasts stopped just respectably short of straining.

Her legs were long and shapely. Men had to look and women were jealous, but she had a knack for making every customer feel special, and her memory! Your name, the names of your kids and your friends, what you liked to eat, what you took in your coffee and what you said about your day the last time she saw you. She had all that down pat. We all loved her, even baby Angie, and Chris was sure he was going to marry her when he grew up. But what a time she gave *you*, calling in sick and showing up late, and that boyfriend with the habit, to say nothing of the mother with the mental health problems coming by the diner and demanding free coffee at the top of her lungs. Rachel poured her sweet love out like sunshine over everyone, but her personal life was always an encroaching mess.

Lily comes from the same pattern, Anna, for better or worse. As far as I'm concerned, the warmth outweighs the weakness, and I love her fiercely, although I don't get to see her very often, because she's a casual.

It isn't just Lily's uncanny knack of guessing what I'm thinking that makes her so special to me—it's the fact that she confides in me. She lets me in to her life, she brings me close, she makes me feel like she needs me. There's a terrible irony here, fit for the unbearable optimist who declares that there's a silver lining in every cloud: the gift in being unable to speak means Lily's secrets are safe with me. Her words fall into a bottomless well. There is no retrieval, no risk of damning indiscretion leaking out at just the wrong time. Lily tells me anything.

It's like a light switch, flicking on and off, two completely different Lilys: the tidy, elegant little nurse with an astounding gift for empathy, and the vulnerable child, whose hurts and fears and insecurities loom like monsters. One second she's reading my mind, and the next, she's emptying hers.

I cherish it. Even though I know it's unprofessional of her to share. She's my Lily.

I hadn't even known Angelina was in the house until she came down the stairs, holding a big garbage bag by its twisted top.

"I'm taking my stuff, Ma."

"Where do you think you're going?"

"Jordan and I found a place."

"What are you talking about? Who's Jordan? A place to *live*? Is that a girl or a boy? You don't need a place. You live here!"

"Mom, that isn't working."

Her gentle words caught me off guard. Angelina was always ready to catch my anger and pitch it, fastball, back at me.

I sat down at the kitchen table with a thump.

Angelina put the bag down on the floor, crossed over to me and, big girl that she was, crawled onto my lap.

It had been so long since she let me hold her, let me love her. My darling Angelina. My baby. Just turned sixteen. She put her arms around my neck and her face against mine, like a child. Her skin smelled faintly of alcohol, but her hair smelled like Angelina and I buried my nose in it. And while my arms were strong around her and my thumb traced circles on her right shoulder blade, everything inside me from my tailbone on the chair to the lump in my throat was tight and brittle, like an old rubber band that has hardened around a package of letters over the years.

I wanted to hold on forever. Angelina's shoulders started to shake, and I heard her catch her breath. When I loosened my arms to look into her face, she pushed herself away, catching me by surprise, hurting me. Snatching up the grey sweatshirt that had spilled onto the floor in one hand, she grabbed the bulging garbage bag in the other and ran out the door without saying goodbye.

For the first few weeks after Angelina moved out, I felt like I'd been cut out of her life completely. The only news I had of her I got from Chris, who counselled me to give her space. It was he who helped her find second-hand furniture, and borrowed the minivan to deliver it to her cheap downtown apartment. I let him take the little table from the patio and some chairs. Pots, extra dishes, cutlery. I pretended I didn't notice when he took staples from the cupboard: half the salt, half the sugar, half the coffee, cans of tuna and jars of jam, cleaning supplies. But I wouldn't let him take Angelina's bed from her room.

"That's for Angelina! When she comes home."

"If she comes home, I can move it back again, Mom."

But I wouldn't change my mind.

Chris told me Ang found a full-time cashiering job.

"What about her education?" I fretted.

"Honestly, Mom, what was the point of her sitting there in school? She didn't learn anything."

"What kind of a job will she ever have without even a high school education? She'll be working for minimum wage for the rest of her life."

"Let her figure that out for herself. Mom, she's doing better than she has for a long time. She goes to work; she wasn't going to class. It's not like she's twelve. She can do this."

It was my busiest season, tax time. One of my clients had lost a whole stack of his expense receipts. I'd completely finished another client's file when I received a frantic call from her; she'd allowed her personal and professional expenses to mingle for her last quarter. My most lucrative client had recently hired a manager so rude and condescending that I was seriously debating dropping them. Although I wasn't reconciled to Angelina's departure, there was a certain relief in having her out of the house. No more pacing the floor at three in the morning, waiting for her to come home and worrying about what condition she'd be in when she finally stumbled up the stairs. No more arguments punctuated with yelling and tears. In fact, there was no bad news from her at all and, in spite of my professional pressures, I was surprised to find I was sleeping through the night for the first time in years.

When Ang finally invited me to her place, I treated the occasion with pomp. I made my mother's recipe for amaretti cookies the day before (they're best when they have time to ripen). I bought flowers and a housewarming present. It was a Saturday morning and Chris drove me downtown.

There were four dark flights of stairs covered with worn brown carpet to climb. Chris stopped me at the top, outside of Angelina's door.

"If you criticize her, this won't go well, Mom."

I was puffing from exertion, or I would have retorted. I pulled an indignant face, but while I caught my breath, Chris reached out and put a finger to my lips.

"Hush," he said.

I belted him as best I could with my arms full of gifts.

Angelina opened the door.

My first apartment when I moved here from Ontario was slummier, but that wasn't what I was thinking. I was thinking, "I worked my ass off to have you live like *this*?"

"Angelina, come home," I blurted. Horrified, I clapped my hand over my mouth, whacking myself with the box full of amaretti.

There was a moment of silence while Ang and Chris registered the regret and pain on my face. Then Angelina laughed.

"Aw, Mom, did you hurt yourself? This *is* my home, do you like it?" she asked, twirling once with her arms spread wide and her hair flying.

It was like stepping back from the curb as a bus thunders by. In my head, I heard the words she'd yelled at me so many times before: *Don't come to my room and tell me I'm wrong! Who asked you? It's my life! You always put me down. I don't care!*

There was an empty twenty-sixer on the counter by the sink and a lingering smell of smoke and mould, but I could also smell bathroom cleaner and I took that as a good sign. The place looked clean enough. Stark but tidy. The bedroom door was tightly closed, and if Jordan was in there, she didn't come out while we were visiting. Chris saw me taking it all in and pinched my arm hard; I held my tongue.

"I made amaretti for you," I said, setting down my packages on the patio table. "I hope I didn't break them to bits. Here are some new towels. Do you need them?"

"Very la-di-da. Thank you, Mom."

All in all the visit could have gone much worse. Angelina wouldn't talk about school, or the future, or her plans. "Just let me do *this* right now," she said. We didn't stay long. Ang had to go to work.

Chris was practically panting with relief. He bounded down the stairs like a ten-year-old and turned at the bottom while I took my time, hand on the rail, careful not to catch my heels on the fraying carpet.

"Let's have coffee at the diner, eh, Mom? It's a beautiful day!"

A few days after she'd returned my altered clothes, Lily brought Sierra in on her day off. Without her scrubs, Lily looked like the black-sheep twin of her work self. The waifish face of a pouty lipped model peeked out from under her loose hair. She wore a short dress made of many fabrics of different textures sewn together. I know that sounds terrible, but it wasn't—it was beautiful and quite remarkable. The bodice was form-fitting and the skirt flared a little, and Lily has beautiful legs. She wore snappy sandals with a little too much heel. Except for the child clinging to her hand, she looked sexy, striking; Sierra could easily have been Lily's younger sister.

Sierra kept her face planted in Lily's side, and when Lily scooped her up into her arms (hitching the hem of the skirt just that much higher on her thigh), Sierra buried her nose in Lily's hair. Then I remembered what we have become so accustomed to that we don't notice it anymore—the smell of an extended care hospital.

Suddenly I saw my room as Sierra must have seen it: the institutional quality and colour of the paint, the grim efficiency of the metal over-the-bed tables, the bedside drawers devoid of beauty or charm. Above all, the smell of urine, old bodies and industrial-strength cleaner. Still, it is my home, and I'm conscious of an unexpected sensation of comfort.

Lily had come to return a vegan cookbook she borrowed from Michiko.

I'm sorry I took so long with this.

You didn't need to make a special trip.

No, I didn't; I needed to talk to payroll.

What did you think?

Well, thank you for lending it to me, but Michi, there's no way I'm ever going to work that hard on my food. I have a new respect for you!

It's not so hard. You get in the habit of taking the time.

Time is exactly what I do not have.

A disc in my back felt out of alignment and I squirmed in my chair. Lily's clear, sweet voice seemed incongruous with the come-hither outfit.

Lily plopped Sierra down again and introduced her to the ladies. Sierra shook hands with Mary and Alice while I waited my turn. I never was that interested in children, except my own. I greeted Sierra with perfunctory interest, then brushed my hand neck to thigh and back and pointed at Lily.

"The dress? You like it?"

I nodded. Lily beamed.

"It's one of my own designs."

I gave her the thumbs up. Sierra was tugging at her mother's hand . . . the "Let's go" code of polite children everywhere. Chris did that. Angelina, on the other hand, would simply pick up something she wasn't supposed to have and drop it.

Being a single mother isn't easy; I have a flash of empathy for Lily and all she has to juggle.

I brought up the dress the next time I saw Lily, repeating the motion I'd made on that day, the sweep of my good hand from neck to thigh and back. I knew she'd remember.

"The dress? You really liked it, then?"

I nodded.

"When I was in high school, I wanted to be a fashion designer," she said. "I dreamed that I would be one of those famous artist creators. The amazing thing is, one of my classmates did go on to fulfill that dream. But her family had money and they backed her. My mother moved up island with some guy. So I moved in with River and had a baby."

Lily had hooked me up in the sling and brought me up over the bed.

"Thank God I took this course right out of high school, or I'd really have been in a jam, moneywise. Mom pushed me to do it. She wanted her freedom so badly, you know; she wanted me financially independent and out of the way."

As she removed the sling, I tapped her with two fingers, asking a question.

"River? He's not a bad person. We stay in touch. He's still got the band . . . Yes, I fell for a bass player. Not my smartest decision, was it? He does kayak tours in the summer. He doesn't make a lot of money, so there isn't a lot of financial support."

I shook my finger at her.

"No. I wouldn't go to court. It's not the worth the hard feelings, Francesca. We were both too young and what's done is done. He helps with the babysitting when he's around."

Lily supported my head with one hand and deftly flipped my pillow with the other.

"Would you like to see some of my other creations?" Lily pulled out her phone with a sly look over her shoulder. "We're not supposed to carry these at work," she said, placing one finger to my lips with a conspiratorial smile. Then she started flipping through pictures of the outfits she'd designed. They were beautiful, functional and creative. I pointed and Lily explained.

"That one? I wanted something that would fill the gap between dressy and casual, something that would be easy maintenance but also look really good. I was thinking of mothers, obviously, because you don't have a lot of time to look after fussy fabrics, but you especially need to look good when you're feeling overwhelmed by motherhood."

I mimed vomiting and Lily smiled. "That's right. Just like extended care! Everything needs to be a hundred percent washable. But when you have a chance to get out, you want to feel like yourself, not 'the woman with the baby,' even when the baby is sitting on your hip. The last thing you want is frumpy. That's what I had in mind when I designed this. But you know what the flaw is?"

I shook my head.

"Solid colours. Solid colours show grease stains."

I nodded solemnly. How true it is.

"Why do children have such greasy fingers?"

I really don't know. Neither does Lily.

That was Lily in the flush of new love, Anna—bubbling and light, warm, understanding and helpful. A crackling fire on a cold day, drawing everyone closer.

Two weeks later, the guy dumped her and the fog rolled in. Lily grew big dark circles under her eyes, her hands shook, and one day she burst into tears in the hallway. Molly grabbed a fistful of my tissues before hustling her into an empty room. "Thanks for the Kleenex," she said to me later. "Lily the Lovelorn needs to learn to leave her home life at home."

It was at least another two weeks before the sun came out, and Lovely Lily smiled again. Most of the fall was calm and clear. Just before Christmas, Lily met another guy and rode the whole roller coaster from infatuation to despair to equilibrium as though she'd never been on that ride before. And in the spring, she did it all again.

But why is it always about the man, Anna? For the first time in a long time, in almost forever, I remember Karl as he was when we first got together. My God, what a good-looking man, all Nordic beauty, blond hair, high cheekbones, aquamarine eyes, long muscles, sensual lips. Every part of my body yearned for him. How proud I was of how we looked together, like sunlight and moonlight, yin and yang. I thought we were perfect for each other.

If we'd just had Chris, Karl might have stayed—at least until I grew the backbone to kick him out. One child is a bump, a blip, a piece of baggage you can wheel along beside you, especially a quiet son like Christian. You could put that boy down and tell him to stay, and as long as he had his matchbox truck in one hand and his magic rock in his pocket, he would wait for hours, like the youngest brother in a fairy tale, following directions as though the wicked witch was waiting to turn him into stone. It was in his nature to be good, and Karl trained him early to sit quietly, taking him to poker games when I thought they'd gone to the park, poor lad.

But two kids, well, that's a family. Unbridled domesticity, responsibility, trikes in the driveway, breakfast cereal. Karl wanted none of that.

We both married such stinkers, Anna.

Your dad was a stinker too.

"Papa thought no one as ugly as I am could be smart," you said, touching your lip. "He thought a damaged animal should be put down."

"What damage?"

"My harelip. He said I am ugly, like a hare."

Did you believe him? Did you marry a brutal man like Anton because you believed him?

Damn it. There are tears on my face again.

"Frannie's crying." Michiko has been doing Mary's care without taking the time to close the curtains. "Do they have her on antidepressants?"

Molly strides across the room. "Aw, Frannie! What's up?"

I shake my head. Nothing. It's nothing.

"She just gets sad sometimes, don't you, Frannie? We all get sad sometimes."

"She cries a lot."

"She smiles a lot too. It's the stroke . . . you're alright, aren't you, Fran?"

I nod vigorously.

"God, she doesn't need more drugs. She's on a bucketful. Let her be sad. She's got a right to be sad. Besides, it's Saturday. That'll take away the tears! Right, Frannie?"

A big grin spreads across my face; Saturday's the day Chris comes in.

"There you go!" smiles Molly. "Want to go to the sunroom, so you can visit in private?"

That's exactly what I want. I have no desire to share Chris.

In the wake of Karl's departure I used to preach to the kids: "Never try to be with someone who doesn't want to be with you. It's no fun." It was the barn door I swung on with the horse long gone, my Cassandra's cry.

But once again I was wrong.

I'm pretty sure this is the last place Chris wants to be, and it's not fun, no, not fun, but it's achingly wonderful just to be with Chris when he visits. Simply to have him near.

I drift off again, and when I wake up, Michiko and Molly are laughing in the hallway, their voices faint but still audible.

So I had him standing at the bathroom bar, you know, getting his pants down, and he said, "Your hair's standing right up, just like my pecker!"

Oh, I bet he was a bad boy!

One time he said to me, all sad-like, "I used to be sooo sexy."

What did you say?

I said, "Dude, you still are!"

Aw, you're good! But y'know, his wife told me he used to say, "If I lose my marbles, let me die. I don't want to live like that."

So I ask him, "Is life still sweet?" and he says, "Life is stiiill sweet!"

Did you tell his wife that?

Well yeah, I did. I mean, it's a comfort to her, right? Like, this isn't easy for her—he's not the guy she married, eh.

True.

"I'd rather be dead." That's what I said to Chris about extended care. I remember it well.

It was Christmastime. Chris's school was paired with an extended care facility as part of an initiative intended to integrate children with the elderly, and his class was giving a concert in mid-December. The kids had practised for weeks. "Bring a Torch, Jeannette, Isabella." "God Rest Ye Merry Gentlemen." Chris had a cameo performance as Santa: "Rudolph with your nose so bright, won't you guide my sleigh tonight?" He took the responsibility very seriously.

I went to a lot of trouble to make sure I could watch the concert. Angelina was in after-school care after kindergarten that day, but I had to see a difficult client who objected to being rescheduled and I had trouble getting away. In the end I was late. I could hear the children's voices as I pushed through the door, conscious of a wall of sensation. The air was overheated, redolent with the smells of urine and boiled vegetables. I could feel the odorants clinging to me, adhering to my nylons, infusing my pores. I became hyperaware of the sound of my shoes, the length of my legs, the sweat on my upper lip as I strode past a gauntlet of hags tied into their chairs; I hurried past. "Won't you guide my sleigh tonight?" Chris's voice rang out clear and pure and all the sweeter in contrast with the putrid air.

I leaned against the wall, faint, as Miss Devon led the class through their final song. The room spun. It took me a moment to regain my equilibrium.

After the music, the children were encouraged to shake hands with the residents before claiming their sugary reward, holly-shaped cookies and Dixie cups of juice. Some of the boys were already horsing around, wadding pieces of their napkins and blowing them across the room with their straws. But Chris had been claimed by a vigorous witch clearly eager to eat him up, so tight was her grip; I walked across the room towards him.

"Christian," I said, and he looked up at me, alert to the usage of his full name, relaxing when I added, "good job."

I pried the bony fingers away, one by one, releasing my son's hand. She was surprisingly strong, and she let out a wail like a wounded cat. Chris rubbed his bloodless fingers on his jeans. "Goodbye now," he said to her, and we turned away.

Outside, free again, the fresh, cold air was sobering as a slap and we gulped deep breaths. "I'd rather be dead," I said. "I'd rather be dead than have to live in a place like that."

And I meant it. At the time.

No one wants their mother to have a stroke. Chris was not only sad during his visits but distant in a way that made me sad too. It was Lily, working Molly's holidays last spring, who helped shift our stagnation.

I wanted to stay up so Chris could wheel me into the garden, but it was raining and the sky was grey and my bottom felt like someone took the citrus zester to it, so when Lily offered, I was grateful to go back to bed. She was just pulling the curtains open when Chris arrived.

It's pretty hard not to stare at Lily, she's just that beautiful, so I was not surprised that Chris wasn't looking at me.

Oh hello, Chris! How are you?

Good, good.

But his back was rounded, and his shoulders drooped.

How are you, Lily?

Oh fine. Francesca will be glad to see you!

I guess.

Lily's attention crackled, like bed sheets snapping when you fold them fast and taut.

You guess? *What are you talking about. It's the high point of her week!*

Maybe.

Maybe?

Well. I just kind of sit here.

Uh-huh.

Like a lump.

Chris. Your visits are what Francesca is living *for. Surely you* must *know that.*

There was an awkward silence while Chris examined the lint in his pockets.

Mom has always been . . . pretty prickly. She was a single parent with a career. My sister was . . . Throwing my mom into parenting my sister alone was like expecting someone with a learner's permit to drive an eighteen-wheeler for the first time on the 401 into Toronto. Or maybe the Autobahn— I've heard that's pretty crazy.

Lily laughed.

Parenting is never easy—that's a given. But Chris, Francesca is fully invested in you. There's absolutely no doubt about that.

Chris shrugged. Lily laid her elegant hand on his arm, and her voice was very low.

Maybe she wasn't able to show how much she cared about you, or maybe she never had the time. I don't know, I didn't grow up at your house. But you can take this to the bank—Francesca loves you. Right now, she's got nothing but time. Take a chance, Chris. She's changed, even in the time since she came here. Anyone who's not dead has got a right to change. You can give her that.

But . . . is she . . . all there? D'you think?

Oh, I'm sure of it. She understands every word we say, Chris. Her cognition is excellent.

Chris looked at me, really looked at me, for the first time in I don't know how long. And his expression was speculative.

I could hardly breathe from the weight of hope.

She's all there, Chris, and she's waiting for you.

Lily put her right hand over her left breast and mimed the opening and closing of a window shutter.

Time is ticking, Chris, she said, turning to go. *Open your heart.*

Turning the wheel on the kaleidoscope—that is one of Lily's special gifts. After that day, Chris's visits were completely different.

The very next week, he strode in with his head up and his shoulders back. I was in my bed. The tube-feed had made me queasy and I'd vomited. I couldn't get rid of the taste in my mouth. The smell on my breath reminded me of babies and sleepless nights and utter, flattening fatigue.

"Mom. How was your week?"

I tipped my hand—comme ci, comme ça.

"So, Mom," Chris said in a low voice, staring into my eyes. "Tell me. Are you glad to be alive? Because I need to know."

To tell the truth, it was kind of creepy. I said nothing, did nothing. I held my breath. Chris took a gulp of air and went on.

"Anna warned me that she was going to kill herself, Mom, when the cancer got so bad. She told me the only time it is permissible to kill yourself is when you won't be *able* to do it tomorrow. She said she was no big fan of pain. You know all that, don't you, Mom."

I nodded, flooded with feelings. A tear welled up in my eye.

But Chris was on a mission. He had a point and he was getting to it.

"You're stuck, Mom. You missed your chance. Even if you wanted to die, you have to live now."

I shook my head and mimed pulling out my feeding tube. Chris looked skeptical—not much of a choice.

Yes. I know.

"The point is . . . Mom . . . are you glad to be alive?"

This time I was ready. I stabbed my finger at my son, willing him to understand. But he didn't.

"Not me, Mom. Not me. I'm just holding on." And he gritted his teeth. His voice lowered to a whisper. "It's the best I can do right now."

I was so sad for my boy, I almost forgot what it was I was trying to say. I grabbed his wrist with my good hand, and held him with all my strength.

It's not a question of glad or sad, or will or won't. My son needs me. Whether he knows it or not. I'm not going anywhere.

So then I knew that you'd talked to Chris, and I was glad. I wondered, Anna, when I called to tell him you were gone and he wasn't surprised. But then, you'd been sick for so long.

You were ill for two years before we pressured you into moving in with me when you got so bad that we didn't want you living alone; we bought an electrical bed with a head and foot raise feature and put it in the living room so that you didn't have to do the stairs. You were with me for almost another year and it was a long haul for you. I don't like to think about your suffering.

There were two years between your death and my stroke. Tidying up your estate took time. I tidied mine too, while I was at it, thinking "just in case." You had eased Chris into the running of the diner shortly after your diagnosis. He had been working with the same company long enough to negotiate for more job flexibility to accommodate his responsibilities, but as a programmer analyst, there were times when he worked gruelling long hours. "Damage control," he said. Somehow he seemed to cope. I tried to bury myself in work too, like I'd always done, but somehow that drug had lost its power.

About six months after you died, Chris dropped by unexpectedly.

"Mom," he said, "you've got to move Anna's hospital bed out of the living room."

"It's my house!"

Chris crossed the room and put an arm around me, not looking in my face. He whispered in my ear.

"It's morbid, Mom. She's dead."

Facing the bed together, I went still as Chris held my shoulders tight, a restraint, and I stared straight ahead, imagining your body propped up, your face catching the afternoon sun that streamed in from the bay windows.

"I feel like she's there. I can talk to her. From the kitchen. From the bedroom if I raise my voice."

"You can still talk to her."

Chris let go, started walking to the door.

"Bought you something, Mom. C'mere."

He'd borrowed a truck and there was a chaise longue in the back.

"Anna's favourite colour," I said. A deep ocean blue. You would have loved it.

"Yup. Help me. We're going to switch these out."

Getting the chaise in was hard enough, but hospital beds are heavy and there was no way Chris and I could lift it. I ended up donating it and hiring men to take it away, but for a while the chaise and bed lay next to each other, crowding my living room. I imagined you getting up from the bed, crossing over to the lounger and reclining there. I brought your quilt out, flung it across the back of the chaise. Something to make you cozy.

Chris was right. I could still talk to you.

It doesn't feel like you've gone, even now, three years later, as I lie here in my own hospital bed. You're still here for me and I still need you.

The family said, "We don't want her to get addicted." Jesus Christ, she's ninety-eight years old and she's in agony. Get her some morphine, for God's sake. She's not going to get hooked and run out and starting doing B & Es to support her habit. Give the poor woman some peace!

I'm beginning to think that Chris isn't coming today, and to wish that I had let Fabby put me to bed after all, but in the late afternoon, well after shift change, he finally arrives. Sitting with his jaw on his fists and his elbows on his knees in the deep chair in the sunroom, Chris addresses my ankles.

"I'm pretty sure Theresa is going to leave me."

I sit like the statue of Queen Victoria on her throne, afraid to wriggle in spite of a terrible pressure spot on the fragile skin over my tailbone. More—tell me more!

Chris lifts his head from his hands and sprawls backwards in his chair.

"You know, we've been together a long time. Seventeen years. I know when she's got something cooking. I mean, the big stuff. She wants a new couch, she's planning a trip, she talks about it for weeks. Months even. But the big stuff—nothing. She just gets quieter and quieter and one day, out of the blue—bam. 'I'm going to change careers.' 'I want to buy a house.' 'I want a baby.'"

Deep sigh.

(More! Tell me more! I hold my breath, staring still and unresponsive as a fried egg on a plate.)

"And there's no baby. There's not gonna be a baby. After everything we've been through trying to make that happen this past five years, no wonder she's not happy. I've accepted it, but you know Theresa. This might be the first time in her life she isn't going to get what she wants. Or maybe the second.

"I guess I should try to talk to her about it. But you know, what's the point? Until she's got it all worked out for herself in her head, she won't talk, and once she's made up her mind, it's a statement of fact, no room for discussion."

Another sigh.

"Whatever I say, she stomps all over it. She's got all the answers."

I have to touch Chris to get him to notice me—he's talking to himself.

You—I point, desperately willing him to understand—*What do you want?*

"Me? You mean me? What about me?"

The words come out without thinking but when Chris hears himself speak, I can see the connections happening in his brain. He makes a bitter, ironic face.

"Yeah. Indeed. What *about* me? What does this have to do with me? That's the whole problem in a nutshell. The whole damn thing's got nothing to do with me. I'm just a freight car on her train."

It's not exactly what I meant, but it's pretty close, so I nod.

Do you remember Chris in love, Anna? One doesn't say much when one's college-age son comes home late or even at eleven in the morning, looking well rested and humming to himself. But this was different. He had been walking around for a week like a man with his own personal source of sunshine, bathed in an aura of giddy happiness so obvious even I couldn't fail to notice it. I was pondering on the cause when I ran into him leaving your diner. With Theresa. Hand in hand.

From the very first I didn't like her.

When I found out that you didn't either, I felt a little better.

By the time Chris brought Theresa over for a proper introduction and a home-cooked meal, I'm pretty sure some of the zing had already worn off. Or maybe it was just that we were all such a bundle of nerves.

I'd gone all out. Roast beef, potatoes, carrot pennies, and salad. Ice cream for dessert. You brought Dutch speculaas and I made amaretti.

Chris had chosen the day of our supper specifically so that Ang could come. She was still cashiering, so her schedule was erratic, but she'd stuck with the same job for two years. She was doing okay, as Chris had predicted. She seemed to thrive on making her own choices. Jordan was long gone, but Angelina had enough work that she was able to manage her rent without a roommate. I theorized that being constantly borderline broke might keep a lid on her party fund, so I didn't subsidize her, except with the groceries Chris still lifted from our pantry.

Ang came over to the house early, looking beautiful with her shiny black hair pulled back and her long legs in clean, fitted jeans. She'd given herself a manicure; her nails had been shaped and varnished with something clear that had glitter in it.

Angelina had opened the wine and was sipping on her second glass by the dining room window when she caught sight of Theresa fussing with Chris's hair on the doorstep.

"Oh, look!" she called to us in the kitchen. "Christian's got a new mummy!"

You kept washing the countertops, but I joined Angelina. Her eyes were sparkling with interest.

"I'd have thought he'd have had enough already between you and Anna, but apparently not!" she whispered in my ear.

As we peered out of the window, Angelina linked arms with me, indicating that we were on the same side.

United, for once, we turned to face Chris and Theresa as they entered the house.

Theresa had taken especial care with her appearance too. Her shoulder-length brown hair was perfectly layered and highlighted. She had a generous figure and she knew how to dress to make the most of it. She wore a tailored denim jacket over a stylish stretchy shirt that came down over her hips. A gold chain of medium weight drew the eye to her breasts. She didn't make the mistake of wearing her jeans too tight, and her makeup was discreetly tasteful. She looked completely poised, but there was nothing relaxed or warm about her.

When I saw Angelina sizing Theresa up and realized we were on the same page, I was meanly glad. Ang and I had spent too much time on opposite sides of an armed battle for me to resist the fierce attraction of a truce against a common enemy. I saw disapproval on your face, Anna, but I ignored it.

All evening I fed Ang lines and she twisted them into barbs.

"Where are your people from, Theresa?" I asked.

"I grew up in Ladysmith."

"So, did you find coming to the city a bit of culture shock, after growing up in such a small town?" asked Ang.

"No, of course not."

"Well, not *everyone* from a small town is a hick."

"You got your degree in nursing?" I asked.

"Yes, and now—"

"You must have a sweet, caretaking personality." Ang again.

"Well, I . . ."

"Nursing is an honourable profession," I said.

"Theresa just completed her master's in health administration," Chris said proudly.

"Oh wow, an administrator! You're going to need balls of steel for that job."

Theresa pursed her lips. Ang's vocabulary was a little crude for her taste.

"The Terminator," said Ang softly, without elaborating. There was an awkward pause in the conversation.

"Well," said Ang, "if you've finished your master's, you must be *quite* a bit older than our Chris here!"

"Only four years, Ang. That's nothing," said Chris.

"Well, you're hardly *matronly*," I said. "Would you like a piece of cake? It isn't as fattening as it looks."

"Not that you need to worry about that just yet," said Angelina in a tone of voice that conveyed it was already too late. "I've heard big-boned women put on weight after thirty no matter *what* they do."

Angelina nailed me too, right after the party.

"*Naturally* you wouldn't like Theresa, Mom. You're too much alike. A nineteen-fifties colour-coordinated cashmere twin set of the Bossy Controlling Woman."

She laughed. "You deserve each other."

Chris pounded down the stairs while I poured myself coffee the next morning. He stood in the entrance to the kitchen, filling it, with hands on either side of the door frame. Although as a rule he avoided conflict, he appeared to feel chivalry-bound to protect his lady.

"You should be ashamed of how you treated Theresa last night," he said, getting right to the point.

"What?"

"Oh come on. You know what you did, don't pretend."

I was embarrassed. At the time I thought we'd been fairly subtle, Angelina and I.

"Angelina is jealous, I expected that, and when she feels bad, she's mean; I warned Theresa that might happen. If Ang finds a needle, she can't resist sticking it in and that's just the way it is, but Mom, you should have known better. Theresa is a sweet girl. She doesn't play those games."

Of course I apologized profusely. But Chris was wrong, as it turned out: Theresa not only "played those games," she turned out to be a master. We got her that once, Angelina and I, by joining forces and sneaking up from behind, but she bested us soundly every time since. She knew where to put the finger to make a body squirm.

"Chris and I will make good parents," she would say sweetly. "Children from two-parent homes are so much more *stable*, don't you think?"

I wanted to tread on her toe and grind it slowly under my heel.

Within six months Theresa and Chris got an apartment and moved in together, and Theresa and I settled into a practical relationship of cold civility. Everything about Theresa was annoying, from her perfect eyebrows to the way she wiped her shoes with a soft cloth when it rained, but it's stupid to fight with your son's girlfriend. I gritted my teeth when she was around, though. She picked at Chris. I didn't expect her to iron his shirts and make his lunches, but I wish she had been more kind.

We were clearing up after a supper, some birthday or another. Chris had gone to look for something in his old room.

"Don't bring any of your old junk back to our house," Theresa told him.

"I wasn't planning on it," he replied evenly as he went upstairs.

"I really think we should remodel the den, but Chris won't give me any input. He is so passive, don't you agree?" Theresa complained in disgust. Although I'd been thinking the very same thing only moments before, I lunged to defend him.

"I'm sure whatever you want will be fine with him. I know he wants to keep you happy." There could be no mistaking the dislike in my voice.

Theresa tossed her head.

"Voicing an opinion and having an adult discussion once in a blue moon would make me happy!"

I felt my neck stiffen and my stomach knot.

"As I recall, you weren't that happy when he refused to buy that house in Oak Bay!"

"That wasn't a discussion. That was just Chris being pigheaded for no reason. It was a perfectly lovely house."

She managed to sound both petulant and self-righteous.

"Didn't the building inspection kibosh that deal?"

"Those problems could have been overcome. Chris was just being stubborn."

Thank God Chris chose that moment to reappear.

"Stubborn about what?"

"The Oak Bay cottage."

Chris's jaw tightened. "That again? By the time we fixed the roof and the foundation, we would have been well over our approved mortgage. We couldn't afford it. It's over. Let it go."

Guiltily I held up the wine bottle.

"Anyone for another glass?"

"No thank you. We needn't all be lushes."

"Well, then."

So what do we think about this, Anna, if Theresa really is planning to leave Chris?

What difference does it make what we think? We don't get a choice.

I just want him to be okay. Whatever that means.

I think the night nurse who does Heather's days off may be slightly crazy. She whispers as she bends over me.

"Every second is so important," she says. "You never know. Sometimes something happens and it stays with me for days, just a little thing, and I think 'When will I ever stop feeling this way? When will I stop thinking about this?' Julie said I'd be good at home support. That wasn't a compliment, you know. That's what those girls say when they mean someone is slow and disorganized. They mean I'm not fast enough to work here. But that's just an example. A homeless woman was trying to get money from the people lined up outside of the walk-in clinic this morning. She said her baby needed formula and a skinny street-guy followed her, yelling, 'You old bitch, you got no baby, stop bothering these people,' and they went away together, screaming at each other. I can't stop thinking about it. Even when I'm moving and doing my job. I take things too seriously. Words stick in my brain. That's why I do nights. It's quieter. There's less to go wrong. There are fewer thoughts, fewer barnacles on the whale. Did you know that whales carry thousands of pounds of barnacles? That's bound to weigh you down."

I don't want to listen, but how can I help it. I keep tracking her with my eyes as she moves from bed to bed, whispering intently to each of us in turn. Before she leaves the room, she catches me, and to my discomfort, we're locked in a stare.

She comes over to my bed, and she's whispering again.

"I know what you're thinking."

I am mesmerized. I can't blink. I can't nod. I can't even shake my head.

Finally she sighs and walks away.

I can't say I'm surprised when I hear the aides saying she's got a medical leave.

DISCONTENT

Discontent spreads through the hospital like the smell of hot new asphalt being laid in summer. It is an offensive odour, pervasive and clinging, affecting everyone.

It was a decent wage when I started ten years ago. But prices go up and our wages don't. It's really not a living wage anymore.

Yeah. Across the board, wages haven't really gone up.

I keep running out of grocery money before payday.

There's never enough moolah.

True that.

Contract negotiations. How unpleasant. I used to be so annoyed when the teachers went on strike. What to do with those kids all day, how to get my work done. I never cared how the teachers were paid, but then I never knew them the way I know the aides here.

Even this shall pass.

In the meantime, the aides grumble to the housekeepers, and they grumble back, and the bad mood spreads like a virus until everyone is miserable.

Nana's family came in today, a group of them. Now I know why they never come!

Bettina had Nana up because she planned to take her to listen to the piano player in the dining room. Molly was working on Mary. As soon as Bettina saw who was coming, she slid out of the room.

The daughter barely made it through the door before the tears started flowing.

Mama? Are you there, Mama?

Naturally Nana didn't make a sound nor a motion.

I know you're in there, Mama, can't you give me a sign?

Anna, it was something to see Molly working like a bouncer controlling a crowd. It was art. She doesn't get paid enough.

Honey, your mama would know you if she could, but she's past that stage. She's moving on to another world. This is just her body, left behind.

Molly had her arm around Nana's daughter, turning her away.

The husband was explaining.

She feels so guilty because she doesn't visit, but she just can't bear coming.

You don't have to come, honey. Your mama is past knowing now. We love her . . . We've got her. It doesn't hurt us that she's not the person that she used to be, not the way it hurts you. It's okay for you to let her go.

Molly murmured all this in her most soothing voice as she ushered the family from the room, and I had a vision of Molly in her scrubs, running a relay, receiving that baton with an outstretched hand, and racing to the finish line triumphant. Molly wins again! Inappropriately, I giggled.

Anna, I sat looking at Nana, still and motionless in her chair. Suddenly, I just didn't want to be there anymore. If I could have hopped out of my wheelchair, I'd have dragged myself across the floor, one-armed and desperate, just to get away.

Of course I can't do that. So I banged my box of tissues against my armrest like a baby in a high chair. It wasn't much noise but it worked. Bettina swooped into the room. "Francesca! What's this!"

Being Bettina, she didn't stop for an answer, but I got what I wanted. She wheeled me into the dining room, a petulant child, removed from the playground.

What a relief.

Now (as if that wasn't enough) as I sit in the sunroom beside Mary after lunch, all the day-shift girls, Molly, Bettina, Michiko and Blaire, troop in and close the big double doors.

The conversation is so heated and everyone is talking so fast that I can barely follow.

Shouldn't we move Fran and Mary?

Nah, they can stay. We're all here, let's get this done.

We need to change the groups.

That's not a heavy group!

But it's such a downer. By the end of the month, I just want to shoot myself.

Yeah, there are too many energy suckers in that group.

Joyce and Calvin should never be in the same group. They're both so negative.

And high maintenance.

And Elaine is no peach either.

But Mark is almost independent.

I like them in the same group. You get it over with.

Yeah, and didn't you book your holidays for the month you're in that group?

Hey! That had no bearing.

Bullshit.

Don't tell me bullshit.

Whatever, Blaire, we need to change the groups.

Put Mary in that group, she's an energy giver.

But her daughter is so awful.

We see her once a week, if that.

Evenings sees her more.

That's their problem, not ours.

And Janet's dying, everything's gonna change.

Janet's dying?

Yup, the doctor was in this morning.

Someone's always dying; this can't wait. We gotta fix this problem.

Because you're going into that group next!

Yeah, and I have lots of sick time, so how about I call in at six fifteen and let you work with a brand-new green casual who barely knows how to tie her own shoelaces every second day? Come on, you guys. We all agree that group is exhausting. Let's split those two kids up, they're wearing us down.

Energy giver. Energy sucker. What does that mean?

Anna, I feel that old part of my brain groaning to life like a rusty old kick-start motorcycle: the survivor part, the observer part, the schemer. The part that gets busy assessing a situation to see how it can be turned to my advantage.

Molly has a paper and pen and she is moving names around like chess pieces, trying to find a workable fit, while the ladies quack and cluck and honk out their diverse opinions in the background. If anyone *could* make the whole group happy, it would be Molly, but I'm not sure it's humanly possible.

And Mary sits next to me, stiff in her chair. I can just barely touch her; I reach over to get her attention. I smile. She smiles back.

Mary is reliable. Guaranteed, if you smile at her, she'll smile back.

The nurses are kinder, sweeter to Mary than to anyone else in this hospital.

My brain hurts. And I'm drooling. Yuck.

And furthermore, I knew Janet was under the weather but I didn't know she was dying.

The girls have been having trouble getting her to eat, but we're used to that. That's normal.

Her daughter came in and I heard her say, "If you want to die, so be it." But I didn't think anything of it, because her daughter's always saying morbid things like that.

However, Janet's curtains have been pulled for a day now, and there's been a flurry of activity by the RN. When the doctor came this morning, I heard him say something about "palliative orders," but I didn't think anything about it until the girls brought it up this afternoon.

So I guess Janet's dying.

After the girls scatter, I sit with Mary, watching the garden, watching my tree from a different angle. The pain in my bottom is worse than the pain in my heart. Thank God, here comes Molly. I'm going for a groan.

"Mmm."

"Frannie! You're in pain?"

I nod. "Mmm."

Molly looks at the time on her pager.

"I bet you just had your afternoon meds . . . maybe they haven't kicked in yet."

I scowl at her with every fibre of my being, white-knuckling the armrest of my wheelchair, trying to heave my ass to a better position.

Molly laughs.

"I know what you're thinkin'! You're thinkin' *I'll show you kicked in!* Sorry, sweetie. I'll call the RN and see if you can have another hit. In the meantime, I'll put you back to bed, okay?"

Oh my God, why is life so damn *hard*?

Then, out of the blue, while I'm literally hanging mid-air, Chris shows up.

My heart does a flip—my first thought is, *Disaster! What could be wrong, for him to be here in the middle of the week?* Anxious, I pant, and have to make a conscious effort to stop myself.

Molly quickly whips the curtains closed as she lowers me to the bed.

"Can I come in?"

"One sec, Chris. Hang on, I'll just be a . . . Okay, come on in."

"Hey, Mom."

I get a peck on the cheek.

"This is a flying visit. I just dropped by to tell you I won't be here Saturday, maybe for a couple of weeks."

I wait, expectant. Chris leans in and lowers his voice. It's personal.

"So, yeah. She left me."

I hadn't realized I was holding my breath until I let it go. I reach for his hand resting on my bed rail. It's a bit of an awkward angle, but I grip the back of his fingers and squeeze.

"It's okay, Mom. Actually. Waiting, uh, for the ax to fall, I think that was . . . worse than the blow."

Well. I guess *that* marriage was even more dead than I thought.

And you know? I think he already seems lighter.

As Chris takes a step back, he straightens just a tiny bit. "So. I'm going to be busy for a while. There are lots of details to be sorted out. I didn't want you to worry. If you don't see me, I mean."

I want to say "I appreciate that."

I want to say "Take all the time you need."

I want to say "Are-you-keeping-the-house do-you-have-a-lawyer what-about-the-diner are-you-okay-really-okay?"

All those words. All that unsolicited advice, the interference, the control. I so desperately want to tell my son . . . what?

What do I know about how to run a life, how to run *his* life, lying here prone in this bed?

I want to say "I love you."

Instead I give Chris the thumbs-up.

"Alright then. Ciao."

I wave.

He's already gone.

During the two years after she moved out, Angelina didn't come by the house very often. We fell into a pattern of meeting every couple of weeks or so. I'd call her up and ask her for coffee or buy her lunch. We never went to your diner. Sometimes we'd try new restaurants together. The pleasure of exploring turned out to be something we both enjoyed, a neutral territory where we felt more like equals and fought less.

After the dinner party for Chris and Theresa, Angelina stood me up a couple of times, which made me anxious. Over the phone, we had agreed on Thai food, and I sat at a booth where I could watch the door. Seeing her sassy self come in, my heart flipped with relief; I sipped my green tea studiously, hiding my feelings.

"What are you having? I'm craving noodles," she said.

"How's work?"

"The same. I'm not going to stay there much longer. My boy-friend says . . ."

"You've got a boyfriend?" I interrupted. "Why haven't I met him?"

"You can meet him if you promise not to grill him," she grinned.

"Does he smoke dope?"

"See, there you go, Ma! Jesus!"

I could never really relax. I felt like a little girl, trying not to step on the cracks, afraid that the wrong thing would tumble out of my mouth.

Fortuitously, the nurse comes in with some painkillers right after Chris leaves.

I sleep so deeply that I barely wake up for my evening tube-feed. I scarcely register Fabby turning me and changing me. The RN must have been generous with the good stuff.

I am awakened by the night shift coming on, two casuals, doing the first round and laying out the linen, talking quietly but distinctly. They're mid-conversation when they walk into our room.

Oh my God, I did a night shift with her on third and the next day I was pooped!

She can't lift.

Can't? Hmph! Won't, more like it. She had a way of standing back so I ended up doing all the rolling, and then she'd step up and slip in the clean pad and think she'd done her half. Then she had the gall to say, "Oh, that wasn't a bad night." My shoulders were so friggin' sore the next day!

Yeah, she did the same thing to me, and Leann was doing the RN position, so I told her about it, and Leann said, "Oh, she's not so bad; you just have to make her take some initiative." I don't have all night to stand there and wait for her to make a move, for God's sake! Chop, chop, we've got forty people to flip here!

So next time I said, "You know what, I'll do the North Wing and you do the East Wing," and she said, "What about 305?" so I said, "Yeah, of course we'll do her together first, but everyone else we can do alone."

So was it better?

From my point of view, I've gotta say it was. I don't know if she did her round, cuz I didn't check up on her, but I know mine were done right.

That's it, eh? You can only do what you can do . . .

And they're out the door.

The new day passes like fingernails on a blackboard. I have bowel care; I am sick and wan. Good God, how does pooping become a day's event? "I'm sorry, Mr. President, I can't do that, today is reserved for moving my bowels!"

Also, this room does not smell like flowers.

The girls, all three shifts, are miserable wretches.

We strike every damn time. If we strike every time, why should they listen?

But we never get ahead. Look at the RNs—they're going to get an increase!

Yeah, everyone gets an increase but us; what's with that?

I thought we got two percent.

It's cuz we're on the bottom.

Yeah, ass-wipers.

Until they have to look after Mom themselves, then it's too much.

They're not big guns if you bring them out every time.

Well, I'm going to vote to strike.

Me too.

Not me.

Essential services.

As long as they don't touch our benefits.

Somehow they manage to put all this aside when they pass behind Janet's curtain. I feel raw, hyperalert to the activity in Janet's corner. Basically, they are doing the same things that they do for me, and I anxiously interpret the sounds coming from behind the curtains. The aides turn Janet side to side every two hours and swab out her mouth with those dampened mint-flavoured green sponge-on-a-stick things. (They taste terrible, but they do get the phlegm out.) Molly puts lotion on Janet's back, combs her hair and flips her pillows. Bettina makes sure the top sheet is fresh and white, and uncharacteristically, Stella murmurs while she works, so that even in her faraway place, Janet knows what to expect.

Janet's daughter comes in the evening, sitting quietly and reading a magazine, the rustle of turning pages punctuating the moments. When she goes home, sometimes the palliative volunteers take her place, playing soft music and sipping cups of tea, keeping vigil so that Janet doesn't have to die alone . . . alone in a five-bed ward, that is.

Even though I think about death and dying constantly, I am struck for a moment by the weirdness of the truth: someday I will cease to exist.

How can something so normal be so shocking?

Like white cells surrounding and neutralizing a virus, my mind takes the idea of death and disarms it, distances it, makes it acceptable. Someday, like everyone, I too will die. My pebble will fall in the stream, making a momentary ripple before settling on the riverbed with all the other stones, and the water will pass inevitably on.

Someday. Not today.

Anna. What the hell am I telling this to *you* for!

Lily has an evening shift and I'm in her group. She must not be getting enough work, because usually she doesn't take the evenings. Evenings are not a good shift for single mothers with school-aged children. Frankly Lily looks haggard. I long to ask how she's doing, but she's moving very quickly. She almost pitches me into bed before supper, and when she comes back to give me a fresh brief before shift change, she is practically vibrating.

"Am I getting burned out?" she asks while she works, deftly detaching the tabs on the disposable diaper and tucking them under my hip so that when she turns me, I won't be lying on the side of the wet disposable and she can pull it out and throw it away. "The new girls look at those rough old hands and they tell themselves, 'I hope I have the sense to quit before I get burned out like her.' But we don't; we're too old to imagine working somewhere else, we've got bills, we need our pension and our benefits and inertia sets in and we're too scared to make a change."

Lily looks anything but old—she looks high-school young and vulnerable, and definitely not old enough to be a mother.

Lily flips me to the other side, and I land right in the middle of the clean disposable. She hooks her fingers under my hip, fishing, and the tabs pull through. Once the disposable is done up properly, Lily begins arranging the pillows—one behind my back, one between my knees, a flat one under my knees just to be certain I won't fall forward, face-plant and suffocate.

"I made Alice cry today," she confesses. "I took too long with Joyce, and it set me behind. I was trying to catch up, so I was rushing Alice. I got her on the toilet and I was undressing her as fast and I could, and she just started to cry. She said, 'It's all too much, it's all too much.' Alice never talks anymore, and that was what she had to say. It's so sad!"

Lily supports my head with her left hand and flips the pillow under my head with her right. The fabric is cool against my cheek.

"I feel so bad," she says. "I didn't go into this line of work to make little old ladies cry."

She's off to her next bed.

As it turned out, the boyfriend's name was Michael. Although he was tall and handsome, Mike turned out to be a big smelly Labrador of a guy, wagging his tail everywhere. When Ang introduced us, he gave me an affectionate hug that nearly knocked me over while Angelina laughed herself sick to see my body rigid with shock and my expression pained. "Sorry, Mrs. Jensen," he said. "Angelina said you like a good cuddle." He threw his arm around her neck in a chokehold and rubbed his knuckles on her head while she giggled hysterically. Even though I knew they were only horsing around, I had to restrain the urge to protect her with my cast-iron frying pan. I was glad when she twisted out of his grasp and kicked him hard behind his knees, buckling them.

I was trying to be discreet when I asked if Michael had any goals, but both Angelina and her new boyfriend saw right through my polite questions.

"I'm too young for big decisions like 'What are you going to do with the rest of your life?' Mrs. J. There's a whole world to explore out there. Maybe I'll start a band. You can be my lead singer, Angie baby. Would you do that for me?"

"I'd do anything for you."

"Anything?"

"Anything."

I cleared my throat. When Ang looked at me, I raised my eyebrows.

"What? Oh come on, Mom, you know I'm not a virgin, right?"

Michael snickered.

"Mom, we're going to take a road trip to Montreal," Angelina said without preamble.

"What about your job?" I cried.

"It's just a crap job, isn't that what you're always trying to rub into me? The plus side of a crap job is you get to quit, no regrets, cuz it's just a crap job."

"But what's in Montreal?"

"Well, Mike's parents for starters. C'mon, Mom, this is exciting! We're going on an adventure!"

Angelina put her arm around me playfully. I looked in her shining face, and bit my tongue.

I wake up on Thursday morning in a terrible mood. I hear Molly's voice in the hallway, but there is a new girl looking after me and I can't make myself understood. It's all I can do to stop myself from snapping at her fingers . . . . literally. With my teeth.

The morning rush is over, and it's almost lunch when Molly lopes in, talking over her shoulder, the new girl at her heels.

It's true, Frannie is particular, but it really isn't that hard to understand her once you know what she wants. She has her ways of communicating. Here, look.

"Frannie, show her 'yes.'"

To hell with that. I stab my finger at her, angry as thunder.

"Moi?" says Molly with mock surprise.

I shake my finger at the casual and stab it again at Molly.

"Oh no, Francesca, this is my day off, but I traded with Bettina so she could do some volunteer work for some church function. You should have had Blaire, remember? She does my days off. But she called in sick. This is Vega."

I make a face.

"So you gave her a hard time, eh?"

Now I'm a little bit ashamed, even though I'm pretty sure the casual is a stupid cow, so I nod.

"There. That's 'yes.' Okay, how about 'stop,' Frannie."

That's easy. I make the cop-stop, with my palm towards her face.

"What about 'no,' Frannie."

I shake my head and flatten my hand, palm down, waving it side to side over the horizon.

"Yeah. How about 'no, goddammit!'"

I smack the table with my fist and the girls laugh.

The casual says, "Yeah, I got a whole lot of that this morning, I'm sorry to say! We were both pretty upset. I had you in a right state, didn't I, Frannie?"

She looks me right in the eye, and at the very least, I have to respect her for that. I nod. No smiles now.

"Oh? What was that all about, Frannie?"

Don't get me started! It makes me mad again just thinking about it. I pick things up from my over-the-bed table and slam them down again, hard . . . my pen, my clock, my tissues, my pile of papers and photos. No, goddammit! The tears come.

"Ooh. Okay, we gotta get a label made for your table, Frannie. We're gonna make it say, 'Please don't touch or move my stuff.'"

"Where am I supposed to put the wash basin, then?"

"Use the bedside table here. Trust me, it's the better way. Happy Frannie, happy nurse. Simple math. In fact, I'll make another label that says, 'Please keep this area clear for the wash basin; do not use the over-the-bed table.'"

"Well, that would be a help, because we did not have a pleasant morning, either of us, and I didn't know what the heck she wanted. I'm sorry, Frannie. Next time I'll know better."

She reaches out to shake hands, and I don't want to, but I notice that she's smart enough to reach out with her left hand instead of her right and I don't want Molly to know that I'm the kind of person who holds a grudge, so I shake, and her grip is surprisingly firm.

Anna, this negative energy is starting to get to me, and it astounds me to think that I used to live in a constant whirlpool of chaos and never thought life could be different. But then, I never had time to notice, and these days, time is exactly what I have most of, although what's the point in noticing when there isn't a darn thing I can do about the maelstrom, I ask you? What's the point in noticing when it's all so frightful?

Shakespeare knew, and so we all learned in high school, Anna, though maybe you didn't, back in the Netherlands.

Tomorrow, and tomorrow, and tomorrow
Creeps in this petty pace from day to day,
To the last syllable of recorded time . . .

The rest of the quote is gone. I can't remember any more of it. Where are the damn words? If only I could lay my hands on them!

There's no way for me to look them up and there's no way I could possibly ask, and what are the chances someone will walk by my bed randomly quoting Shakespeare before I die? Or that it will come on TV? Even if it did, the aides would change the channel, immediately. No. Those words are gone and I can't get them back.

Damn it all to hell.

I am in despair and I sob quietly.

If the nurse hears me, she will think I'm in pain. She will come with Tylenol.

I *am* in pain. But Tylenol can't fix it.

I ran my own accounting business. And you ran the diner. You had staff, and I had the kids and we both had endless work and long days and we were busy all the time. And now I'm flattened when someone fiddles with the stuff on my table? Mother of God.

I can't call Chris. I can't call you. And I can't help Lily at all.

The very thought of my impotent anger exhausts me even more. I am heavy as sin.

I close my eyes and sleep.

I dream that I am able-bodied.

I am young, but at the same time, I am aware of what a miracle my fully functioning body is. Look! I bring both hands to my face, run my palms from the sides of my jaw down my entire side: over the front of my shoulder, down my rib cage, my extended fingers lightly touching the sides of my breasts. The heels of my hands nip into my waist and my full palms and fingers spread over my hips. Oh, how I love my body!

I have a first-day-of-vacation luxurious feeling . . . What shall I do first? Run? Stretch? Drink coffee in the sun? Make love?

But as I reach across my pillow, I begin to wake up, and I remember that I have two children to raise and no man to love or loathe at all, and I have to get up and make myself work. Here comes another day.

Angrily I sink into sleep again.

It's Friday. Molly's second day off. Or would be if she'd been off, really off, yesterday. I remember. I should have Blaire but I guess she's still sick, because I have another casual I don't even recognize.

She's young and totally green, and scared stiff of looking after Janet.

Michiko is clearly unimpressed.

I've never taken care of anyone palliative before.

No difference. Wash her. Turn her every two hours. Talk to her. Watch out for the butterfly.

Butterfly?

Yeah. She's getting a lot of meds by injection, so they insert a semi-permanent needle and tape it down against her skin, so she doesn't have to get a poke every time they need to give her a needle, get it? But you can get a needle-stick if you're not careful.

Does that happen?

Course. Accidents happen.

Then what?

Then sucks to be you.

Mich flings Janet's curtains aside and points to the wall at the head of the bed.

See this decal? That butterfly sticker tells you this lady's got a butterfly somewhere. Look for it.

She whips Janet's coverlet off, and Janet doesn't move, not even a twitch.

There you go. Right thigh. That's a butterfly. Avoid it.

Then with one quick flip, Michi brings the coverlet back over Janet's shoulder and stalks away.

But when the casual does my care, I find I like her. Her hands are shaking and she keeps dropping things and she's slow as waiting for rain in a drought, but I can tell she's trying hard.

"You've got muck in your eyes," she whispers to herself. "Is that the cloth I used for your bits?"

She makes a face. "Ew. I better not risk it." She tosses the cloth into the dirty linen and looks around for another one, but she's used them all, and she stands there hesitating like a fool at a four-way stop. I grab a tissue and swipe at my eye.

"Other one," she says. "Here. Let me." She wipes my other eye gently, gently, baby tender.

She must be all of nineteen years old. When I pat her hand, she gives me a look of profound gratitude.

There you go, Anna. I did my good deed for the day. I think you'd be proud of me. Inside, I smile.

Evenings aren't impressed either.

Oh my heavens, what was that little girl thinking?

Which little girl?

The day-shift girl. Mary is sitting on her seat-belt buckle. No wonder she was making that face.

Oh dear. She's going to have a buckle-shaped imprint on her butt!

Harvey was sitting on his scrotum.

Ooo. You've gotta give that junk a little scoop when you put on the brief, or that happens. Gives a new meaning to the expression "numb nuts."

Do they even train these new girls? Sometimes I wonder.

Ha ha, Stella, you know they do!

It was a rhetorical question. I didn't recognize the wee thing. She was brand new. She said it was her first shift. Of course it brings to mind when I was hired, right off the street, mark you. Back then there was no course or any suchlike for this job.

Well, I took the course and I remember being so scared every time they called me that I wanted to vomit. I'd wake up from dreams where I was turning people and putting in slings and trying to get the brief centred properly. There was months of that! It took me a good two years to be the nurse I am today.

You're a good wee nurse, my dear!

Well, thank you, Stella. Coming from you, that's a real compliment. But it's hard when you're new.

It is indeed. I mustn't forget that. Mary will live.

That she will.

Molly is back. Thank God. She complains to Michiko as they set out the breakfast trays and feed Mary and Nana.

Lord, mercy, who was here yesterday?

Some total newb, why?

Chaos. I can't find the socks, there are clothes everywhere. And my hair-brushes are in the kidney basins with the toothbrushes and the toothpaste. I mean, who the hell does that? Hair in your toothbrush and toothpaste in your hairbrush. God!

She was pretty green.

Green, sure, fair, but where's the common sense?

What happened to that new one you trained just back?

I saw her working at Starbucks. Said she wasn't getting the shifts and besides it's too stressful.

She had a little one, didn't she.

Yeah, five years old.

Seems like a pity.

It does, doesn't it? There's another four training shifts down the tubes. But on the other hand, if you're not getting the hours . . .

No money, no candy.

No candy for the baby. Bottom line.

Molly turns to me.

"Francesca, at morning report the RN asked us to tidy our resident rooms a bit—get rid of the mismatched socks and the old Christmas cards and such. I guess the housekeepers have been complaining about the clutter."

I'm pretty sure this isn't coincidence, given my temper tantrum with Vega the casual over the things on my table two days ago.

Molly sighs.

"I wish family would do it. Some people just seem to have no idea. They bring crap in and dump it. They think Mom's still gonna slap their hand for sneaking candy from her purse; they'd no sooner go through their mom's things than fly to the moon, and we can't throw it out because it's not ours. So it sits there, totally in the way."

I nod sympathetically.

"Anyone who can keep their own damn room tidy probably doesn't need to be here. Anyway, the point is, Fran, please go through the stuff on your over-the-bed table."

Immediately I take offence, and Molly knows it. She pulls her stern face.

"None of that, Francesca! Make it neat. When I move the table to do your care, I don't want a trail of crap flying off it."

I mime speed, shake the table for good measure and then hit it. If the nurses didn't move so bloody quickly, things wouldn't fly off!

"Yes, Fran, I know. But reality check: I'm in a hurry. There's six of you and one of me, and let me tell you sister, if Mrs. X is covered in poop from her ass to her eyeballs, it's more pressing to me than your darn stuff."

I can't yell, but I can roll my eyes and toss my head and send her *blah blah blah* right back to her. But I guess the effect is ruined if you're drooling, because Molly starts to laugh.

"I bet you were a piece of work before your stroke, weren't you, Ms. Francesca? I'm freakin' glad you weren't my boss. Be a doll. Clean up your table. Think of it this way: better you do it than someone else sneak in and do it while you're in the dining room like we're gonna deal to our hoarder down the hall. You with me, sweetie?"

Molly gives me a hug, the nerve! And flounces off.

When Molly and Michiko are putting Nana and me back to bed after lunch, Michiko shuts the door and lowers her voice.

I heard Lily came in loaded yesterday evening.

Oh no! Did they fire her?

Well, I guess she wasn't loaded, per se, or Holly would have blown the whistle on her, you know how straitlaced she is . . .

Lucky Holly was her partner then; she's soft-hearted.

That's it, but Lily'd obviously been drinking. I guess Holly told the RN Lily was sick and had to go home.

She's never done that before?

Not that I know of. And she better not do it again.

Who was the nurse?

Sue. She came down and apparently Lily didn't say much, just looked ill, and Sue said she'd replace her and sent her home. But they had to go into overtime to cover her.

I figured they were at the bottom of the list, considering who was in for Blaire yesterday. But do you think Sue knew?

Well, if she suspected, she didn't let on; you know Sue. She's not going to rock the boat unless she really has to, and there was no real harm done.

Sugar! Damn that Lily. I love her, but . . .

I know. I love her too. But she sure picks losers, and then she bleeds. Where does she find these guys?

Like flies to honey.

Sure glad I'm *not honey.*

Molly laughs.

No, you sure aren't. And in case there's any doubt, you have your clari-fication bumper sticker to set 'em straight, don't you?

I have no idea what Molly means. Catching a glimpse of my expression, Molly laughs again.

Look at Frannie, Mich—she doesn't know what I'm talking about. Show her! Oh c'mon, Frannie won't tell.

Michiko makes a "maybe not—oh okay, then" face. Molly pulls my bed curtains around the three of us, and Michi turns around and exposes her right buttock. Her skinny, muscular bum is almost covered with a fierce tattoo of a snarling tigress. A caption in flowing script reads "Hard Assed Bitch."

I make an effort to close my gaping mouth.

Molly thinks I'm hilarious.

"What do you say, Frannie? Does she make her point clear?"

They are turning to go, laughing, off to the next task. "Wait!" I think, but the only sound that comes out is a little choking note, like a duck being squeezed to death. Desperate, I bang the table.

"Hey," says Molly, "relax!"

Sure. Relax. Like dropping a carton of yogurt on the floor of the express queue at the grocery store and watching it explode. I don't know how to make myself understood. Flailing, I finally think to mime drinking shots.

"Oh. Lily. Yeah. I'm going to call her tonight. You want me to let you know how it goes?"

Sick at heart, I nod.

I ignore Molly's request to tidy up all day on principle, and besides, I have other things on my mind. But by evening I'm tired of worrying about Lily and Chris, I'm fed up with my memories and ready for anything that will take my mind off my troubles.

It's not like I don't have the time.

So after Fabby puts me back to bed, I start sorting the things on my table, and putting them in order. But you know, Anna, if I had a tray with a ledge . . . or even the lid of a box.

Without thinking it over, I ring the bell. As soon as I see Fabby's harried expression, I regret it. I start to try to explain, but within seconds, Fabby's done.

"I don't know what you want. I'm up to my . . . This obviously isn't urgent. I'll deal with it later, whatever it is."

She's gone.

The truth is, I'm afraid I'll forget what it was that I wanted to ask. Things slip away so quickly now.

Besides, how was I supposed to know she was so busy?

Cow.

It's hard not to take it personally.

I don't feel like sorting anymore.

I'm having trouble with my bottom—it's very sore. Molly says I'm breaking down. The skin is getting fragile. So she puts me back to bed right after lunch, and I try again to organize my things.

I'm able to make Molly understand and she brings me the lid from a box of photocopy paper. It's a little deeper than what I had in mind, but at least my things won't fall out. I start sorting through my papers. Grudgingly I have to admit Molly was right: there's a lot of useless crap here. There are letters from the hospital management—they look like satisfaction surveys; how do they expect me to fill those out? There are advertisements and promotions and a few personal cards that Chris brought in for me, there are photos and darn, are those bills? Surely not; Chris looks after my mail, but even so this paper garbage multiplies, apparently.

There are far, far too many words for me to read in my present condition. I can read . . . that is, I can pick out words, but for some reason my eyes won't scan a line, and by the time I've come to the end of a sentence, I've forgotten the meaning of the beginning. I want to scream with frustration and humiliation.

A memory pops into my mind, of sitting at the kitchen table with Angelina. See Jane run.

"Try it again," I urged her. "Sound it out, from the beginning!" Thinking *how can you not do this?*

Angelina tore the book from my hands, ripping the pages as I held on too tightly. I feel the anger now, both hers and mine, in my bones—a superpower emanating energy, a cartoon character steaming from the ears.

I leave the papers scattered on my bed and pull the quilt over my face.

When the girls come to put away the personal laundry, I can hear them talking about me.

Molly, look at this.

Oh dear.

Did you ask her to clean up her stuff?

I did. My mistake. I guess it's too much for her.

Y'think?

Okay, okay, I'm on it.

"Oh, sweetie! Such tragedy!"

Molly pries the quilt from my fist, peels it from my face.

Personally, I don't think it's very funny.

"C'mon. I'll help you. Are you ready to let me help you?"

Molly starts picking up papers.

"Okay. You're not going to be switching internet providers, so . . . I'm going to take everything that's obviously useless and chuck it, alright?"

I nod.

"You put the photos in a pile, Frannie, cuz I don't know which of those is valuable, and I'll make a pile of anything that looks important and we'll get Chris to go through it later. We'll be done in five minutes, honey. It's really not so bad."

For her, maybe.

I stack the photos in a pile without looking at them. And Molly organizes my stuff like I'm a kindergartener with a hot temper and a bruised heart.

Just when I get used to the rhythm of Janet's palliative care, she dies.

Heather and Julie, the night aides who prefer to work together, are methodically making their way around our room, starting in Mary's corner and ending in Janet's. They've been a team such a long time that they have their job down to a science. Heather flicks on the dim night-lights while Julie presses the buttons that raise Mary's bed to working level. While Heather folds down the blankets, Julie is already pulling out the pillows from behind Mary's back and between her knees. Heather is the right hand and Julie is the left, and they are fast and quiet. It's an aberration when they move out of sync, and when that happens, they laugh about it and complain about being all thumbs.

The privacy curtains give the room a claustrophobic, stuffy feeling and the noise of pulling them wakes us all up, so the girls don't use them at night, but Janet's curtains have been closed ever since she started dying. Julie is bringing my blanket back up around my neck when Heather disappears behind Janet's curtain.

Oh. I think she's gone. Call the nurse, will you?

Okay. Shall we wash her up now?

No, you go on your break.

Okay, but wait for me. We'll do it together.

I am truly awake now, all drowsiness faded. A few moments later, Leann, the night RN comes in to confirm that Janet is dead.

Are you going to phone the daughter? Heather asks.

Already did. She's on her way.

Too bad she couldn't have been here.

Pretty hard when you work full-time.

This has been going on, what, five days now?

About that.

So did you call the funeral home?

No. I'll wait to see how much time the daughter needs.

Well, give us some time to wash her up, okay? I don't want to be doing it on last round. Joyce is going to start ringing about five . . .

I know. Can you do it before the daughter gets here?

Yeah, I guess.

Where's Julie?

She went on her break.

At this point that Julie walks in with the palliative kit.

Hey!

I'll take my break later. Let's get this done.

Heather smiles and I feel that current of energy pass between her and Julie, the connection between members of a good team.

It makes no sense to me that they're washing Janet. Evenings just washed her a few hours ago. But I guess that's just what you do. Now I know.

I can hear Heather and Julie murmuring to each other and, of all things, to Janet.

Goodbye, sweetie.

Safe journey, Janet. You be good now.

Oh, she'll be good. She's in the land of all good now.

Mmm.

Should we put the ID tape on her now?

It looks so institutional.

But I might not remember to do it before the funeral home comes.

We'll remember. One of us will.

Heather empties the basin of water in the sink with a splash.

Frannie's wide awake.

You okay, Frannie?

I nod.

She's alright.

I don't know whether Julie is talking about me or about Janet, but either works.

Take your full break, Julie. I don't want to see you.

You call me if you need me.

Someone's coming.

Yeah, good timing.

It's odd to think this is the last time I'll hear the click clack of Janet's daughter's heels coming down the hallway. They echo especially in the stillness of the night. Janet's daughter always has great shoes.

I don't know why I'm here. I can't do anything.

Lots of people need to come. Some don't. It's whatever you need to do. Take as much time as you want. Can I get you a cup of tea or something?

No. I'm okay.

The daughter bursts into tears.

She's fully dressed in day clothes, and her makeup is perfect. But she falls into Heather's ample arms and cries like a baby just the same. Heather holds her, humming condolences softly, making a duet with Janet's daughter's sobs.

The problem with crying is that you have to stop sometime.

Sorry about that.

Your mama just died. I think you're entitled. I'm going to get that cup of tea now.

Yeah. Thanks.

Janet's daughter slips behind the curtain and the room is suddenly so still that I can hear Alice's snoring, delicate as a southern lady's summer fan. Mary the Energy Giver is smiling slightly even in her sleep. Nana doesn't move.

Well, Angelina. Here is a scene you will never have to go through.

My pillow is wet with tears.

It's Monday morning. A new week. Janet's bed is empty, neatly made and starkly institutional with the hospital bedspread and two plain pillows.

I slept beside her, but I hardly knew her. What did I know about her? She had a daughter with fabulous shoes. Brilliant. Well, it's not like she could see me, and it's not like I could make polite conversation, was it, now?

No. I really didn't care.

I listen to Bettina, washing Nana in her plodding way, without enthusiasm, behind the curtains. Bettina is not my favourite. She's very vanilla pudding. She does her work quietly, the minimum, without much enthusiasm. Yet I can hear her behind the curtains, murmuring to Nana, who cannot answer or respond at all.

Lily says Nana isn't easy. She is hard to turn, dead weight, stiff and contracted. And yet the girls treat her like a favourite pet, caring for her with a warmth and gentleness that defies my logic. It seems to me the purest form of love, to look after someone so totally passive, from whom you can expect no benefit, praise or gain. I would never do it.

On the other hand, Nana will never bite you back. She will never report you, or fight you, or gossip about you, or make snide comments that make you feel small. I heard Michiko tell Molly that she finds it restful looking after her, an oasis in the war zone, and then I imagine it is a cowardly kind of love, caring for someone who does not have the power to hurt you.

Anna, why did you love me? Why did you open your heart to me and to my family? Yes, I did your books for you, but you gave your heart. Secretly, inside, I considered myself the superior one, and you *knew* that I thought that. You saw me for what I was: a grown woman with the mentality of a grade two girl who thinks she's smarter because she gets a hundred percent on her spelling quiz, who thinks she's better because her clothes are nicer. And all the while, you were wiser, kinder, more generous, more giving—in every meaningful way a better person. And yet you loved me.

In my mind I hear your voice answering me. "Oh, stop whinnying like a horse. You are making a self-pity party out of nothing. How can I get along without you? I will have to *pay* someone to do my taxes! I won't like *that*." You knew how to stand up to me; you knew how to laugh at me, how to make me laugh at myself.

Oh, my dear friend. I miss you so much.

My God. It's only Monday morning. There is still so much of this damned day to get through. When will I feel better?

Interestingly (and I can't think why this is so) it turns out that the general mood has shifted since Janet's death, and, susceptible, I float in the current.

Michiko is singing old Cole Porter songs while she dresses Mary.

"I've got you . . . under my skin!" Actually, what I really want is a clean undershirt to put over your skin. God, where are all your undershirts? Okay, we're just going to put this one on again cuz it's not really dirty, and even if it was, it wouldn't kill you.

No.

No, we don't worry too much about these things, do we? But suppose it did kill you, Mary! Just think of the headlines: "Resident Killed by Dirty Undershirt." "We don't know what happened," says the director of care. "It is certainly not our policy to dress people in dirty undershirts. A full investigation is underway." The obituary: "In lieu of flowers, donations of laundry detergent will be accepted!"

Mary the Energy Giver is smiling, because Michiko is smiling, and that's what Mary does, but I am laughing myself sick over here.

Michiko keeps playing it up, and I know it's for me.

The next headline: "Care Aide Gets Two Years for Laundry Abuse." "I don't know what made me do it," sobs the repentant aide. "May God forgive me for my sins!"

In fact, snot is pouring down my nose, and I am now snorting. It's disgusting, but I don't care. Molly walks into the room, just as Michi says, *Oh my God, who put this away?*

She holds out the cardigan that she took from Mary's closet, her nose wrinkled in disgust.

Is that . . . gravy?

Don't ask! Just wash it!

I shouldn't laugh, but I do. It's better than wine . . . all my sorrows are floating away.

Look at you, Mary, you are just so sweet! You are just so nice! How come you're so nice?

My mama taught me.

It has become unusual for Mary to make full sentences; Molly and Michiko are thrilled. They lean in, attentive and fully present.

Oh my God. She taught you? How did she teach you? What did she say?

She said, "Mary, be nice."

Oh my God. If only it was that easy! Imagine. "Mr. President, be nice." "Ayatollah, be nice." Oh my God! I effin wish!

I howl. Molly laughs too.

Be nice. Don't lie. Change your socks. It should be so easy.

I was seeing a client, and Angelina went home with a school friend, so I told Chris to go to the diner after swimming practice. It wasn't uncommon, was it, Anna? Really Chris spent more time with you than he did with me. More quality time, certainly. The diner was almost empty. Through the window, I saw you sitting across from Chris in *our* booth—he looked like an angel, with his blond hair just starting to darken and his serious blue eyes. I noticed the delicacy of his fingers holding the pencil over his math notebook, and the way his used napkin was neatly folded, not crumpled, on his empty plate. My heart skipped with love, crunched in on itself, a painful hiccup.

You were relaxed, half smiling, leaning forward with your chin propped up on the palm of your hand.

The doorbell startled you both; Chris began gathering up his belongings and you rose to greet me. I hadn't eaten, and I was distracted by the smell of ketchup and fresh french fries and malt vinegar; my mouth watered. As I held the door open, Chris turned to you with open arms and you enveloped him in a wide embrace. Your cheek rested on his golden head. My son.

As he buckled himself into the front seat of the Toyota, I asked, "What were you and Auntie Anna talking about, Chris?"

"Nothing."

But then a moment later: "Mom, is it always right to tell the truth?"

"Tell the truth? Have you done something wrong?"

Sighs. "No Mom, it's an *ethical* question. Are there times when it's right to tell a lie?"

"Don't lie, son. You tell the truth or I'll smack you!" I reached across the gearshift stick to punch him in the thigh.

When he looked at me, I had the feeling that he wasn't listening to what I said, but assessing who I was, like taking a reading on a temporal thermometer.

I focused on the road.

"What are we going to have for supper?" I said.

It's a beautiful evening. Quiet.

I think I've finally got the energy to sort my pictures. There aren't many. Just a few snapshots that Chris must have chosen for me.

Here are my parents, on their wedding day. Henry Smith and Enrica Lagudi. My goodness, Mama looks like Angelina! She looks fierce, even in her bridal whites. We certainly didn't specialize in soft, yielding princess-types in our family; no wonder, looking at Mama.

I don't know this person. Who the hell is this? She looks familiar but I can't place her. Should I know her? It's upsetting not to remember.

Here are the kids, when they were little, looking like a pair of angels. I can't remember why I had them all dressed up, but I do recall Angelina throwing a fistful of muck at Chris and then wiping her filthy hands on her dress. It's a miracle they stayed clean long enough to take a picture.

Lord, I was mad. I came close to killing them both then and there.

There you are, Anna, in the diner. Chris took this picture. Even if I didn't remember him buying the camera and bringing it proudly to the diner, I'd know he took this picture because I recognize the expression on your face, that look of pure love you reserved exclusively for him. Look at you, Anna. You are the very picture of pride.

Chris was the picture-taker in the family. I wish I had more pictures of him, but he was always the one behind the camera. Here is a fuzzy picture of our backyard. Why did Chris give me this? I try to slip this picture to the bottom of the pile, but it feels thick. Oh, there's a second picture, accidentally stuck to the back. It takes me a moment, one-handed, to detach it. It's a photo of someone's thumb and the hind quarters of a cat. Now I remember yelling at Angelina from the patio, "Leave your brother's camera alone!" while Chris, halfway across the yard, advanced softly, slowly, like a fireman talking a jumper off a ledge, hands outstretched. In the end she threw the camera, but Chris was quick enough to catch it.

The cat was long gone.

Here is my favourite set of pictures. In the first, Angelina, about eight years old, is nestled against me, her cheek on the front of my shoulder, my chin against her glossy hair. Chris snuck in and took it while we were absorbed in the movie we were watching on TV. He took a second shot quickly; it's a little out of focus. The instant Angelina caught sight of her brother, she made a goofy face. There I am, reacting slower, looking stunned. "Look at me, Mom, I look cool! I look like a monkey," crowed Angelina when she saw the picture. "And you look like I just stole all your bananas!"

Here is a picture of Theresa and Chris.

I can't stand her face.

I'm struck with a wonderful idea. I set the picture aside; there is no point in ringing the bell and risking the wrath of that little witch

Fabby for something like this. I wait patiently until I see her, and then I ask for scissors. Scissors are easy to mime.

Fabby comes back quickly, but when I hold out my hand for the scissors, she hesitates.

"Are you sure you can handle these?"

I want to smack the table, but there's no point getting snotty when she's just done me a favour. I motion *give, give* but when the scissors are in my hand, I see what she means. I can't hold the picture and cut too. I set the scissors down, trace a line between Theresa and Chris with my finger and pick up the scissors again.

"How about you hold the picture and I'll cut?"

So I plant my thumb and finger right on Theresa's face, and hold up the picture, and Fabby cuts for me.

"Look at this, Stella."

Stella peers over Fabby's shoulder.

I take the picture of Chris and put it carefully away.

"What do you want me to do with this half?"

I take great pleasure in crumpling Theresa's face. I press it into Fabby's palm.

"Huh. Wouldn't want to get on *your* bad side, Francesca!"

I guess it *is* kind of funny. So we all laugh.

There is a picture of Angelina's goodbye supper somewhere.

I tried to talk Mike and Ang into putting their trip off until the spring, but having decided to go, they were eager to be off. They wanted to stop in Banff and ski for a couple of weeks on their way across the country. When I inquired, Ang assured me they had the budget for that. I watched with surprise how practical and responsible she was preparing for her trip. She gave notice at work and on her apartment, and donated most of her things. What she decided to keep, she boxed, labelled and stored in the basement at my house. Mike had been living out of a backpack with friends until he began spending all this time with Angelina, so he didn't have a lot of stuff. The plan was for them to spend the night at my place after Ang handed in her keys and collected her damage deposit. They would catch the first ferry the following day.

I wanted to make an event of it, so I invited Chris and Theresa to come for supper too.

Mike and Ang had been cleaning her apartment and packing the car all day. They were both dirty and tired, and also a little glassy-eyed.

"Are you *high*?" Theresa said in disgust.

"Are *you* high?" Angelina countered, making eye contact with Mike, who immediately said, "*Are* you high?" and then he and Angelina giggled.

Chris stiffened visibly. I hurried to bring the lasagna to the table.

While everyone mopped their plates with the garlic bread, Ang and Michael chattered about their plans. Chris chimed in from time to time.

"You drove out here, didn't you, Mike?"

"Hell yeah, I did! It was amazing!"

"I've always wanted to drive across Canada," he said. "That's an epic journey."

I was still trying to show Chris that I was sorry about being rude to Theresa, so I asked her if she'd ever travelled across Canada.

"My parents drove the whole family from Vancouver to Toronto one summer," she said. "It was an incredible waste of time. Everyone talks about how big and flat the prairies are, but the Canadian Shield is just as boring in its way."

"You're going to take the Trans-Canada, aren't you?" I asked, anxiously changing the subject. "There may be cherry blossoms in Victoria in February, but for the rest of the country, it's still winter!"

"Don't you worry, Mrs. J., you don't have to school me on winter! I'm from Montreal, remember?"

"Aren't you going to stay for dessert?" I asked as Theresa rose to go.

"Chris and I have other plans for tonight."

If they had plans, it was clear Chris didn't know about them. He folded his napkin deliberately, took his time pushing back his chair.

Angelina got up and walked them to the door with me.

"Hey, aren't you going to hug me goodbye?"

Theresa was already down the steps, but Chris stood in the doorway with his coat on. He turned and opened his arms.

"Take care, little sister."

"*You* take care, brother. That cat might eat you up!"

YOU DON'T KNOW HOW GOOD YOU HAVE IT

Excitement! We're going to have an admission! Family—I assume it's family—are here with boxes . . . too many boxes. They'll never get all that stuff put away.

The RN is doing the honours with the daughter, a fussy little dumpling with curling hair.

This is your mom's bed.

We brought her favourite duvet; can she use that instead of the hospital one?

Oh sure, but we strongly suggest that everything you leave here be machine washable. Your mom is incontinent, correct?

Well, yes.

Please ensure that all your mom's personal belongings, especially clothes, are marked. Here are her labels. There's an iron in the laundry room if you want to use it. Make sure it's good and hot or the labels won't stick. This is your mom's locker and this is her side table. Please try to keep the over-the-bed table free for trays and wash basins and so on . . . you don't want wash water splashing all over your mom's things.

I can see the woman glancing at my bed table, and the RN follows her eyes.

Francesca is tube-fed. We do try to maintain some flexibility with regard to individual needs.

How diplomatic!

Mom has an easy chair . . . we were hoping . . .

The RN is shaking her head.

We can revisit that when your mom gets her own room. But as you can see, we are really limited as to space, and the more crowded the room is, the more hazard to both your mom and our staff.

Do you have any idea how long that will be? Before Mom gets her own room?

I'm sorry; I can't even guess.

I chuckle quietly to myself. What a nice way to say somebody has to die first. "Excuse me—how long do you think that old girl in the single room is going to last? She's looking a little peaked, wouldn't you say?"

Meanwhile the nurse is talking on.

If you plan on bringing your mom a TV, you'll need a table, preferably on wheels. Also, your mom has hearing issues, doesn't she? You might consider getting a set of headphones. The nurse makes a gesture encompassing the full scope of the room.

Oh, Mom is very considerate. She has a caretaker personality. She was a nurse too. She worked at the Jubilee for years before going into community care.

Did she? That's lovely. I hope she'll be very happy here.

Again I find myself snickering quietly. This should be interesting. I've heard the girls say, "Old nurses make the worst patients—they're fussy, impatient, bossy and opinionated. They know just how every little thing should be done."

Just like care aides, actually.

Just like me, for that matter.

Molly comes to wash me behind closed curtains, so I miss the arrival of our new roommate. Molly isn't interested.

"It's not our turn," she whispers. "Everyone else gets a go at her first!" I think of my own admission and shiver involuntarily, remembering the many people I met that day and how overwhelming it seemed at the time.

Molly slaps a bracing cloth across my back. I can feel her tension. "I finally got ahold of Lily."

I stiffen; the new admission rockets off my radar. Instinctively I strain to see Molly's face, and she pushes hard against my hip. "Don't roll back," she says, "I'm not finished yet."

I smack the side rail.

"I think she's doing okay."

Molly is choosing her words carefully, speaking very quietly. "She told me she took some time off to get herself together. Which she can do, because she's casual. But financially . . . there's no money. She can't stay off work long. Come back, Frannie, I'm ready for you now."

Flopping, my momentum helps Molly bring my weak side over. She says nothing while she washes my hip and pulls the sling through. When I'm flat on my back again, she looks me full in the face.

"She needs a break. She needs support, and mentoring, and a whole lot of unconditional love. But I ain't Jesus, Frannie. I can't save her."

I feel my eyes welling up. Molly hands me a tissue as she swings my table in place so I can reach my things.

"I'll get you up when the gridlock clears, okay, Fran? Just wait a bit for me, darlin'. I'm going to my next. You've got the bell for emergencies. I'm keeping the curtains closed."

Molly leans in.

"I told her you'd be saying a little prayer for her. So you better get on that."

There's no humour in Molly's eyes.

A prayer? That's quite an assignment for an agnostic like myself, but I'll do my best.

I hear the daughter telling the new lady that's she's going to take her for a tour, and a moment later Molly blows in, gets me up, and parks me in the dining room.

When Fabby puts me to bed after shift change, our room is empty except for Nana, but Fabby draws the curtains around my bed anyway.

"Stella's going to put your new neighbour to bed," she says. I'm dying of curiosity—after all, we'll be living together—and I bang on my table and point at the curtain.

"No, Frannie. Keep it closed. Just for a bit. Give the new lady some privacy."

I would like to pout, but Fabby keeps talking.

"You haven't met her yet?"

No.

"She's quite with it. I think."

I make the *more* sign with my hand.

"Um. They call her Tiny."

Tiny? What kind of a name is that? I shake my head.

"I'm not sure what to say, Frannie. Best you see for yourself soon enough."

Fabby smiles kindly. "I know you won't tattle, but it's unprofessional for me to gossip about the other residents."

Now I'm smirking.

"Yes. I know. We do it all the time. But we shouldn't. It isn't right."

Maybe so. But I'm straining to catch every word when Stella brings Tiny into the room.

Are you pretty tired?

I really am, dear. It's been a long day.

The OT says you can stand at the bar. Would you like to sit on the commode before I put you to bed?

Well, I don't know, dear. I think maybe I'd better.

Alright then.

I can hear Stella wheeling Tiny into the bathroom.

Both hands on the bar. Bring your feet back from the wall.

I don't want to slip.

Yes. But when your toes are against the wall, you're water skiing. Step back so that you can stand upright, and your legs and back will support you, not your arms. Here. I'm putting my foot between your toe and the wall. You won't slip. Now try again.

I'm . . . can't you help me?

You have to be able to do this by yourself. I'll give you a little boost on the tailbone but that's it. One more try. Or we'll have to use the lift.

Not the lift!

Very well, then. I want to see how strong you are. One, two, three. That's it.

I hear Stella's rapid scuffle; I know the drill. Pants off, wheelchair whipped away, commode whipped under . . . and plunk, bottom down.

Well, my lady. We won't be doing that again.

That was hard!

Tiny is almost wailing.

Indeed it was. According to the OT you're fine on days, but not when you're tired by my eye, and I'll not let you be a danger to me. You were a nurse. You know what's what. I'll not injure myself.

I would never hurt you!

And I shall never let you, love.

Stella marches into our room and begins the bedtime preparations. She likes to pull the covers back her own certain way—one side folded back neatly, then the other, forming a point that Stella then pulls back, making a fan fold of the blankets at the end of the bed. It looks like origami. While she's working, she calls to Tiny, still seated on the commode in the bathroom.

Do you wear your own nightgown?

Yes, my daughter just bought me a new one.

Sweet Lord. Days will never get this off her, Stella mutters to herself. She stomps off, impatience radiating like a halo.

Hello? Hello? I think I'm done now.

Forgetting I can't tell Tiny that Stella's gone, I squawk like a seagull. It's no help at all.

Tiny begins to sob. When I bang my table, she cries louder. Then I remember my bell and ring it just as Stella comes back. She pokes her head around my curtain, eyebrows raised, and I jerk my thumb towards the bathroom. Stella stabs the off switch, tsks at me and disappears. I hear footsteps, and then Stella calls into the hallway.

Fabby? I've got that bell.

Then she swoops into the bathroom.

What's all this, my lady? I've brought you a hot blanket and a gown.

I thought you'd left me here!

No, my dear, that would never be. Now you'll kindly wash your face, and I'll attend to your back.

Thank you, dear. You couldn't find my nightgown?

I found one, Tiny, but it's too small. This one is nice and warm. Lift your arms, please.

Do you have to put that on me?

Stella must be putting the sling around her.

Of course. How else am I to get you into the bed?

I'll walk there, of course.

Indeed.

I always put myself to bed.

We'd best use the lift tonight. You're very tired.

No! I'll get into bed myself!

Leaving her on the commode, Stella wheels Tiny into the room, next to her bed.

So, put yourself on the bed, my lady.

I'm holding my breath, but nothing is happening. Tiny starts to cry again.

That will be all. It's time for bed.

No! I don't want that! I don't like it.

One, two, three.

Tiny shrieks as Stella uses the lift to move her from the commode to the bed.

That was awful! Don't you ever do that again!

Now a quick wash down below.

Stop! Didn't you hear me?

I heard you. You'll wash just the same.

Leave me alone! What are you doing?

I'm attaching the brief, my lady, so you don't pee all over the bed, for then I'll have to come in and change you, and you'll not like that.

I don't pee the bed. Don't be so ridiculous!

And I've a nice hot blanket for you. There you be.

Tiny's answer sounds like a moan.

Here's your bell, my lady. Call me if you need me.

I hear Fabby's footsteps, and then her voice.

How'd it go? I heard the yelling.

I did but a lick and a promise down below, and she's resistive with the lift, but she'll do.

Did she pee on the commode?

No. Exercise in futility.

Oh no. Is she another Gladys?

Don't you be worrying, Fabby. It's too soon to judge. She'll settle. Most of them do. Have you finished?

I think I'm done, except for last round. But oh, I'm so tired!

Stella is suddenly all attentive concern.

You go rest then. I'll finish up here. I don't want to see you for twenty minutes.

When will this end! It's so exhausting.

In about twenty years, love. Unless you decide to have more.

Oh my God, no way. This is it. I'm never doing this again.

Stella laughs.

You'll forget all about it when you've got that babe in your arms, you'll see.

Fabby is pregnant! Oh my goodness!

Tiny rings several times in the night. The conversation is always the same.

You rang?

Yes, dear, I need to use the little girls' room.

I'll give you the bedpan.

The bedpan! I can't pee lying down.

I can roll your head up a bit.

Why can't I go to the little girls' room?

Honey, we don't have enough staff on nights to use the lift. It's not safe. Only people who are independently mobile get up at night.

I don't need a lift. I can get myself up!

Sweetie, I don't think so.

What are you talking about? I always get myself up!

Julie lets her try to show her that she can't, and that makes her cry. Julie rolls her over, puts her on the bedpan and tells her to ring when she's done. Which she does, but, forgetting she's on the bedpan, she asks to use the little girls' room again. Finally she manages to wake Alice up, and then Julie is really angry.

The night shift staff carry phones because there are so few of them and they could be anywhere, so Julie calls the nurse.

Do we have anything for our new lady? She won't settle.

—

Not even an order for Ativan? Does she have a sleeping pill?

—

I can't get a spec. She's not peeing in the pan at all, she's wet when I get there. I guess she could have a UTI but days will have to spec her, and that's not going to help me here and now.

—

Okay, fine then. Can you throw some milk in the microwave for me? And Alice is up.

—

Yeah, fantastic. I'm really enjoying myself, thanks.

Julie gives the phone a vicious poke with her middle finger as Tiny pipes up again.

Dear? I need to use the little girls' room.

Tiny, you've really got to get some sleep here. What do you usually do when you have trouble sleeping?

Well, usually I get up and I do a little tidying . . .

So glad I asked. I'm just going to roll you up a bit here. How about a nice cup of hot milk? Sometimes that's just the ticket when you can't sleep.

Well, that sounds . . .

Oh, Heather. Thank God. Let's do up this room, cuz I swear, if we ever get them settled, I'm not coming in here again!

I hear the dream team changing Nana's brief and positioning her on her flip side, then moving to Mary before it's my turn.

"Poor Frannie," Heather whispers. "Did you get any sleep at all?"

A wave of exhaustion rolls over me—I hadn't realized how tense I had been feeling.

"Don't worry, Frannie, my love. She'll settle. They always do eventually."

"One way or another."

"Now, Julie. Try to let it wash over you, Francesca. Do you want an Ativan? We can't give *her* any, but I know you've got orders for one if you want it."

What I really want is a cold glass of Chardonnay and a cigarette . . . but what the heck, Ativan will have to do. I nod.

Dear? I need to use the little girls' room.

Jules, grab a hot blanket, would you? Get one for Alice too.

Heather slips between the curtain and the wall.

Now, Tiny. How's your hot milk?

Oh! It's just delicious.

Well, you drink that while it's nice and warm. I see you've got a teddy bear here, that's a comfort.

Oh! Give him to me.

Here you go, lovey. Here's a hot blanket. Isn't that nice and cozy? You go to sleep now, Tiny. It'll be morning before you know it.

They leave the door open a crack on the way out. I can hear the dirty linen cart being rolled down the hall. Alice is muttering to herself, but at least she's in bed for the moment, and Nana is almost snoring. Tiny's plastic cup upsets on the table with a little clatter.

"Oh dear!" she says to herself, and starts to snivel, but after a few moments, her whimpering stops, and the whole room is rich with sonorous breathing.

When the pill nurse comes in silently, I open my mouth and she pops the Ativan under my tongue. She puts a finger to her lips and slides away; my consciousness is right behind her.

I wake up groggy and I can feel how wet my brief is. I must have slept through breakfast. Molly is getting Tiny up, and from what I can hear, she's a different person on days. She knows where she is, she knows it's September and she accepts the lift without making a peep. I hear Molly praising her for how well she stands at the bar, and when Molly washes her bits, Tiny thanks her and tells her how nice it is to be clean. Then she sits at her bedside table in her wheel-chair, brushing her own teeth and fussing with her curly hair. She looks just like an older, miniature version of her daughter.

Michiko comes in to do Mary's care while Molly is making Tiny's bed.

Ugh. She's so wet.

Yeah, I expect they're all wet. Heather told me they did their last round at three, because they didn't want to risk coming in here and waking everyone up. Apparently they had a hell of a time getting this one settled.

Which one, dear?

You, Tiny. You had a hard time getting to sleep last night.

Nonsense! I slept right through the night. I always do.

We're going to have to be careful what we say in this room now. Hearing issues, my ass.

What did you say, dear?

We were commenting on how good your hearing is.

Yes, I'm very lucky that way. I should have a headband . . .
Is this it?
No, a blue one . . . could it be in the drawer?
This one?
Oh. Well. Maybe that will do. Could you put Teddy at the head of the bed? In the middle? That's right, he looks quite nice there.
Okay, Tiny, is there anything else?
Could I have a glass of water? It's very dry . . .
There you go.
May I have my notebook and pen?
Okay, Tiny. Are you set? I'm going to start my next person . . .
Ohh. Yes, dear. What should I do now?
Well, Tiny, you can write in your book, or you can wheel yourself down to the sunroom and watch the squirrels in the trees, or there's a TV in the dining room, if you like TV.
Will you come with me?
No, honey, I have work to do here.
I could help you.
I'm sorry, lovey, this is something I need to do by myself.
I used to be a nurse, you know.
I did *know that. Now, lovey, I'm going to push you down to the sunroom and you can sit there for a bit.*
Molly is back in a minute.
Her care is easy, I guess we can be grateful for that.
But she's going to be a huge energy suck. I bet she sundowns big time.
Oh Lord. I can just imagine.
Well, you must be glad it's almost group change.
Do you think that group shuffle we did helped?
It's hard to say . . . no matter how you cut it, 105 is a piece of work.
Harrumph. As if I didn't know who *that* is!
You said it yourself: mentally, you just have to put on your protective all-weather gear when you go in that room.
I said it and I meant it. She's hard on me. I don't think I've ever worked with a more vindictive, manipulative woman.

But you know, thank God she refuses to leave that room of hers . . . she'd infect the whole floor.

There is that. You know, I do better with dementia. Those cognizant types, I find they can be very demanding.

Frannie's pretty with it. If she could talk, we'd have to be just as careful what we say in front of her as we are with 105.

Yup, that's true.

Molly smiles at me.

But Frannie would never be like that. She's kinder.

"Aren't you Frannie? You've got a loving heart, don't you?"

Do I? Is that what she sees in me? No one has ever suggested such a thing to me before. All I can do is stare. Shoot, my eyes are filling with tears.

"Aw, Frannie! Did I make you sad? Haven't you ever had a compliment before? You're my darling . . . you're my chocolate chip cookie!"

Now, that's a bit much; I bang the side rail with my fist.

Not a chocolate chip cookie. That's way too plebian for our Francesca. More like a nice fat slice of that German Bundt cake you make. Loaded with almonds and apricots and brandy. Mmm.

Are you hungry, Michiko? You sound hungry.

I'm starving to death. I forgot my smoothie.

I've got a granola bar in my bag if you want it.

Ooo . . . is it vegan?

Now, really, would I offer it to you if it wasn't vegan, darling?

Once again you save my life.

No worries, take it.

Dear? What should I do now?

It's Tiny, wheeling herself back into the room.

Take her too. Let's see if she can fold face cloths or something.

Yeah, or maybe she can sort the button box. C'mon, Tiny. I'm going to try to find a job for you.

Well, that would be lovely. I used to be a nurse, you know!

A loving heart?

Is that what they think of me? That would be a first!

What I remember is yelling.

Standing, fists clenched, mirroring my mother, both of us shrieking. Papa, hat in one hand, the other on the doorknob, slinking away.

In my office clothes at the kitchen sink, dumping coffee dregs while yelling at Karl stumbling in from God knows where, his face emptied and boarded up like a failed business.

Yelling at teachers, specialists, the checkout counter girl, the gas jockey.

Yelling at Angelina, and her yelling back, just as I had done with my own mother, both of us hoarse. Caustic bile in our throats.

And yelling at Christian for leaving crumbs on the table. He was fourteen.

"Mom, you're tired," he said. "When you're tired, you yell. Go rest."

He had a natural ability to step outside of himself, to think of someone else. Who taught him that—was it you, Anna? Because it sure the heck wasn't me.

I reached for him, choking on shame and fatigue and anger and pride, but he ducked under my arm, eluding my embrace, and disappeared into his own space.

A loving heart? I don't think so.

Good thing I have lots of tissues. All my yelling has dissolved into tears.

It is afternoon, the lull just before coffee break, and the girls are hanging out in the sunroom while Bettina, a fervent Christian, tells Molly and Blaire an involved story about her congregation. Molly is clipping and filing my nails. Bettina is very gentle, but she makes me uneasy. She has an unnerving habit of praying under her breath while she works.

When Chris walks in, I notice that Molly is quick to turn the conversation.

Chris! It's nice to see you back!

Yeah, it's been a while. Sorry.

Hey, no "sorry" required. It's your life. We knew you were going through some stress.

Chris raises his eyebrows. Molly reaches over for the half photograph that was once Chris and Theresa and holds it up.

"Mom! You did that?"

His tone is accusatory but also amused, and a half-witted grin spreads over my face.

Chris turns to Molly.

She never did like my wife. My ex-wife.

Oh well. It happens.

I'm embarrassed but it's wonderful to see Chris smile.

Your mother doesn't have many visitors.

No. Her best friend passed away just a couple of years before the stroke, and she has no extended family.

That must have been hard as a single mom. She was a single mom, right?

Yeah. She worked like a dog, all the time.

Your Mom's social history in her chart says that you had a sister?

Yeah. She's . . . uh . . . she's dead.

Chris and I exchange a look. We are conspirators. Angelina may or may not be dead, but we're checking each other to make sure that we're both okay with this simpler version of the truth.

My eyes are welling and Chris puts his hand on my shoulder protectively.

She's in a better place, says Bettina piously, and without censoring myself, I instinctively jerk my hand from Molly's and smack the table with it, making everyone jump with surprise, and my stomach clenches from indignation and grief.

You've got to understand, says Chris. *For my mother, there was no better place for my sister than right by her side, no matter what.*

Now the tears come from surprise. Is that what Chris believes?

"Francesca, I'm sorry that I mentioned your daughter," apologizes Molly formally. "Even the thought of losing one of my children is unbearable, and I can't imagine what you must have gone through. Please forgive me."

Even though Molly means well, her words do nothing to soothe the ache in my throat that comes from trying to control my tears, and Molly is astute enough to realize that is what I'm fighting to do. She changes the topic abruptly.

I've been meaning to mention this anyway, Chris. If you think your mom needs more social interaction than you can provide, why not hook her up with a companion? I mean, I don't know how finances stand ...

Quickly: *Finances are fine. I'm just not sure how Mom would take to a stranger. She never was that outgoing.*

My sister is looking for clients, Blaire pipes up.

Ugh. Anything to do with Blaire! I'm making a face. I know I'm making a face.

You could give it a try. Introduce them, see how it goes.

Maybe.

Huh. Maybe *not!* Does this mean I'll see less of Chris? I don't like this idea at all.

Molly finishes my nails and she and Bettina and Blaire drift away. Chris has a lot to tell me. He and Theresa have put their house on the market. Theresa is living there until it sells, and he is living at my house with the other renters, who are friends of his.

I knew about the renters, but I'd forgotten. They're using my furniture, which is significantly more bearable to think about than imagining it all sitting on the front lawn with a big yard sale sign and a couple of balloons.

"I suppose I could sell the house for you, Mom, if that's what you want. I'm pretty sure I could get more income from investing your money than you're getting for rent after taxes."

I shake my head.

"On the other hand, you're not pressed for money. You're okay. I really don't want to, um, slam that door shut. On our past. We've ..."

Chris cleared his throat.

"We've had that phone number as long as I can remember. I've got the land line forwarded to my cell phone. Angelina knows that number. I mean, she knew that number."

It makes me angry that he's put me in the position of having to shake my head at him, to remind him what we both know.

"I know. She's not coming back. But it's the only number left that she'd know."

I grimace and Chris ignores me.

"Anyway, it works out, and I'm grateful to be able to stay there now. Daisy and Abdul are good roomies. Actually, it's really nice to have them there. They're good people."

I'm pleased with the arrangements; a house shouldn't be standing empty.

Angelina disappeared fifteen years ago somewhere between Revelstoke and Montreal.

She called Chris collect one day from Revelstoke, sounding excited and happy as she told him they were thinking of heading down to Radium Hot Springs, one of many picturesque side trips Michael made on his way out west from Montreal last summer. Listening over Chris's shoulder, I hissed out my worries. "Tell her to be careful, the Rogers Pass is dicey to drive, tell her to check the weather report, tell her . . ."

"She can hear you, Mom."

"Let me talk to her," Ang laughed, and Chris passed the receiver to me. "Hi, Mom! Are you being a good girl?"

"Angelina." Now that I had her on the phone, my throat was dry.

"Have you been yelling at Chris enough? You better practise on him while I'm gone, I don't want you to lose your scolding skills!"

"Don't you sass me!"

"That's the ticket! That's the mom I know and love!"

"Do you think she was high?" I asked Chris when she hung up.

We waited a long time for the next call, and when it didn't come, I got angrier and angrier, cursing her for her negligence, cursing her for not knowing or caring that we needed to know she was okay. Still there was no news, and finally Chris went to all of Ang's friends, asking if they'd heard from her, and when that drew a blank, it occurred to us that we didn't really know Mike very well. Chris starting tracking down his friends, but they didn't have much information to give. Mike hadn't been in Victoria for very long. He was a great guy, lots of fun. Yes, he smoked dope; no, no hard drugs as far as they knew. Yes, they knew he was planning a trip with Ang, lucky guy, she was a hot babe. No, they hadn't heard from him.

Finally we called the police. When they started looking for Michael and Angelina, we learned that the last time Michael used his credit card was when he gassed up in Revelstoke, the same day Angelina called us.

By this time we had connected with Mike's frantic parents in Montreal. Mike had told them about his new girlfriend but not that he was planning to bring her for a visit. They guessed it was meant to be a surprise. That would be just like Mike: he was a bit impulsive, a big kid, really, a lovable clown, the kind of guy who'd try anything once. When Chris asked if that included drugs, there was a hesitation that stopped my heart.

"This isn't a judgment," said Chris. "I just need to know."

"Does Angelina do drugs?" Mike's father countered.

"She smokes pot," said Chris, "but that's it, as far as I know."

"Mike too," said his father. "As far as I know."

It wasn't reassuring to any of us.

Against Theresa's bitter protests, Chris used his spring break to fly to Montreal, where he talked to Mike's family and school friends.

"I told you so," said Theresa, when Chris came home empty-handed.

There were posters asking for information all over Victoria; only cranks responded.

The police found no evidence of foul play. No one remembered seeing them in Revelstoke or Radium. Their vehicle was never found.

I had trouble sleeping because of the imaginary films that played on repeat in my head. Did they decide to take a scenic route, a back road? I saw a dark night, deep powdery snow, Angelina and Mike hitting a patch of black ice, skidding into a canyon in a remote part of the mountains, fresh snow quietly, fatefully covering their tracks. That was the best-case scenario. What if they picked up a hitch-hiker? Would that be "just like Mike" too, guileless and oblivious to danger? He wouldn't be thinking of Angelina's protection! Or what if Mike was not the harmless buffoon his friends and family made him out to be? Why hadn't he told his family that he was bringing Ang to meet them? That seemed suspicious too. Maybe he intended to head down to South America all along. What if he was involved in trafficking? Could Ang be hunched in some alley with a needle in her vein? Or prostituting herself? At first Chris tried to reassure me: these were wild, crazy thoughts, but at night they crowded in, intruders making themselves at home in my head, and I got up and paced myself to exhaustion with the lights on and the television blaring. As time went on, and the police had nothing new to tell us, my despair deepened. It was harder and harder to hold on to hope, and eventually Chris and I realized, even if we did get news, whatever it was, it couldn't be good.

She didn't run away. She would have called. She'd have called Chris if she did something so stupid that she was too ashamed to call me. Eventually, she'd have called.

That's how we know. Unless she has amnesia and is living as someone else somewhere, she must be dead.

As it turns out, Tiny hates water.

Michiko's shoes are squelching, and Molly points.

You're leaving tracks. You showered Tiny? How?

I bullied her.

Oh no.

Yup. She said, "I don't need your help, I've been washing myself for ninety years, I'm a clean person, blah blah blah," and I said, "Stop making such a fuss and acting like a big baby, and you'd better hold this cloth over your eyes if you don't want soap in them."

Oh my.

Uh-huh. She backed right down. Last week, I tried to sugar her up and it took me forty-five minutes and I never did get her hair washed, so this week I thought, "Fuck it," and I tried a tougher approach and it worked. And you know what? I'm glad. She reeks.

She does have a strong odour.

Yup. Some people are just like that, and she'd be one of 'em. She probably did wash every day when she was herself. She'd probably be appalled to know she stinks. I did her old self a favour.

And you'll do it again next week.

Oh my God, I sure the hell hope not. I'm praying for a miracle.

Did they ever get her an order for Ativan?

Yes they did, but it doesn't seem to touch her. Maybe it would help me. It's not my idea of a good time, bullying people. Even if she is acting like a stubborn bag.

The sky is blue and my heart leaps up to meet the sun as Molly adjusts me in my chair.

"I want you looking especially nice today, y'know why?"

It's Wednesday—surely Chris isn't coming today? What else would I care about? I shrug my shoulders.

"Today you're going to meet your companion, remember? Blaire's sister?"

Immediately I scowl. Blaire is so . . . disengaged from her work. It's true that she's capable, I give her that, but I feel like a slab of brisket in her hands. I just know she wants to be here approximately as much as I do—which is to say, needs must. This is much better than the General Hospital or some dirty overcrowded facility, but it's a far cry from standing at my kitchen window with a nice glass of white wine looking out over the tulips in my own backyard.

Molly reads my face.

"I've never met her," she says, "but I can tell you this: my sister and I, we're from different planets, you know what I mean? You have a sister?"

I shake my head.

"But you had two kids. Were they alike?"

Is the wind like the sun?

"There

 go. Give Nadine a chance."

Molly puts a string of fake pearls around my neck and reaches into her pocket.

"Look what I found in my stuff when I was cleaning out!"

It's a watch bracelet, set in an elasticized weave of beads so that Molly can easily stretch it over my wrist . . . lovely.

"I won it in a Christmas draw and it's sure the heck not my style. Don't know why I didn't get rid of it ages ago, musta been waiting for you, eh, Fran?"

I know darn well Molly has chosen this moment to butter me up deliberately. She wants me to get along with Blaire's sister.

Molly laughs at my expression.

"I know one thing, Miss Francesca. I'm pretty confident that if you don't like her, you'll find a way to get rid of her! I have faith in that. You'll find a way to get the job done!"

I don't quite know how to take that comment.

"Oh, it's not an insult," Molly says lightly. "I have a mighty admiration for strong-minded women. Planning on becoming one myself! You look great. Gotta fly."

Something's not right with this girl, I can tell you that right away, and I'm not just being a fashion snob. The impression goes beyond the frayed jeans and the pastel windbreaker over the red T-shirt. It even goes beyond the nicotine-stained fingers and the smell of smoke. It's her eyes.

Oh. She's stoned. And I'm pretty sure it's not recreational because Molly would never send me off with someone who was high. Now I get it. I know why Molly really wanted this to work out. Blaire's sister has mental health issues, Blaire's looking out for her, and Molly can't resist playing Mama Fix-It for a work-sister.

It would be funny if I wasn't being bundled into one of those all-weather ponchos and sent out with Nadine for an excursion.

Molly is waiting for us expectantly when we get back.

"How'd it go?"

"Fine," says Nadine. It's the first time I've heard her speak.

Molly looks impatient. Apparently she meant me, not Nadine. Good. So I top Nadine on Molly's mothering priority list. I'm pleased about that. But my bottom is incredibly sore from the inevitable bump I got every time the wheelchair hit a crack in the sidewalk. Nadine took me directly to the churchyard, where I sat with the sun in my eyes while she smoked on the bench until it was time to come home. It was a long, long hour, thank you, Molly, for the watch.

Nadine has swiftly disappeared without saying goodbye. I point to my bed, but Molly is already swinging the lift towards me.

"How are you really?"

She sounds worried. I shrug my shoulders. I'm too tired to care. Molly lowers me to the bed, rolls me on my side and folds the sling under. She's got a fresh brief. She detaches the tabs on the old one and squeals, "Oh my God, look at your butt!"

Molly dearest, I think reasonably, how can I possibly look at my butt?

"It's open. Get the nurse," she snaps to whoever is behind me. I look out the window at my tree, with my bottom exposed, feeling oh-so-grateful to be back in bed with Molly at the helm. Behind me the girls have collected and are clucking like hens.

Forget the companion, what she needs is a Roho.

What the heck is a Roho, I wonder?

She's got money, she can do both. (I think that's Blaire.)

Does OT have a spare? We could trial one.

I think the finances are there.

I'm gonna slap a dressing on that, just let me grab my . . .

D'you think a Roho will help?

Can't hurt.

Looks like hamburger.

Poor Frannie.

Molly comes around to my side of the bed to talk to my face.

"Poor Frannie, you've got a problem with your fanny! Don't worry, sweetie, the LPN is gonna put a dressing on that, and we'll see if we can get you a special chair cushion that'll keep this from happening again."

I can't help it. A tear comes rolling down my cheek. But Molly says nothing, just wipes it away with the fat thigh of her thumb.

"It's okay, sugar. You'll see. It'll be okay."

Sometimes I wish I could just black out.

By the way, Michi, how are you finding our little lady next door?

You're talking about Jane? Oh my God. She's having so much pain during a.m. care. Her arms are so stiff. And her hands are getting really contracted too.

Yeah, the doctor reduced her painkiller. Husband complained that she's too sedated.

Well, she ain't now. She's in pain. She's calling out "Hey! Hey!" Today she said "Damn you!" as clear as a bell while I was washing her up.

Oh no.

Uh-huh. I feel so mean. I said, "Look, I'm only trying to help you. I'm sorry that it hurts."

Why are we fighting her into those pants? Can't she wear dresses?

Family says she's never worn a dress in her life. They lie: I saw her wedding picture.

Ha ha. I seriously don't think that counts!

Dear God, when it's my turn, please give me the good stuff.

Amen.

The crazy night nurse is back. It isn't until I see her that I remember she's been missing.

Julie refuses to work with her. They've split the workload and they're both doing half alone.

It's a rare night: both Tiny and Alice are sleeping. I'm terrified that the nurse's rambling will wake them up—I hold my breath while she talks to me.

"Did you ever read the story about the toys that came alive in the nursery when the children went to sleep at night?" she whispers. "Sometimes I think that's what happens here."

She gestures with her hand, including all five beds in her circumference.

"When I close the door, Nana slips her feet over the side of the bed and walks over here to talk to you, and Alice and Mary practise a waltz. Some nights you all play poker, and Tiny cheats, so she always wins. And she gossips about us, the way the nurses gossip about you. *Apparently . . .* she says, and *that's what I heard, anyway.*"

I shrug my shoulders. Why would anyone stay here, if we could walk away. But Cuckoo-girl is ready with the answer.

"You see," she says, earnestly, "you're all volunteers who've sacrificed your lives to create an opportunity for us to be of service.

So you're the real heroes. But even heroes get bored. Even heroes want to dance."

Maybe that's why Cuckoo-girl is so very gentle. When she rolls me on my side, the room never spins and her hands are quick and sure removing my disposable, sliding the new one under my hip in exactly the right place so that the centre line runs up my spine. She arranges the pillows perfectly every time, and her hands smell like lavender. Every breath releases a whiff of fennel, sweet, the kind you get coated in candy, pink-yellow-orange in Indian restaurants. I imagine her sitting at the nursing station in between bells and rounds, keeping awake chewing the licoricey seeds one by one, thinking her next crazy thought. In the shadowy darkness, her presence is surreal, but I am comfortable now, the pillows plumped and cool beneath my cheek, and I fall asleep quickly, dreaming Alice-in-Wonderland-type dreams until Molly's bracing gale drags me into stark reality at seven o'clock, the start of a new day.

Lately I've been so tired I can barely think straight. Nights haven't been able to solve Tiny's nighttime behaviour, and it's affecting Alice, who had been sleeping pretty well before Tiny started waking us all up. Julie and Heather are afraid Alice is going to fall.

Tiny's restless on day shift too, making many demands for attention. We've had group change, which means Michiko and Bettina are working with Tiny . . . a net loss of patience where Tiny's endless list of requests is concerned.

Tell me what you want right now, Michiko scolds Tiny. *I'm not going to interrupt giving care to someone else to go look for your stuff.*

Well . . .

Look, Tiny. You see that lady in the corner? She's just as important to me as you are, but she can't ask for help, so I haven't touched her yet, and yet I've answered your bell four times. You're taking more than your share!

I'm not that kind of person!

Yes, you are.

But Tiny is far past that kind of logic, and even if Michiko wheels her into the sunroom, it takes Tiny less than three minutes to bring herself back.

Dear? I used to be a nurse.

Michiko rips the tabs off my brief in her impatience. *Damn it to hell!* she mutters, hurrying to get me up.

Lily is back at work but not in this wing. I saw her in the dining room, but I have no idea how she's doing. There doesn't appear to have been any fallout from her misadventure, and I'm conscious of the irony in my gratitude. If I'd been the boss, my younger self would have fired her stat, no questions asked, as I used to counsel you to do with your diner staff. You cut your workers a lot more slack than I ever would have. Reflecting on that doesn't make me feel very good. Fabby is on vacation, so I don't know if she is still tired and nauseous. I'm spending a lot of time in bed, being turned side to side, waiting for my bottom to heal.

The aides have stopped talking contract negotiations, so I guess there's that to be grateful for.

I've made up my mind about one thing: if they try to send me out with that stupid companion Nadine, I'm going to refuse to go. I'll kick. I'll hit. They can't make me.

But they can. That's why my pulse races every time I think about it.

So far it hasn't come up.

I feel like I'm treading water waiting for a rescue, and I'm getting very tired.

It's time for something good to happen.

Did you shower Tiny again?

No, I didn't. There's no mistaking the way she's saying "no," so if anyone hassles me, I'm going with her right to refuse care.

But she smells.

Yes. Yes, she does. That's not going to kill anyone. Look, I'm sorry, but I'm just not going to do it. It's bordering on abuse. Hers and mine! After last week's performance, I went home and had two stiff shots of Scotch straight out of the bottle and then I cried. Screw that! I didn't become a vegan to prevent cruelty to animals just to turn around and torture little old ladies. I ain't doing it!

Don't mess with Michiko!

That's right. Damn straight.

Michiko cried? Over a resident?

Huh. So much for "Hard Assed Bitch."

Seriously, you guys don't know how good you have it here. This is paradise.

Funny kind of paradise, if you ask me!

No, seriously. At my other job, we have minimum eight residents to your six, and if someone calls in sick, which we obviously do because we're exhausted, they don't replace. We're expected to pick up, so we usually end up doing eleven or twelve.

But you must have some mobile residents.

No! It's all end stage dementia, plus we've got MS and rheumatoid arthritis, you name it. No mobility, that's my point, and we've got some heavy, heavy people, and no overhead lifts, all Maxi. Try moving those XL people with the Maxi lift, you feel that in your back, believe me, sister. And we serve both breakfast and lunch as well as doing the feeding, and baths and bowel care and getting people ready for activities and outings. By three o'clock, you're done in. Plus evenings have double the workload you have here.

How in God's name do you give good care?

Well, we don't.

What do you cut? Teeth?

I try to get to them at least every second day. Try. It isn't always possible.

Jesus.

Uh-huh.

My God. I don't think I'd want to be a care aide if I had to work that way. I mean, where's the job satisfaction?

Why do you think I'm here? I'm just trying to build up enough hours here that I don't have to ever go back there!

They'll miss you—you're a good nurse.

Huh. Good nurses fry up nice and brown too!

I shudder. I've escaped horrors I didn't even know existed. I think of the loving care I'm given and the respect I'm almost always treated with, and I'm thankful for the pure, sweet luck that brought me here.

I didn't die; I'm grateful for that too.

But this is nothing like my old life, that's for sure.

So I guess I could say it's a funny kind of paradise for me too.

SHIKATA GA NAI

Happy October. It's group change day.

Camille, one of the ladies who had a single room, died suddenly in the night, and in spite of the fact that a death in extended care should come as a surprise to no one, we are all aflutter here.

In the sunroom after lunch the girls discuss the death. Everyone has a story.

Heather said when she went in there to change her, she noticed her feet were mottling, but she decided to change her anyway, and when she put her on her side, she gave one last breath and that was that.

God, it's so weird when that happens!

You've had someone die on you like that?

Yeah, when I first started. I was doing a night shift.

Nights always seem to get the deaths.

Well, they're doin' fifty people, we've got six or seven each.

Yeah, that's true.

I've been doing this ten years now and I've done lots of palliative care, but I've never seen someone actually die.

But that's good, right, because that means we've been able to get the family in and they're the ones at the bedside.

Yeah, that's good.

The ideal.

But sometimes there just isn't time to call. Poor Camille.

You know her family was just in.

No way!

Yup. Coupla weeks ago. From California.

D'you think that's what gave her the courage to die?

Ha, you believe that?

The girls all talk at once.

Who knows? Maybe!

Oh come on, Camille was long gone, she'd been here what, ten years? There weren't many tools left in that shed!

You don't know for sure!

You'd be surprised.

Michiko's strong voice dominates:

I've seen people go after the family gives them permission to go on ahead. Lots of times.

And I've seen people hang on long after they shoulda let go, too.

Later, when Molly and Michiko are putting me back to bed, Molly asks Mich if she really believes that someone could die just because a family member gave them permission.

Yeah, I do. I really do. I know it doesn't always happen that way, but when it comes down to it, what do we really know? Weird shit happens. Like, my mom came to me in a dream after she died.

She did?

Oh yeah. I had this big trip planned, I had some gigs with my band in England and I was superstoked. Mom and Dad wanted me to go; you know, they thought it would be good for me. But Mom was really sick with her cancer and I struggled with the decision, right?

Of course.

But I went and while I was over there, I had this dream. It totally freaked me out so I called home right away. Dad picked up and I said, "How's Mom?" and he said, "She's fine," and I said, "So can I talk to her?" He said,

"Well, she's too sick to talk right now," and I said, *"Don't bullshit me, she's dead, isn't she?"*

And she was?

Yeah, she was. They didn't want to tell me. They didn't want to spoil my trip. I said, "Well, if Mom didn't want me to know she shouldn't have brought Grandpa to visit me last night, all full of joy and saying shit like 'All times are equal now,' and how she'd see me very soon."

Molly can't suppress a laugh.

Oh my God, Mich, what did your dad say?

He said, "Shikata ga nai. She must have changed her mind."

He speaks Japanese? What does that mean?

No, he doesn't speak much. He's second generation. But "shikata ga nai" is one of Obasan's expressions. It kinda means "it can't be helped." Poor Dad. A wacky wife and three headstrong daughters—he loves us like crazy, but life is just one long string of shikata ga nai as far as he's concerned.

Oh my God.

Yup. He said, "Well, baby girl, that's not on me. You know your mom. She does what she wants."

The apple didn't fall far from the tree, did it?

Mmm. No.

I wonder if Michiko misses her mom. Maybe they weren't close. But they were close enough that Michiko dreamt about her. So maybe they were.

I have never once dreamt about my mother, but I had terrible nightmares for about two years after Angelina went missing. Sometimes I dreamt that I was compelled to train Angelina to jump through a hoop of fire or sit up and beg like a circus dog. She was afraid of the fire, too restless to sit and too proud to beg, and our struggles left me frustrated and repentent for trying to make her perform those silly tasks in the first place. In another vein, there was a horrible recurring nightmare where Angelina would come towards me, smiling, and I'd open my arms filled with love and relief, but at the last moment, she'd place both hands on my shoulders and shove, sending me reeling backwards. But mostly I dreamt of car crashes and snow, and I'd wake up sweating or even screaming.

Towards the end of the second year, I had a different kind of dream. Angelina and I were sitting in the backyard in the sun, browning ourselves and sipping iced coffee. I looked over and saw that she had cut her glorious hair into a chin-length bob.

I could have cried.

"What have you done to your hair!"

"I cut off the split ends."

"All the way to your *chin?*"

"I like it like that."

There was that saucy grin, challenging me, *daring me,* to put up my dukes and get into it, and I bit my tongue.

She saw me holding back and laughed.

"It's just hair, Ma. Next time you see me, it will be long again," she said.

She put her hand on the nape of my neck, squeezing a little bit. "If anyone tries to hurt you," she said, "I'll pull their fingernails out."

I turned to her in surprise, but she was gone, and so was the sun, and the coffee and the backyard, and I was lying in my bed, wanting more, yearning for something elusive. But I wasn't sweating and I didn't weep.

For a long time after that, I went to bed hoping that I'd fall asleep and find myself in my backyard, sipping iced coffee with Angelina. But although the nightmares stopped, I never had that dream again.

Alice and Tiny hate each other.

It always starts with Alice getting into Tiny's stuff, and Tiny goes off like an angry bird. The more she quacks, the firmer Alice gets, and you can see what kind of a parent she must have been.

Today they got into a confrontation over a glittery piece of jewellery on Tiny's bedside table. Like a magpie, Alice grabbed for it, and Tiny held it out of reach, scolding away. Finally Alice leaned over with her long, bony arms and slapped Tiny's face.

There was a moment of perfect silence before Tiny started to scream and swing back. I rang the bell, but footsteps were already pounding down the hall, drawn by Tiny's shrieks. Alice, with the advantage in mobility, was well out of reach, and in frustration, Tiny winged her box of Kleenex at her. In a brilliant moment of comic timing, the box hit Alice square in the forehead at the very moment the nursing staff came bursting through the door.

"Take Frannie out of here," said the RN, and that's when I realized I was banging my fist on the arm of my chair like an unruly spectator at a hockey game. If I'd had something to throw, I'd have nailed Tiny back, but Michiko grabbed my chair and I missed the rest of the party.

"Wow, *you're* worked up!" said Michiko.

Of course I am! Who does she think she is, Miss Snooty Pants Ex-nurse, coming in here and stirring up the pot.

Anna, last night was the worst yet. The evening girls couldn't get Tiny to settle down. She went up and down the hallway complaining loudly that she had been told she was responsible and where was the doctor? She wouldn't be distracted by music or old TV shows, warm blankets didn't comfort her and she flung her hot milk across the room. None of the usual tricks worked. She didn't wind down; instead she got more and more agitated. Stella told Fabby she didn't want to leave her up for night shift, so they put her to bed together, and when they used the lift, Tiny literally screamed.

She was still ranting when night shift came on. Alice kept getting out of bed, making her rounds, scolding us all; Mary's eyes were deer-in-the-headlights open wide and for once she wasn't smiling.

Finally Alice got into Tiny's things, and that brought the house down. Even Mary was yelling, "Be quiet!" Heather and Julie stormed into the room, talking loudly to each other over Tiny's shrill litany of threats.

This is ridiculous, Heather!

I need the little girls' room!

Should we get her up?

I'm going to call my MP. I have friends in high places, you know!

And put her where?

Don't think you can get away with treating me like this! I used to be a nurse!

Oh my God! I've got an idea! Let's use Camille's room!

You wicked, evil people! God will punish you!

Yes. Let's!

Don't use that thing on me!

Not the lift.

Huh?

I can't believe anyone could be so inhumane! This is supposed to be a five-star hotel! Don't think I won't report you to the consulate!

The whole bed, Jules. Let's move the whole darn bed.

Oh my God. You're brilliant.

Heather kicked the brakes off Tiny's bed, ignoring her wails and shrieks. Together she and Julie pushed her out of our room.

The room was like a tuning fork, vibrating. Checking on us all, Alice drifted over and stroked the velvet on my quilt before turning briefly to Nana.

Ow, said Mary as Alice sat on her. Alice shifted, muttering, picking at the bedspread.

Please get off, said Mary kindly.

Alice wandered away.

We could still hear Tiny's protests down the hall and behind closed doors.

A few minutes later, Julie and Heather returned, bringing Alice with them.

"Warm blankets for everyone!" Heather announced. They tucked Alice into bed, changed the rest of us, wrapped us up, and when they left, they shut the door.

I think Alice was trying to sing a lullaby but the words were gone and the tune was shaky too. Trying to make it out, I finally fell asleep.

Tiny doesn't come back, but the next day they bring in an empty bed, and in the afternoon, the aides and the housekeeper swoop in and remove all of Tiny's things. They wheel the crowded over-the-bed table down the hall and return with an empty, clean one. They take Tiny's clothes on their hangers in big bundles in their arms. All her shoes. All her pictures. The calendar. The clock.

I'm next to an empty bed again.

It would be kind of sinister except that, from time to time, Tiny forgets that this isn't her room anymore and she wheels herself in, looks about in a bewildered way and wheels herself out again. "Oh dear!"

I've discovered I can hiss. So I do.

Oh wow, they moved Tiny?

> *Yeah, she went into the single when Camille died.*
>
> *You're kidding! Why'd they move her?*
>
> *She's totally disruptive on nights. She kept waking Alice up.*
>
> *She's a pill on days too.*
>
> *Nooo. She's sweet!*
>
> *She's manipulative.*
>
> *Yeah, well. Aren't we all?*
>
> *I've got no patience for that.*
>
> *Do you think she acted out on purpose? To get a better room faster?*
>
> *Oh no. She's not that with it. She's still ringing all night long.*
>
> *She's sundowning on evenings big time, too.*

She's fine on days.

What planet are you on? She's so demanding!

She presents well, but . . .

Big *but. And family is totally clueless. They think she's all there.*

Uh-huh. Denial, big time.

But why reward that behaviour with a single?

Because she was such a crisis. Nobody was getting any sleep. She totally bumped everybody on the list for a single. She went straight to the top.

Yeah, that's not fair. I mean, why not move Alice? She's been here longer.

I think they thought Alice is pretty settled, why shake the pot, since family are satisfied.

Frannie's been here longer than Alice . . .

"Frannie, wouldn't you like your own room?"

You know, if you'd asked me before Tiny moved out, I would probably have said yes just to get away from her.

But if I was in a single, I'd miss all this.

I smile and make an inclusive circle with my finger.

Oh my God, she likes to watch!

She likes the drama.

"Are we entertaining, Frannie? Better than TV?"

"Look at her grinning! You don't miss a trick, do you?"

The casual, whose name I don't know, reaches over and gives me a smacking kiss on the cheek. I push her away.

"Frannie doesn't like physical affection, do you, Fran?" says Molly.

Chris gives her an air kiss, like this: mwaa, mwaa.

That's Michiko.

Aw, everybody needs to be touched. It's the human condition!

I wouldn't say that. Everyone is different.

Michiko starts to sing:

"I don't want my arms around you, no, not much.

"I don't bless the day I found you, no, not much . . ."

Y'know, Michiko, I'm looking forward to your first CD. I think you should call it "Michi the Tattooed Vegan Warrior Sings the Oldies!"

Everyone laughs.

Lily is working with me the afternoon that the OT sets me up with a deluxe cushion for my fragile coccyx. (*That took long enough!* Molly whispers to Lily.) She shows me how my weight is distributed over the little rubber fingers of air. This is the Roho they'd been speaking of.

Not only that, we are trialling a new wheelchair, a "tilt-in-space." It's much sleeker than my old wheelchair, less of a bucket and more of a vehicle. The OT shows me how the handles on the push bar can be squeezed to recline or right the chair.

"Give it a try," Molly enthuses, using the lift to hoist me into it.

The OT takes out her tool kit and makes adjustments to the head and foot rests. Molly tips me and then brings me back up-right, showing me my options.

"Look at you in your new Cadillac!" she says. "This wheelchair is way easier to manoeuvre than your other one, you'll see. Lily, why don't you take her for a spin? It's quiet here, I've got you covered."

Lily grabs the quilt you made me from the bed and quickly wraps it around me. Let's go!

I am riding smoooth! I feel like . . . I'm riding in a convertible. Out, into the cold clear fall afternoon.

As Lily wheels me along, I have a vivid memory: I am a passenger in a sports car, and the colours are as bright as fireworks—aquamarine sky, ocean blue as glass with whitecaps like toothpaste, but my lover's teeth are whiter and his skin is a delicious, edible brown. I have a yolk yellow sundress on and, flashing on my finger, a bright diamond ring.

I want to call out to that girl in the car, "Hold on to this moment." But my words are lost in the wind.

Then I remember that my words are lost, period. I notice that Lily is talking to me.

". . . and oh, Francesca, I thought maybe this was the one. He's kind and he's thoughtful and he's handsome too. We had a lovely date. We went for supper and then for a long walk, and we talked and it was so easy. I thought we were really connecting. He came back to my place and . . . you know. But afterwards, we were lying in bed together, and just as I was thinking, 'I like this guy, I *really* like this guy,' he tells me he's not interested in any kind of traditional relationship. That's too *restrictive* for him, he wants to experience life to the fullest, including his sexuality—he wants an *open* relationship."

Lily stops my wheelchair abruptly, slams on my brakes. We've walked up to the church, where the trees are in their full riotous fall colours. Lily perches herself on a short stone retaining wall.

"Well, at least I have the sense not to go down that road, Frannie. I know what 'open relationship' means. It means he can have sex with whoever he wants and if he doesn't have anything more *exciting* going on, he'll have sex with me, and every girl I see, I get to think, 'What about her? Is she the one he's going to have next?' Fuck that! Fuck that!"

Lily swearing! My goodness!

The angry tears start filling her eyes. "I'm trying so hard! Why can't I find someone who'll love me? I'm not asking for the moon. Just a decent, faithful man, who'll be there for me and Sierra. Is that too much to ask?"

For once, perhaps, it's just as well that I can't talk. I couldn't even begin to know what to say. I reach out. With a hiccuping sob, she allows me to take her hand in mine. I will her to know how special she is, and how much I love her.

She says, "Oh, Francesca! I know I have good skills. When it comes to work, I have excellent intuition and empathy. I'm grateful for those gifts and I try to use them consciously for the highest good, to help my residents and make their lives better. So why can't I do that for myself. Why can't I tell what a man is thinking? Why can't I find one who's thinking *good* thoughts? Every time this happens, it just rips me apart. You know, for a smart girl, I sure am dumb!" And she weeps.

I want so badly to tell her to take care of herself. I point to my ear and then to my heart. But she doesn't get it.

"I *do* listen to my heart. I *do*! Look where it gets me! My heart tells me I want someone to love me. I want it so much!"

Now I'm mad. I jab my finger at her. You, Lily! You love yourself!

Lily wipes the tears off her cheeks with her thumbs.

"Come on," she says. "Let's go back."

That's when I realize it doesn't matter that I have no words, because I know in my heart, she's not ready to hear.

Chris comes in while Stella and Fabby are turning Nana. I'm so excited to see him!

How's the Roho working?

Very well, Chris. That was five hundred well spent. She's healing up nicely indeed.

Five hundred dollars? Oh my God! For a cushion?

That's great. If there's anything she needs, please let me know . . . anything that would improve her quality of life . . .

I gather you were informed that the companion didn't work out.

Molly told me.

You could always try again. There are several excellent companions.

I guess that sounds . . .

Chris drifts off. It used to make me crazy when he did that. And five hundred dollars! I feel nauseous thinking about how Chris has to take care of this for me.

How small my world has become! How distant the millstone that I turned to grind away at the minutiae of my life . . . utility bills, managing my work schedule, servicing the car, the guidance counsellor, the rip in the armpit of the cream-coloured silk blouse, the hot-water tank, the swimming coach, fiscal year-end, Angelina's ongoing difficulties at school, it never ended. Even after the kids grew up and I lived alone, it seemed there was always something. A problem client. A hole in the roof. A poor investment. Plantar fasciitis.

The moments fell faster and faster, like grains of wheat pouring into the flour mill, and I just kept working away.

It's all on Chris now. He's talking to me and I'm reading his body. The careful tension in his posture. The amount of pressure as he pushes his fingers together, leaning forward in his chair, elbows on my table. But . . . there are kind lines around his mouth. Goodness. I never noticed that before. There are little crow's feet in the corners of his eyes.

"Okay, Mom?"

Oh dear. I wasn't listening, and now it's too late.

Another admission!

This lady is so old she looks like Methuselah's widow. Her *children* look ready for extended care, I'm sure. Molly respectfully brings a chair to the bedside for the daughter.

Are you comfortable, Mother?

I'm fine.

Standing at the foot of his mother's bed, the son leans his forearms on his walker.

Are you in pain?

I'm fine.

The new lady is lying on her side, towards the wall, but her daughter, looking over her mother's bed, faces me and she doesn't look very happy. The son clears his throat, but doesn't speak. His sister lifts her hand helplessly.

Mother, she says. *We'd best go.*

I'm fine.

It appears we have permitted a presence into our midst. There is no more joking around, and even Alice is minding her p's and q's. The aides change her position every two hours, working two by two instead of on their own, as they usually do. The new lady grits her teeth. She refuses food, and even Stella doesn't push her. Who is this person, Queen Elizabeth's aging auntie? I'm so intrigued that

when Stella comes to take care of me, I mime eating and point to my
new neighbour.

"She's one hundred and three years old," says Stella, as if that
explains everything.

I smack the table, but very lightly so as not to make a ruckus, and
glare at Stella, who obligingly glares back.

Night staff flip my neighbour gently and I hear her refuse their
offers to get her "anything," but while they tend to me, Heather tells
Julie in a low voice that until two days ago this lady was living independently in her own home. She fell and broke a hip, and she hasn't
had anything to eat or drink since.

How did we get her? How'd she get a bed so fast?

I don't know, Jules. It seems to be one of those things.

Well, she sure doesn't want to be here.

No. She's doing her best to go.

So I am simultaneously unsurprised and astounded when nameless Madame One Hundred and Three Years Old manages to die
silently and unnoticed sometime between Heather's last round and
day shift's first check.

Goodness. I didn't know you could do that.

Maybe you need to be one hundred and three years old with a Will of Steel.

I guess.

That makes three. Maybe we're done for a while.

Janet, this one and . . . who?

I was counting Camille.

Oh, Camille.

Three good ones, really.

Mmm, not too bad. Mind you, Camille was lying there long
enough.

But the actual dying process.

Well, this one takes the prize.

If only it would always be as sweet.

If only we could all die in our sleep.

Amen.

Tiny's bed stays empty over the weekend. (I don't even think of it as belonging to Madame One Hundred and Three Years Old; it's more like she rented it.)

An empty bed buys me a little time, says Michiko cheerfully, and she buzzes around singing "With a Little Bit of Luck" and "There Is Nothing Like a Dame." All happy tunes.

It's almost as though Michi was working magic, summoning sunbeams, because Monday morning, we get an admission, and the first thing our new arrival says is, *Well! This looks lovely!* We lift up our heads as though the Captain of Our Soul had announced, "Land ahead!"

Yes. I think this will be fine, don't you, Milton?

It will take some getting used to.

Yes, dear. We were expecting that.

This apparition of practical optimism wheels over to me and extends her hand. I have to shake with my left, and I see her calmly assessing my bum arm. She notices the tube-feed too.

"I'm Ruby," she says, and I withdraw my hand to point to my throat and shake my finger.

"Well then," says Ruby, "I'm sure someone will introduce us properly very soon."

At this, Milton steps forward, shakes my hand and, looking at the writing on my over-the-bed table, says, "May I?" He has to put his reading glasses on before saying, "Francesca, is it?"

I nod.

"Mother, this is Francesca."

"Pleased to meet you," she says, and I hope I'm not drooling as I smile back, because her own smile is lovely.

Alice is off somewhere wandering, but with Milton's help, Ruby solemnly introduces herself to Nana and Mary before reiterating, "Yes, this will do very well."

The RN comes in.

There you are! We still have some paperwork to do. Would you like to come down to the team centre?

Certainly, Milton and Ruby speak together, and then exchange an amused wink. Their obvious affection for each other lights up my day.

I wake up in the night because Ruby is weeping. There is an unmistakable odour in the room. I reach for my bell and, a few minutes later, Heather appears. I'm so glad it's Heather; she is sturdily, steadily, dependably kind. Right away, she knows why I rang. She catches my eye as she flicks the bell off and turns to my neighbour.

Oh dear.

I've soiled myself!

Oh, honey. Don't cry. It happens. I'm sorry, ladies; I'm going to have to turn on the light.

Heather steps into the washroom and returns with a wash basin and a pile of face cloths.

I'm so sorry. I'm sorry for you, sobs Ruby.

For me? Oh, sweetie. This is my job! If I can't handle a little incontinence I'm definitely in the wrong field. Now, lovey, you need to do me a little favour here. I've got your hands clean, and now I want you to keep them out of it; there's no need to make this worse. I'm gonna whip this gown off . . . okay, cross your arms over your chest . . . perfect. Now, honey, close your eyes and think about something peaceful; I'm going to make you feel like this never happened.

Heather hums softly. Oh. I know that tune. It's from *Hansel and Gretel.* I saw the opera on a field trip with Chris when he was in grade four. "Now I Lay Me Down to Sleep." Goodness! Does Heather like opera? I took her for a country and western kind of woman.

Turn on your side now. Okay, back this way. Beautiful. Sweetheart, you are clean as a whistle. I'm going to get you a hot blanket; I'll be right back.

Heather shuts the lights off on her way out. I'm still thinking about the witch in the opera and I'm starting to dream in a half-awake way that it's Angelina and Chris instead of Hansel and Gretel who are lost in the woods when Heather comes back.

Thank you so much! God will bless you for your kindness.

Aren't you a darling? Like I said, it's my job, lovey. Don't you worry about a thing.

It all turned out in the end. Hansel was resourceful—or was it Gretel?—and shoved the witch into the oven, where she magically turned into a big cookie. I fall into a deep sleep thinking about gingerbread, the memory of sugar icing on my tongue.

When morning arrives, it's like last night never happened.

Ruby and I are sharing a mutually satisfying silent moment of admiration for my chestnut tree when Alice's daughters breeze into the room, carrying a big package. We see Josie all the time. She's warm and friendly, and from what I've observed, unflappable, but she always looks like she has temporarily stepped off the field from some sweaty team sport. Her sister, whom I haven't seen before, is Lady Vogue.

Michelle said she was sending some new clothes for Mom's birthday.

Well, let's hope she sent something Mom can wear!

You don't think she's changed sizes that much?

Oh no. Size isn't the problem.

Well, I do hope she sent something decent. Mom looks so shabby!

Meaning what?

Well, track suits, Josie? Mom would never have worn track suits! What happened to all her good clothes?

Susan, get a grip! What you call "good clothes" aren't appropriate for her anymore!

You get a grip! If you're the one choosing her clothes, for heaven's sake, why don't you choose something a little . . . dressier!

Her clothes are appropriate.

Something more in keeping with her taste.

Jesus, Susan, Mom doesn't have taste anymore!

Come on! She's old, she's not dead.

Look, sister. Mom's needs have changed. She's incontinent, for Chrissake. The pants need to go down fast, and they need to come back up easily. She's not Mrs. Oak Bay Tea Party Hostess anymore. She spills food on herself, she dribbles, she . . .

You're dressing her just like you dress yourself.

Thanks, Susan. Screw you too. Let's just see what Michelle sent her mama, shall we?

Ruby is more discreet than I am . . . I'm practically falling out of my chair in my effort to see what's in the box. New clothes? Count me in!

Okay. Well. These are lovely underwear, but . . .

Yes, Josie, you keep telling me, Mom's incontinent. Must you rub it in?

D'you think Emma could use them?

Thongs, sister. The girls wear thongs.

Oh. Okay, then.

Is this cashmere?

That's no good.

Whyever not? It's lovely.

Everything needs to be machine washable.

Surely they wouldn't throw a good cardigan like this in the machine.

Everything, Susan. Ev-ery-thing.

And these pants are linen.

Plus, Mom can't handle zippers anymore.

Three for three. What a pity.

The irony is, Mom would have loved these things.

Where is Mom? She's drifted!

Susan scoops the clothes off the bed back into the bag, as Josie ducks into the hallway. Her voice floats back.

She's right here. Pilfering the snacks from the trolley.

"Well!" smiles Ruby as Susan follows her sister out of the room. "Wasn't *that* interesting! I love clothes, don't you?"

I nod. Both of us raise our eyebrows and grin.

Molly fairly bounces doing my care.

"Frannie, guess what? Bettina took that night position on third! She said she needs full-time, and it's better for her family and her church activities."

I knew Molly wasn't particularly fond of Bettina, but this degree of enthusiasm surprises me.

"So her position is going up next week . . . wouldn't it be awesome if Lily got it?"

Oh!

"Lily's got lots of hours, Frannie. She could have had an evening position a long time ago, but she needs days for Sierra. It's kind of ironic—when the kids are little, you really need days, but by the time these girls have enough hours to get permanent days, their kids are all grown up. But Lily started working here when Sierra was a baby."

I had no idea Lily had enough seniority to be in the running for a day position. My heart is pounding.

I'm not sure where Alice's daughter Susan comes from, but clearly she's breezed in on a duty visit and she's putting in her time. Every day she comes and stalks the hallways, two steps behind her wandering mother.

I am sitting in the sunroom when Susan and Josie come in together. Susan has Alice in tow and a box of treats from the Dutch bakery in her other hand, and Josie balances a tray of proper teacups and a pot of tea with cream and sugar in a matching set.

"Do you mind if we make ourselves at home here?" Josie asks.

I shake my head vigorously.

All politeness, Susan offers me a cup of tea, but Josie, who knows me, explains my tube-feed *sotto voce*.

Susan is embarrassed; she doesn't know how to meet my eyes.

"Oh. Well then," she says.

I enjoy watching the pouring of the tea, the laying of the cups and saucers and tiny spoons. On the pale blue paper plates with matching paper napkins, the cakes are pretty little snowy castles, sprinkled with sugar flowers.

Mom is in her element.

Oh my God, I can just hear her saying, "Two lumps and lemon, please . . . you do have lemon, do you not?"

Josie laughs. *Oh, Mom!*

I miss that version of her so much, says Susan. *That elegant lady with just a hint of bitch; it shatters me that she has changed.*

We all change.

Yes, but . . . I don't know her, Josie. This isn't my mom. It bores me to death hanging around here. It's dismal and I can think of a million better ways to spend my time. I can't wait to go home tomorrow. Frankly, I don't know how you do this week after week.

I don't think of it like that. It isn't about intellect; it's more about how you feel. Emotional communication. Not to be disrespectful, but it's similar to how I relate to my dogs.

Ugh. I never was an animal person.

Odd, isn't it? Of the three of us, you were always the closest to Mom. But now . . . maybe it's a good thing that I'm the one who lives here.

You definitely handle this better than I do, if that's what you're saying, I give you that. And Michelle . . . forget it. Let's not even bring it up.

Ha ha, I think we've built a fragile bridge on that subject over our wine last night, but for heaven's sake, let's not test it with any heavy trucks.

Foot traffic only.

Absolutely. A hanging bridge with vines. No army vehicles!

The sisters laugh, and I feel a current of energy pass between them.

I simply can't imagine Angelina visiting me here. She didn't have a caretaking bone in her body, that girl. *Christian* was the considerate one. That was the story I told myself, anyway. But although Angelina wouldn't hesitate to bait her family, she wouldn't tolerate anyone else doing it. Maybe over time, that loyalty would have developed into thoughtfulness.

I wonder what would have happened if I'd given them both more space to step outside of the roles I put them in.

I always believed Ang needed the people she loved to be sturdy rock-and-mortar walls that wouldn't crumble when she threw herself against them, like crashing waves against a breakwater.

I believed Angelina needed me to be strong. Now I wish I'd been more flexible, that I'd made a softer place for her to land.

Molly pulls the curtains around Mary's bed; she comes back with the RN and she's got the binder that holds the bowel records in her hands.

I don't know what I'm going to do with her. Look, you can see it's getting harder and harder to get anything out of her.

Did you commode her?

Don't insult me! I gave her the Dulcolax, I waited a half-hour, and then I gave her the Fleet and I put her on the tilt commode, and she sat for another half an hour. I couldn't keep her on there any longer. She's so stiff, her legs are going to go to sleep!

Alright, I'll give her a check.

—

There's nothing up there.

Like I said. You guys are going to have to push from above.

Are you on tomorrow?

It's my Monday.

Okay. We'll give her more laxative. You give her a break tomorrow, and then the next day we'll try again.

Fair enough.

Poor Mary.

I have a bad feeling. She's going down.

Well, it's bound to happen.

Not my Mary. Not my darling Mary.

Even your darlings, Molly. If we kept all your darlings, there'd be no more room on the planet.

Ouch.

I think it was guilt more than affection that made Molly bake a cake for Bettina's last day.

"We've been partners a long time, Frannie . . . long before you came here," she says.

The cake looks amazing, a shining dome of chocolate, and I can smell the Grand Marnier in the ganache from my corner of the dining room.

We'll miss you, Betts, call the girls, and I think Bettina is touched. She's so phlegmatic, it's hard to tell.

Alice, sitting quietly for a change, is holding a teacup with her pinky out. I can see Tiny on the other side of the room—she thinks the party is for her. Molly is spooning bird-sized bites into Mary's mouth.

Didn't they put her on full-minced?

Come on. This is fine for full-minced. She loves chocolate. Don't take this away from her.

She's getting thin; she needs the calories.

Oh my God, did I tell you what she said the other day? I was washing her up and I said, "Mary, you've lost a lot of weight!" and she said, "It was borrowed."

Everyone laughs.

Sometimes she still comes out with stuff like that.

It makes me wonder if she's still thinking those zingers but she just can't get them out.

"Well, isn't this lovely?" says Ruby, daintily eating her cake.

They've taken to putting Ruby beside me in the dining room at lunch; what a pleasure it is! Ruby's way of speaking to me . . . but wait . . . she speaks to *everyone* as though they are sentient beings, not brainless, drooling *things*.

When the cake is done, the girls clear the dining room. Being in the corner, Ruby and I wait for the others to go first. Maybe that's why they put Ruby near me . . . she is patient, and does not try to leave before there is a clear path, as some of the residents do, banging their wheelchairs hopelessly like a football mob leaving a stadium. When Molly comes to us, Ruby thanks her.

Did I hear correctly that you made the cake?

I did indeed . . . did you enjoy it?

It was wonderful! That icing! What was in it?

Grand Marnier.

Ruby's face clouds.

That's not . . . that's not booze, *is it?*

Molly sees that she's troubled.

You can eat vanilla, can't you? In your religion?

Oh yes.

Well, this is just the same. It's a flavouring.

Oh, I see. Well, it certainly was delicious. That was a very kind thing you did. In fact, you are kind to us all.

I love my job.

Yes, I can see that you do. Did you always know you wanted to do this kind of work?

Oh God, no. I never knew what I wanted to do; I never chose or made an active decision in my life. I fell into this, like a canoe going over a waterfall. You couldn't get a job washing dishes, those days, let alone find a good job, and I had two kids and then my husband got laid off, and my aunt, who's a nurse, said, "Honey, why don't you go and take your care aide course, it's only eight months." She said, "Trust me. I'll help you." It was just one of those times in my life when I was so desperate that if the Devil himself had offered me a trip to Georgia, I'd have taken it, y'know? I had kids to feed, I had to have work. It turns out I just love working here, I love this job . . . I love believing I can make somebody have a better day, just by being glad myself. No one wants to see a crabby face. The kids are grown up and I'm still here. I almost feel like it happened for a reason.

Ruby reaches for Molly's hand.

I'm sure it happened for a reason.

My cup runneth over.

Well, thank God your cup runneth over on me!

I haven't seen Chris for a couple of weeks, and when he comes in on Saturday, I have so much to tell him. I point frantically at Ruby's bed. Chris has no idea what I'm on about.

"Where's Janet?"

Good Lord, has it been that long? Some floating memory from my childhood latches onto my motor skills and I draw one finger across my throat.

Chris reels back, shocked, and a gurgling laugh escapes from my gut. I try again: I make the "dismissed" gesture . . . Janet is long gone.

"She *died?*"

This old man came rolling home . . . I try to indicate "turnover" but Chris isn't keeping up at all. Fortunately Ruby chooses this moment to wheel in, and I beckon her near and point to Chris.

Chris and Ruby shake hands and introduce themselves.

"You're Mom's new roommate?"

"Yes. You must be Francesca's son. I recognize you from your mother's photos."

Chris looks stunned. In my previous life, I was unapologetically and vocally scornful of people who showed off pictures of their children and grandchildren. I shrug away Christian's questioning glance. He should try making riveting conversation without a voice.

Chris gathers his wits and smiles.

157

"Very pleased to meet you. When did you move in?"

Ruby frowns. "I can't recall. My memory is not what it used to be. But I think fairly recently."

"You're adjusting?"

"Oh yes. Everyone is very kind. Your mother is a good friend." Ruby touches my sleeve. "My son visits."

"You have just the one son?"

"My daughter died of cancer. Many years ago."

Ruby's voice is steady but she surreptitiously wipes the corner of her eye. A tear escapes every time Ruby mentions her daughter, and she always keeps a tissue in her pocket.

Chris puts a gentle hand on her shoulder, and Ruby reaches up and covers his hand with her own.

"You and my mom both lost a daughter."

"Yes, that's what Francesca indicated. Your sister's name was on the back of her photograph. A beautiful girl. I pray for her when I pray for Connie. Well. I just stopped in for my Bible. If you'd reach it for me? Thank you. It was a pleasure to meet you. I'm sure I'll see you again soon."

Ruby wheels off. Chris gives me a considering look.

"You showed her Angelina's picture?"

I shrug.

Chris shrugs back.

"She's lovely."

I nod. Yes, she is.

"You've changed."

Really? How?

Chris pulls a chair next to me and puts it at an angle, so that we're not staring face to face. He sits on my left. I can reach him if I want to.

"Remember Janice?"

I shake my head.

"Janice. Our next-door neighbour."

Oh God. Janice. The Pentecostal. Ghastly.

"You had no time for her at all."

Surely Chris would not equate Ruby with Janice . . . they are nothing alike! Again I make the sweeping dismissal gesture and grimace for good measure. Why would I ever think about Janice?

"She wasn't so bad, Mom. She had a good heart. She was . . . but now your roomie is *praying* for Ang?"

I shrug. Apparently it's the gesture of the day.

"You've changed. You . . . pay attention. No offence, Mom, but you never used to listen. You were always so busy. So sure you were right."

I'm holding my breath. Quietly, keeping my eyes on Chris's face, I let my hand fall open, palm up.

"What's going on in that head of yours, Mom?"

Chris leans back in his chair, smiling.

"Guess Lily was right, huh, Mom . . . you're never too old to change. How about that?"

Breathe.

After Chris is gone, I think about what he said.

Is it true that I never used to listen? Is that why Angelina yelled so much? Is that what she felt she needed to do to make herself heard? Oh God. The irony.

Like a sliver in my thumb, like a pain in a tooth that the tongue keeps seeking, I find myself thinking again about an insignificant moment, an unimportant conversation that lately keeps rising to the surface in the stew of my brain.

Angelina was in grade five. Her class was taking a field trip to Sooke Potholes Provincial Park, which should have been less than an hour's drive, but Ang and her best friend, Raven, missed the school bus. They took the city bus downtown, then walked over a mile to get to the highway. The police picked them up just outside of Victoria, with their thumbs out, trying to hitch a ride. I got a call from the police saying they were bringing the girls home, and I stomped around the kitchen, slamming cupboard doors, choking on anger and fear. Chris was home with a mild flu that day. He was propped at the kitchen door, sipping on a can of ginger ale but, deliberately, he didn't sit down—he was protecting a clear exit path.

"Why doesn't she *think*?" I ranted. "She's almost eleven, she should know better! Why does she *do* these things?"

"But that's just the point, Mom. She doesn't think. Angelina is not like us. She doesn't need a logical reason. She just acts."

"But surely even Angelina can see there could be consequences, *dangerous* consequences . . ." I had much more to say, but Chris was leaving.

"Have it your way," he said, disappearing down the hall.

It wasn't just Angelina that I misjudged. I didn't realize how much Chris identified with me. "Like us," he'd said.

I didn't listen to Christian either. I didn't even acknowledge that we were on the same team.

The wave of sadness is nauseating. Love and anguish, sharp as a fresh cranberry.

But here's the thing about being a survivor. You get to try again.

It's with listening in mind that I observe my conversations with Ruby, and I do feel every bit as much an observer as a participant.

"Milton was in yesterday. I don't believe you saw him."

I shake my head.

"He brought me this."

It's a candid picture of Connie and Milton as young adults. They both seem to have a fair bit of paint on them, and Connie is gesturing with a brush in her hand. Both young people are crinkly-eyed with laughter, facing each other, sharing a moment of mirth. They look like they're enjoying each other's company, and I point from one to the other to indicate the warmth between them, but Ruby doesn't get it.

"Oh, that's Milton and this is Connie. Milton was two years older, you see; Connie always adored him."

I mime painting, to keep up my side of the conversation.

"Yes. My husband and I moved into a condo here when the children grew up, but it needed quite a bit of attention; Milton and Connie gave it a fresh coat of paint for us. Gordon was already unwell by that time."

I point to various parts of my body.

"Breast cancer. We didn't know what it was for a long time . . . he just felt sick. People don't think of men getting breast cancer, but they do. Treatment was not as effective as it is now. I believe they've made great strides in that department. Connie died of cancer too. But I told you that, didn't I?"

I nod.

"My memory is so poor. Is that how Angelina went?"

I shake my head. It's so complicated. We've been through this before. Ruby doesn't remember. I try for a journey, and then a car, but it's obvious that Ruby is confused. She gives up.

"It's hard, isn't it? The Lord giveth, and the Lord taketh away. Blessed be the name of the Lord. But children aren't supposed to die before their parents; it's not the natural order. I kept myself busy after Connie passed away. My congregation was a great support to me. And I had my work. Did you work outside of the home?"

Suddenly I have a burst of my old confidence. I nod vigorously. I had a business! I was very important and very responsible, and for some reason, I feel strongly that I want Ruby to know this about me, right now. I am gesturing wildly.

"You must have enjoyed it," says Ruby. Just as quickly as my enthusiasm rose, I am deflated. I *didn't* enjoy work, per se. Rather, my work defined me. I wasn't particularly friendly with my clients, but I liked the person I was with them—a professional. I was confident, reliable, dependable and trustworthy. My role was to ensure that my clients paid as little taxes as possible while staying strictly within the law. You know where you are with a good tax accountant. *I* knew where I was. But how to explain?

Ruby is moving the conversation forward.

"I think most people have mixed feelings about their work. It takes so much time, my husband used to say. He was the type who would much rather be reading . . . not that he was lazy. He simply resented the time that took him away from the worlds in the pages of his books."

For me work was a necessity, a distraction and a source of security. Work was predictable compared to the chaotic backdrop that was my parenting life. Later, in the long years after Ang disappeared, work was the drug that kept me from going crazy, the preoccupation that made the long, agonizing hours disappear. Now I am struck by the sudden realization that I invested more in my work because I cared *less*, and I invested less at home because I cared *more*.

How absurd!

I feel my stomach knotting up, my face furrowing with frustration. A word flashes in my mind like a neon sign: agitated. That's what the aides call us when we're upset. I imagine a washing machine, thumping the clothes this way and that. It shakes something loose in my head and suddenly I'm free. So what if I can't tell Ruby what a big man I was! That information wasn't going to impress her anyway. She doesn't care. She's lovely and she's polite, but she has her own fish to fry.

Indeed, she's still talking.

"Milton took after his father. He's a college professor now. But Connie had a more playful nature."

How like real life, I muse. We are stuck in our own worlds, with our own thoughts. Yet we're friends. We wave to each other across a football field . . . look at me! Look at me!

"People said she took after me."

There's the silent tear on Ruby's cheek.

Breathe. Carefully, like I'm stepping onto ice, I reach for Ruby's hand and squeeze.

It's true . . . she can't read my mind, and I may be getting her all wrong too, for all I know. But we're here together now and this will have to do.

We're nearing the end of October. Almost group change . . . I'll have Molly, and Blaire on Molly's days off, for a month. In the meantime, Bettina's job has been posted and will be up for a week, and it will likely be another week before the lucky owner of a brand new day shift starts, so there is a casual named Jennifer doing Michiko's days off. Today she's working with Molly.

These groups are too hard! On third floor, we're done by ten thirty.

This is a heavy wing.

Evenings should be putting away the laundry. It's not like they have a lot to do.

They have their own workload.

Come on! It's way easier to throw them into bed than it is to get them up and dressed, and we have bowel care and outings. Days are much heavier than evenings.

Evenings have to deal with sundowning.

It's not that bad. Really. They take long breaks on evenings. And there's no administration around.

You do a lot of evenings, Jennifer?

Oh no. I haven't done evenings for years.

Jennifer's been my nurse for two days, and Anna, if I counted the number of times she's said "It's good enough," you'd be shocked. Or maybe you wouldn't, because every now and then you'd hire a girl like this at the diner: a hustler. A girl whose mission it is to work hard at avoiding work. You'd recognize the type.

"I'm not killing myself here," she says, while she gossips and complains about the other staff.

Yesterday she gave me "a bed day" without asking me if I wanted one, saying, "What does she have to get up for?" Today she rushed to get me up and "out of the way" before breakfast, barely washing me and skipping my teeth. She left me up after lunch.

When Stella comes on at three, she puts me to bed first.

"Molly told me you were up early. You have a good cushion, but your bottom isn't that great yet."

I could hug her. I definitely need a sign for "thank you." I pat my heart.

When Michiko's days off are over, I'm extremely grateful to have her back. I give her my best attempt at a grin and grab at her sleeve.

"Glad to see me, are you?" Michi grins wickedly. "I'm not going to pretend I don't know why!"

I raise my eyebrows.

"I've worked with her before; I know what she's like."

Michiko leans in and whispers.

"Crappy casuals have their purpose."

I smack my side rail.

"Yup. They make you guys appreciate the little extras we do for you. Keep you from taking us for granted."

Now I'm listening.

"You're actually pretty lucky here. No one could be better than Molly—she's on her own level. But Blaire is a good, solid aide, and your evening staff are good too, right?"

I nod.

"Stella? She's the grande dame. And Fabby is a sweetheart."

She's right.

Furthermore Michiko herself is one of the best. I decide I'm going to try to tell her so.

"What?"

I point at her, then give her a thumbs-up.

"Me?"

Thumbs up!

"Aww! A compliment, right?"

I nod, grinning. I did it!

"Well, thank you, Francesca. That means a lot to me."

"You know," she confides, "I wanted to change the world with my music. I wanted to write songs that inspired people to be the very best they can be. But—"

Michiko straightens up and shrugs. "An artist has a hard life. I had a couple of low-down, dirty Lily-style love affairs and I ended up writing a lot of redundant crap about good love gone bad, and the years went by."

I point to my buttocks.

"That's right, honey. Hard Assed Bitch. But you know, Frannie, I think this might be my real gift after all . . . my work here. Looking after you guys. There's something profoundly spiritual about showing up, day after day, staying present, staying compassionate, staying real. I'm still making music, yeah. But this is a pretty important part of my life. I spend a lot of time here."

This is the most personal Michiko has ever been. I wish I could tell her that it makes a huge difference to me, the fact that she's emotionally invested in her job. Thumbs-up just doesn't cover it.

Michiko smiles and poses thumbs-up back to me, with her elbows at her sides and her spiky hair sticking straight to the sky.

"Let's get you up, shall we?"

I nod.

Blaire and Michiko are venting in the sunroom. Ruby and I sit, fawns-in-the-tall-grass quiet, listening.

When Molly and Michiko work together, I have no trouble identifying who's speaking, no matter how quickly they talk. But when Michi works with Blaire, I have a hard time telling their voices apart. Michiko mimics Blaire a little. I don't think she knows she's doing it.

Elaine's daughter was in complaining to the RN again.

What was it this time?

Oh, she said we aren't brushing her mom's teeth well enough.

Well, if her mom didn't spit at me, maybe I'd do a better job!

Yup. I call that the right to refuse care. I think she makes herself pretty clear.

She's better if you get down on her level.

What, you mean spit back?

Ha ha, no, stupid! Bend down, so she doesn't have to look up!

Sometimes nothing works.

Yeah, I know. Anyway, that daughter has complained so many times about so much random shit that it's not likely they're gonna pay a whole lot of attention.

She's kind of like one of those small yappy dogs. You just wanna misstep and accidentally crush it.

You can't please her.

All the time Elaine's been here, she hasn't had one good thing to say.

She likes to try to pit us against each other.

She's a splitter, for sure. I just smile and nod and try not to engage.

But it makes it hard to deal with Elaine. I get so mad at how her daughter treats us that it's hard not to go in that room with a bad attitude. Especially when Elaine can be so resistive.

Uh-huh. Not doing one little extra thing. Not one.

I don't want to be that way. Elaine is an old lady with dementia; her daughter's attitude is irrelevant.

Maybe not. Maybe Elaine was a terrible parent and role model. Maybe she's responsible for that daughter being such a pill.

Irrelevant. She's old, she's uncomfortable, she's confused and she's nasty. She needs care and that's my job. If we only looked after the people who deserved kindness, it'd be a skinny job.

Well, it's not my *job to be treated like shit!*

Yeah. It's a tough thing to be a good advocate, though. If you want the best for your mother, you certainly don't want to antagonize her caretakers.

Or your kid's kindergarten teacher.

Yeah, how's that working out for you? Is Stephen doing any better?

Oh my God, it's a nightmare. I can't wait for this school year to end! I just hope Stephen isn't scarred for life.

It's pretty sad when your kindergarten teacher is a bitch.

An effin sadist!

When Michiko and Blaire leave, Ruby and I exchange glances.

"They're good girls," says Ruby.

I shrug. I touch my right arm, where Michiko has her dragon tattoo, and make the thumbs-up sign. Then I make a circle with my thumb and finger and bring it to my eye to indicate Blaire's glasses, then wave my hand back and forth to say "no." I won't go so far as to make a thumbs-down sign, but Blaire is hard. And tough. She should be the one with the tattoo on her ass.

"We have to pray for that girl."

I am doubtful.

"She has many sorrows. She works two jobs, you know."

I did *not* know that.

"When she's done here, she goes to another place and works until nine."

No wonder she's so short with us.

"I worry about her son. The sister lives with her, but . . . from what she said, I gather that's another burden."

Ruby's eyes are kind but very serious.

"If she had faith and community, her life would be easier."

I look at Ruby with new respect. Could it be that Blaire confides in Ruby? Goodness knows it sounds like Blaire needs a friend.

I know I didn't treat you well after Angelina went missing. Pain makes a person selfish, that's a fact.

You were such support during the first couple of years, while we were still hoping, fearful and anxious, for any word at all. You were as absorbed as I was, not only out of concern for Angelina but because of the toll her disappearance was taking on your Chris. I leaned on you, and you leaned on me. For a long time, no other subject could interest us in any meaningful way, and we went about our work mechanically.

But you moved on, and when you did, I buried myself in work.

I always found it easier to work than to feel. Client problems have solutions.

It was work or take up drinking seriously, and I couldn't do both. So I worked.

You called. "I made fresh poppyseed bread, come for coffee." Or "There's a show I want to see, let's go together."

"I can't, business is thriving, I'm buried. Let's get together soon."

Finally you showed up on my doorstep, a bottle of wine in a bag hanging from your wrist.

"I am trying to help you, but you must help yourself or this will kill you. I need you. Chris needs you. You must keep on living."

It was a much-needed slap in the face, and we drank the wine, all of it, plus another bottle that I had stashed away for emergencies. I had a terrible hangover the next day, but I worked for sixteen hours anyway.

It took me another six months to act on your advice. I'm surprised you put up with me that long. I called you up and said that I valued our friendship, that I was sorry I hadn't made time for you. I lied and told you I could imagine having zest for life again, someday in the future, and you said, "That's the first step." It turned out that you were right.

I made myself stop thinking about what might have happened to Angelina. But that didn't mean I stopped thinking *about* her.

Many times over the fifteen years since Angelina disappeared, I hoped I had her tucked away, only to find that, because of some new experience, every memory of her screamed to be re-examined.

I think about her as though she is some kind of puzzle, and if I could only drop the pieces into the right place, there would be a loud click, and something mechanical would abruptly whirr into action. I think about my daughter as though by thinking about her, someday I will find the switch that I need to pull to reach into the past and make the whole freight train go down a completely different track.

I made myself stop thinking about what might have happened to Angelina. But I can't forgive myself. Her time was so short, and even though I tried, I know I didn't help her to become, as Michi puts it, the best that she could be. For years and years after she disappeared, I believed in my heart that she'd come back and I'd get another chance to get it right with Angelina.

Shikata ga nai.

CIRCLING

Lily comes dancing into our room with a face like sunshine. Both Michiko and Blaire look up, start, and drop what they're doing. They bounce over, trampoline joyful, matching her mood.

You got it!

I got the position!

You're one of us now.

Oh my God, it's going to be so great. No more daycare hassles.

You'll have steady, predictable income.

And benefits.

Oh my God, benefits.

And sick time.

Oh, Lily. This is going to make such a difference to you.

I know. Oh my God.

Michiko sounds a little wistful. *I'm going to miss working with you, Lily.*

Oh shoot, that's right . . .

You'll be doing my days off . . .

I'll be following you . . .

But I'll see you when you're down the hall . . .

You can leave me nasty notes saying "What kind of loser puts the tooth-care stuff right under the soap dispenser?" and "Who took the last damn brief and didn't replace the package?"

Yeah, you watch it, I'm gonna ride your ass.

Michi and Lily hug, and Michi holds her tight.

Oh! Michiko loves her. I guess it's no surprise. It's Lily, after all. I just never noticed before.

Blaire hugs her too, smiling.

I'm so glad, Lily.

Oh, Blaire. Me too.

Lily bounds over and throws her arms around me. I can smell her shampoo. Lavender. How delicious.

"Did you understand, Francesca? I got Bettina's job. Permanent. I'll be doing Michiko's days off and then Pat's days off down the hall. Almost full-time, Francesca!"

Lily breaks away and spreads her arms wide, catching manna from the sky.

We'll be able to eeeat!

The girls laugh.

When do you start?

Tuesday.

So we've got Jennifer for a couple more days?

I thought she said she was done . . . I thought Amit's coming.

Did he go casual again?

So I heard.

No freaking way! I love working with that dude.

Okay, guys. I had better run . . . I'm on coffee.

Bye, Lily.

Thanks for letting us know.

Congratulations.

They're like tropical butterflies, all aflutter, flashing their beauty. I think, "More of this please. More."

Chris comes in to see me, his wet hair slicked back, glowing with energy, a furtive grin on his face. Oh my goodness! He just had sex and a shower! He just had sex and a shower and I can't make enquiries. Not that I *would*, but still. He pulls a chair across the floor from the hallway, scraping it just a bit, just enough to set my nerves on edge before picking it up properly, swinging it around and straddling it backwards. He crosses his arms over the chair back, leaning in towards me and I get a whiff of chlorine. Oh! Not sex, he's been swimming.

He used to swim on a team when he was in middle school. I remember when he quit.

The phone rang as I walked in the door in my pale lemon linen suit, with an armload of groceries. Diving, my stomach already knotting, I dashed the receiver against my teeth, holding my breath. (*Angelina!*) But for once it wasn't all about Ang. Chris's swim coach was calling to talk to me about inviting Chris to try out for the provincial team.

I hadn't realized he was such a talented swimmer. Once again I had been so preoccupied, I hadn't even noticing he was becoming so accomplished. I just paid up the fees and sent him off, grateful that he was productively occupied. I felt a wave of guilt, euphoria and pride. I hung up the phone and turned around; Chris was standing there, swim bag in hand, and I noticed with a pang a wide pale band of wrist between his hand and the cuff of his jean jacket. "Chris, we should celebrate! Congratulations!" As I stepped forward to caress him, my beautiful son, almost a man, he instinctively stepped back, and the blood rushed to my face.

"I don't want to do it," he said.

"Don't want to—?" Stupidly. Aggressively.

"I don't want to swim competitively. It takes all the fun out of it. It takes too much time."

This, I don't understand. The only thing better than doing something well is beating someone else at it.

"Time? What do you need time for?"

Chris was very good at keeping his face flat, but I caught a glimpse of stubborn scorn as he turned on his heel, and I crossed the room in a bound, catching him by the arm.

"Don't walk away from me! I'm talking to you."

One, two, three beats of silence as we stared each other down.

"Let's get this straight, son. I've paid your team fees and I'm not wasting my money. You *will* swim, and you *will* do well!"

Five minutes before I hadn't cared how Chris was doing at swimming—now in my mind's eye I already had him standing on a podium, medal in hand, thanking his mother, and I would have something to be proud of, proud for a change (*oh, Angelina!*), and I wanted it so desperately my lungs hurt.

"You've got lipstick on your teeth."

As my hand flew to my mouth, Chris made his escape, stopping only to throw me a grenade over his shoulder. "I'm not Angelina, Mom. And you can't yell me down."

My hand fell to my side, leaving a streak of red lipstick on the sunny yellow of my tailored blazer.

I never did get that stain out; the suit was ruined and, as far as I know, Chris never swam again.

I reach over to touch Chris's arm, smiling, then pantomime a one-armed crawl.

He smiles back. "Yeah, I've been swimming every day for a while now. Trying to get back in shape."

I make a bicep and grin.

"Yeah, I'm getting stronger." He looks sideways, and I know he's thinking about our argument, just as I am. Quickly I reach out again, bringing his eyes to my hand on his sleeve, and then to my face. I mime a frown, pass my hand from chin to forehead dragging the corners of my mouth up as if by a string, and then smile anxiously, willing Chris to understand.

"Yeah. Yeah. It makes me happy. Endorphins, right? I'm feeling good."

Relief floods me, and dammit, my eyes fill with tears. I fight to hold them back, rigid, the smile on my face wooden as I struggle to contain myself. I reach out to stroke his sleeve again, barely breathing.

"Don't worry, Mom," he says. "It's no big thing."

Amit, the casual who's bridging the gap between Jennifer and Lily, turns out to be a lot of fun.

At first, I could tell that Ruby was really dubious about having a male caregiver, but Amit has her as out of character as a tipsy librarian in no time at all.

Where to, m'lady?

The dining room, please.

Why, that's simply boring. We should go to the moon. We'll take my Ducati. You can ride on back.

Oh, Ruby, says Molly, *you've found yourself a good-looking guy!*

Eat your heart out, says Ruby.

That's okay, I've got one at home.

But that's at home! says Ruby, her cheeks pink at her audacity.

Who'd have thought she had it in her to flirt like a girl? It makes me smile.

Amit tailors his presentation to each person.

I am Mrs. Jensen and he straightens his back for me, but then he calls me "boss" and gives me the kind of a cheeky wink I would never have tolerated in my professional life, and I find myself winking back.

When he's working with Blaire behind Mary's curtain, I hear him pull back the blankets and say, *Oh God, I'll never eat gravy again,* while Blaire doubles over with laughter.

When he works with Molly, she tells him Paul didn't get his bath last night because he was sundowning out of control again. *If you cover me, I'll try him,* Amit says and Molly nods with satisfaction; it's what she expected.

I'll do the bed change for you, she says. *I won't leave you hanging if you get behind.*

Sure, Molly. Feet up, finger up your nose, every day, all day . . . I know you!

You're one to talk, she laughs, and they high-five.

Amit talks about "the wife" and "the kids" all the time.

Amit, how does an accountant end up married to a care aide?

You have to ask! Who could resist all this?

Amit poses like a model, sucking in his cheeks and pulling in his belly, one hand behind his head, fingers pressed lightly against his bald spot, in spite of which he is noticeably and incredibly good-looking.

Molly laughs.

Yeah, you're pretty hot, Mr. Bollywood. So you're taking the fam skiing this winter?

Oh for sure. It's the one thing that coaxes Shianne away from work.

Well, if you're casual, you can pick your time.

That's what Shianne said. Plus she wants to go back east for Christmas and there's no way I'm gonna get Christmas off.

You pretty much have to be born here to get Christmas off. But I can't imagine you're too bloody sorry to be leaving your position up there. Word is it's getting pretty hard to work on third.

Oh, there are some heavy people up there, but the work is straightforward enough.

No, no. I meant your co-workers.

There's some pretty intense conflict happening. But no offence, I don't want to spread that energy around.

Fair.

Molly takes the hint and changes the subject.

So Mount Washington for a week?

Even better. Two weeks in Banff right after we get back from Montreal.

Oh my God. Heaven on a stick.

And they're gone.

Oh, how you used to love skiing, didn't you, Anna? "When you come from a flat country, it's easy to fall in love with the mountains," you said. You took a week off every year to get on the slopes. The two days we went together wasn't part of your week. We pulled the kids out of school and drove up to Mount Washington together; what fun we had! Chris learned quickly and you were so proud of him. But Angelina was a whiz. Chris and I couldn't keep up with her. When we got to the bottom of the hill, she wasn't waiting by the lift as she'd been told to do, so you and Chris stayed there while I went up on the lift, my gut roiling, scanning the slopes anxiously from my ride in the sky. There she was, zipping down, a flash of incredible beauty in motion, and I thought, "Oh, if only she could always be here."

You caught her at the bottom and the three of you came up together and met me at the top. Then you took Angelina, because you were the better skier, and Chris and I skied together for the rest of the day. It must have been hard work for you. The first night we ate out, but coming home after the second day, we ate sandwiches in the car, delicious after the day in the open air. We all had snow tans. Angelina fell asleep with her head on your lap in the back seat after crowing about how good she had been. In the mirror, I saw you and Chris winking at each other.

It was a perfect getaway.

"Milton is coming to take me out to tea," Ruby tells me, flushed and excited into a state of polite formality. "My dear friend Pearl's son is in town for a visit, and the four of us are going to the Empress. Pearl can't get out her own now, and obviously neither can I, so our get-togethers are necessarily curtailed. This is a lovely and rare opportunity to share her company!"

I smile brightly.

"It is an unfortunate hazard of a long life that the ranks of one's friends sadly diminishes," she says. "But one must not dwell on unpleasant thoughts. Especially on this occasion. Pearl and I have been friends since grade school. Our parents used to call us 'the Jewels!'"

As Ruby is struggling to put on a pair of gloves, I am spared the effort of responding. *Blast,* she mutters under her breath.

"Ah, Mother," says Milton, coming up behind her. "May I help you with those? Hello, Francesca. I hope you are well."

I nod while Milton gives his attention to the gloves.

"It's the arthritis. It does limit one so."

"I know, dear. Well then, Mother. Are you ready? Have you got your purse?"

"Side table, bottom shelf."

"Excellent. We'll be on our way, shall we? Au revoir, Francesca." Ruby waves gaily.

They are off, but Milton is back in a minute, searching in Ruby's locker for her hat.

Molly comes in with an armful of towels.

"Oh, Milton. I was hoping to catch you alone. Do you think your mother would enjoy having a TV? We have a donation."

"Ah! She does have a TV. Rather, it's simply that . . ."

He pauses and Molly waits expectantly, like a collie with pricked up ears.

"Technology defeats her. Also some of the programming upsets her terribly."

Molly nods. Milton decides to elaborate.

"When she was at home, by accident she managed to turn on one of those rather explicit crime shows and she found herself unable to change the channel or lower the volume, which was at its maximum. Fortunately I happened to come by and found her locked in the bathroom, weeping. I have no idea how long she had been sitting there, nor was she able to say. It was exceedingly unpleasant."

"I see," says Molly.

Milton straightens, hat in hand. "Some studies suggest that television exacerbates dementia. Mother presents well, but her memory is poor. You will have noticed that, I am sure." He looks about the room. "In fact, we are grateful that there is no television in this room. There is little one can do to escape should the tastes of others fail to coincide with one's own."

"I will keep that in mind," says Molly, smiling.

"Well, we'll be on our way."

"You'll remember to sign out?"

"Of course," he says from the doorway, nodding slightly as he leaves.

Molly grins at me, and whispers in my ear. "You sure can tell he's a professor!"

I grin back.

"You know what's really funny?" Molly says, tugging on a corner of my bedspread to subdue a wrinkle. "When Michiko has been with him for ten minutes. Michiko sounds like whoever she's been talking to last, did you ever notice that? She's a real parrot. She can't help herself."

Amit comes blasting into our room while Molly is getting me up.

I need to use a bitch coupon!

What's a bitch coupon?

Molly! You don't know what a bitch coupon is? I'm shocked!

Well, what is it?

It's when you just need to get a little something off your chest.

And you need a coupon for that?

Well, sure. One a day, maximum. I can't just be bitching non-stop, Molly . . . everyone would start thinking they're entitled to the same, and then where would you be? Swimming in a sea of negativity, baby!

Molly is laughing hard. She finds Amit hysterical always, but I think he just makes sense.

Okay, Amit. Here's your coupon. Whatcha got?

I've forgotten.

Oh my God. I'm going to give you an award for being the best whiner ever.

Nice! I'll put it with all my other awards.

Such as?

Oh, you know. Most studly. Best coiffed. I've got a whole collection.

Worst memory?

What are you talking about? All my memories are the best!

A few days later, I am sitting in the sunroom when I hear a dog barking and Blaire and Michiko's excited squeals down the hall. And then ... oh my God! Is that Chris laughing? I crane my head around, but I can't see.

The girls follow Chris into the sunroom as if he was the Pied Piper, twittering like birds.

He's got the cutest little boxer pup you ever laid eyes on. Even Blaire is delighted.

Oh, you sweet little guy! How old is he?

Eight weeks. I just picked him up today.

Chris always wanted a pet.

I just couldn't handle the extra responsibility. I think Chris understood that I couldn't manage one, because he never begged, but I know he secretly yearned for a dog of his own.

Chris lifts the puppy onto my lap and I defend my face as he tries to lick me. I can't help but smile. He's so irresistibly soft and so wiggly, it's like trying to hold water.

I throw my hand up, raise my eyebrows, squawk.

"You're surprised?"

I nod, grinning.

"Me too, I guess. I told Theresa I was planning to get a dog and she flipped her lid. You know how she feels about animals. She said a dog will devalue your property and a whole lot of other crap that's none of her business now that we're not together."

My mouth is wide open. I shut it with a snap. I'm pretty sure steam is going to billow from my ears.

Chris thinks it's funny. For a split second he looks like Angelina stirring the pot, with his mischievous grin.

"I told her she can't have it both ways. She can't split up with me and keep on telling me what to do, like I'm some kind of a trained eunuch."

My eyebrows shoot off my forehead.

"So you're okay with me having Astro at the house?"

Are you joking, my love? You're offering me an opportunity to thwart Theresa? Why don't you just go ahead and get a whole pack of pit bulls? Thumbs up!

Chris grins.

Snuff, says the puppy, slobbering on my lap.

Good boy.

Lily has started her new position and she's clearly riding a wave of sunshine. She's beaming.

"I received the nicest compliment. Would you like to hear it?"

I nod vigorously.

"I was portering Ruby out of the dining room. She took my arm, and she said, 'Look at them, Lily. They've lost so much. Their homes, their careers, their pets, even their families.' She said, 'You brighten their lives.' Isn't that sweet, Frannie? What a lovely way to think of my job!"

My face is stiff. I'm having a hard time composing the necessary smile. I'm . . . I'm jealous, that's what I am. *I* want to be the one to tell Lily how wonderful she is.

"Things are looking up, Francesca. Sierra likes her teacher, I've got a steady day job, I've got more time to work on my designs . . . and I get to see more of *you*! Isn't that great?"

Like an impetuous child, Lily flings her arms around me and presses her cheek next to mine. With my one good arm I hold her close, feeling her ribs beneath the soft cotton scrub. And breathe.

The wicked feelings are gone.

Whatever makes Lily happy, whoever turns the light on in her eyes and makes her shine, that's the person or the thing that makes me grateful. I swear.

It's okay that I'm jealous of Ruby. It doesn't stop me from appreciating her.

Don't you mind about Ruby, Anna. She'll never take your place in my heart.

Later, what Ruby told Lily about loss comes back to me, and I start thinking about something that happened shortly after I came here. I had a temper tantrum after a run-in with one of the aides. I have an image of the snippet who was working with me, but I don't know her name and I don't think I've seen her since. But Michiko was there. With her sword and shield. Defender of the faith.

What the heck does she want?

Oh, she wants her box of Kleenex. She likes to keep it with her. She drools out of the right side of her mouth.

Yeah, I know, gross. I gave her a handful of tissues.

She doesn't want your wad of snotrags. She wants her own box.

Well, she needs to learn that she can't always get what she wants!

Michiko marched over to me crackling with rage.

"Hey, Frannie? You want a nice hot fresh croissant?"

Still sniffling, clutching my bum arm to my chest like a teddy bear, I nodded—a tearful child offered treats.

"How 'bout, maybe you'd like to do a little dancing?"

Michiko started a little soft-shoe shuffle, while she talked.

"Little two-step? Meet some nice guys, maybe have a couple of drinks? You wanna, Frannie?"

I had to grin.

"Or maybe just walk down to the corner store and buy a paper and a coffee, sit in the sun, waste some time? Sounds nice, right, Frannie?"

"Okay, Michi," I remember thinking. "I bet she's got it."

"Yeah. I thought so. Me too. I want all those things. Here. Have your goddamn box of Kleenex."

Michiko stomped out of the room.

What a bitch! said the Snippet bitterly.

At that point I had to wipe the drool off the side of my mouth. I remember that especially. Disgusting.

On third floor, a ninety-eight-year-old woman with dementia has been sent to emergency with chest pains, and the girls are all buzzing with the news of it.

How does that happen?

Didn't she have a Degree of Intervention form?

Her family filled it out and they want all hands on deck, pull out all the stops, including resuscitation.

Oh my God! They'll break her ribs!

My Lord! I do *not* want that to happen to me. Do I have one of those forms? I'm going to check with Chris the next chance I get.

What is it that you don't like about being alone?

I feel so . . . terribly empty. And then I panic.

See, Lily, that's the thing. You've got to stop thinking of this as a problem that can be solved from the outside. You've got to heal that hole from within.

Good advice, maybe, but I notice you're still single, Mich.

Yeah, but honey, I'm okay with that.

I don't want to be single.

That's cool, Lily. But single or not, you still have to deal with that hole inside. Nobody and nothing can do that for you but you.

I have a brilliant idea. Wouldn't it be lovely if Chris got together with Lily?

I start to scheme. Maybe I could get Chris to buy me some clothes. If he got Lily to tailor them for him, maybe he could pick them up at her place . . .

I'll have to think about this.

God knows I have lots of time.

When Chris comes in, I try to make him understand about the Degree of Intervention form and get nowhere. Fortunately Lily comes in, and it occurs to me this might be a good chance to bring them together. I ring my bell even though she's walking towards me.

"I guess that means you want to see me!" she smiles as she shuts off the bell.

"Lily! Thank God. Can I impose on you for a minute?"

"Of course."

"Something Mom wants . . . I can't figure it out. She keeps flipping her calendar. What am I missing?"

I've already taken the calendar from my over-the-bed table, ready to show. I turn the page, sweep the squares with the back of my hand, turn, sweep, turn, sweep, and Lily understands almost right away.

"The future? What about the future? *Your* future? Is it a will? No? The Degree of Intervention? Okay." Lily turns her sweet face towards Chris.

"Man, you're good," he says admiringly.

"I cheated. We were talking about that in her hearing just the other day."

"So, what now? I'm pretty sure we filled that form out when Mom was admitted."

I tap my head. I don't remember!

"Do you want to go over it again?" asks Lily.

I nod.

"I'll get the RN to bring you a copy and you can look over it together."

"But . . . Mom is pretty stable, isn't she?"

"As far as we know, Chris, but it's always good to be prepared and clearly Francesca is thinking about this. She may have changed her mind about certain things. What if she gets pneumonia? If that should happen, does she want aggressive antibiotics, or 'comfort measures only'? What if she has another stroke? What if she has a heart attack? Does she want to be resuscitated?"

I am shaking my head like crazy.

"She knows what she wants, don't you, Francesca? I'll go talk to the nurse."

"I don't have time to do that right now, but," Chris turns from Lily to me, "I promise we will attend to it soon."

"As you like," says Lily.

"Thank you," says Chris, and we watch her go.

"She's a good kid," says Chris.

I use my good hand to mime "shapely."

Chris shakes his head firmly.

"Don't even go there," he says. "One, she's just a baby, and two, she's not my type, and three, I may not have made the best choice last time, but it's my life and none of your business."

He stands up, smiling to soften his words, and his shoulders are back. "Gotta go. Love you." He leans in and kisses me on the cheek.

I was angry, but I guess I'm not anymore.

Hey, Lily, what happened to Elaine's clock?

Oooh. That was me. Was her daughter upset?

Steaming. You know how she goes off about every little thing.

I was trying to park the power chair and I hit the wall, and I guess the clock wasn't very secure up there because it just bounced right off and shattered. I was meaning to replace it but I was busy last night.

You shouldn't have to spend your own money to replace Elaine's clock! That family has buckets of money.

Yes, but that's not the point. I broke it, I'll fix it. I just didn't get around to it. I'll run to the drugstore on my lunch break.

Don't do that. Honestly. You can't make that woman happy.

She's not a bad person. She's just . . . having a really hard time accepting that this has happened to her mother. She's grieving. It's not about the clock. Or the socks, or the teeth, or her mom's twitch. She complains about what she can afford to complain about. What she's really saying is that she's in unbearable pain.

You really believe that, Lily? Because I think she's just a terrible whiner, and grief is no excuse for treating people badly.

The leaves on my tree are starting to come down in the rain, and the high-wind storms we get in the fall have begun. Lily shows us pictures of the special costume she made Sierra for Halloween. Sierra looks very serious, all dressed in yellow with bright red spots on her cheeks and a hood with black-tipped ears. Ruby clucks like a perfect grandmother.

"Isn't she darling? What is she supposed to be?"

"She's Pikachu!"

"Pikachu?"

"It's an anime character. A Japanese cartoon. Very popular right now." Lily uses her phone to show us a picture of what Pikachu supposedly looks like in real life: a cartoon animal with a lightning bolt for a tail.

Ruby and I smile and cluck, but we have no idea what she's talking about.

Mary has been having a lot of trouble eating lately. The dietitian changed her meal texture from minced to purée with thickened fluid, and she's still choking. Feeding her turns out to be stressful for the aides, and both day shift and evenings discuss Mary's decline anxiously, saying the same things over and over, as if to convince themselves.

I want to be a good nurse, and I sure don't want her to go hungry, but I feel like I'm force-feeding her.

I figure when they stop eating, that's Mother Nature's way of trying to tell us something.

Yeah, like they said in that course. "She's not dying because she's not eating. She's not eating because she's dying."

But the problem is knowing the difference between someone who wants to eat but takes forever, and someone who takes forever because they're basically done with eating. That *is the crux of it.*

When Mary starts coughing yet again, Molly says, *Oh, Mary! This is no fun, is it?*

Mary shakes her head.

Okay, I'm done here. We love you, Mary; you know that, right? Molly kisses her cheek and Mary smiles because that's still what Mary does.

Emotions are contagious, and I feel anxious too.

Michiko traded a shift with Blaire, so she's working down the hall in the East Wing today, but she explodes into our room while Molly and Lily attend to Nana.

Oh my God, it's the best day of my life!

Why, what happened?

Remember a couple of weeks ago I was telling you my buddy and I went for a picnic and a Great Dane came bounding up and scarfed down three-quarters of our lunch?

Yeah yeah yeah, and the owner was so rude about it. Yeah, so?

So, the dude was with this young woman, I mean young, *and hot, right?*

Yeah, you told us.

So the admission comes in to 107 with this lovely middle-aged woman, "Hi, I'm Ayesha, blah blah blah," and I'm helping her put her mom's stuff away, and in walks Wah-zoo of the Great Dane fame.

No way!

Yes!

Did he recognize you?

Damn straight he did, right away. He gave a little start, and he went white. So I said to Ayesha, all sweet, "Oh, is this your brother?" *and she goes, "Oh no, Geoff is my husband; Nancy is my mother-in-law."*

What did you say?

I said, "Really! Even better!" Then I walked out. Oh my God, best karma ever!

Why, what do you mean? You wouldn't take it out on a resident, just cuz the son is a jerk, would you?

God no, what do you take me for? As if! I'm gonna treat her sooo good. I'm just going to make sure every time I see the guy, one way or another we end up talking about dogs.

Oh, Michi! You're incorrigible! Did you?

Is the Pope Catholic? I said Nancy might appreciate a calendar, animals are always a hit, maybe a specific breed, like Great Danes for example. Ayesha said, "That's an odd choice!" Geoff looked like he was going to puke, so I guess the dog belonged to the bimbo.

I thought you said you walked out.

Yeah, baby, I went and got Nancy a nice warm blanket so I could walk right back in again. Damn, I'm enjoying this! Thank you, Goddess!

I can't believe a Great Dane ate your vegan lunch.

Well, he didn't bother to unwrap the sandwiches, did he? He just wolfed 'em down. So maybe he was as disappointed as we were. The point is, your dog eats my lunch—not the time to be a prick, am I right?

Molly looks troubled but Michiko raises her hand and Lily meets her with a high-five.

Don't worry, Moll—I'm only down there for a day. I'm not gonna shake the tree . . . much!

She flounces away, calling over her shoulder *Places to go, pots to stir,* leaving Molly laughing in spite of herself.

I wonder if Geoff (whoever he is) loves his mom. I wonder if he cares. I wonder if it crosses his mind that she is vulnerable, totally vulnerable, and he's made an enemy of the woman who's going to be doing her most personal care.

Not that Michiko would ever harm a resident, but Geoff doesn't know that, and she looks daunting too, with her spiky hair and tattoos. If I was him, I'd be sweating.

No, Michi would never treat a resident poorly, but she does have dramatic flair, and she's going to thoroughly enjoy telling this story to everyone. She's liked and respected, and the aides will all side with her.

It occurs to me that Victoria is a very small city.

I wish I'd been nicer.

It's too late to be nicer to the people in my past: the teachers, the checkout clerks, the butcher, the baker, the candlestick maker. That ship has sailed. But it's not too late to appreciate my girls here. Mama Molly. Lovely Lily. Michiko the Warrior. Stella the Grande Dame. Fabby, neat and tidy, with her big belly stretching out in front of her. Even Blaire with all her cares. The night nurses. The casuals.

Christmas is coming. I have to find a way to get Chris to help me.

I'm worried that I'm going to forget. By the time Chris comes on Saturday I've fretted myself into a tizzy and everyone knows it.

"Your mom's got something on her mind," Michiko tells Chris.

"Oh? What's going on? Is it the Degree of Intervention? Because we'll get to that, I promise."

I shake my head furiously.

"She's been trying to write something all week. But. You know. She kinda can't."

Michiko shows him the list I was trying to make. Squiggles on a page, nothing more. My face burns with shame and I snatch the paper from Chris's hands and scrunch it up, glaring.

I try so hard. I squeak and flap and Chris tries too, but I end up in tears and he gives up. It's the worst visit we've ever had.

"I don't know what you want, Mom. I'm going now; I'll come back when you're calmer."

I'm not sure I'll ever be calmer. I think I might explode.

By a stroke of luck, Alice's daughter Josie brings Alice a small box of good chocolates. She leaves them on Alice's bedside table, and after

Josie leaves, Alice sits on her bed, warming the chocolates in her hands and smearing them all over everything. When Michiko walks in, I swear her hair doubles like a cat's tail bristling.

"Oh my God!" she shrieks.

Molly comes running.

"Oh no. Someone's been digging. And painting."

By this time I'm laughing so hard that tears are rolling down my cheeks. Michiko gives me a dirty look.

"What say *you* wash her up, Francesca!" she huffs, taking Alice by both wrists, and gingerly raising her hands.

"Chocolate! Oh, Molly! I thought we had a major Code Brown!"

"Oh my God. So that's why Frannie is splitting a gut over there! You are so naughty, Francesca! But it's still a mess."

We all laugh hard together, releasing our tension. Michi walks Alice to the bathroom, washes her hands and changes her clothes while Molly strips the bed and remakes it.

I point to the empty box and beckon.

"You want that, Frannie? It *is* kind of pretty. Let me wipe it for you, it's a little sticky. But it smells like chocolate!"

We giggle again, and I put the box carefully on my table, under my calendar.

I've got a plan.

When Molly gets me up the following Saturday, I have the chocolate box in my hand.

"What the heck, Frannie? You want that?"

I have to let go of the box to get my hand through my sleeve, but I make Molly give it back and I clutch it while she hoists me through the air.

"Okay Frannie. Whatever," she says.

Chris looks a little tentative when he comes in, so I give him my best smile and the thumbs-up. Then I show him the chocolate box.

"What's that?"

I make a circle with my hand.

"Chocolate?"

Thumbs up.

Chris looks uncomfortable.

"Mom, you can't eat chocolate."

Oh brother! Geez! I know! I bang the box on the arm of my wheelchair.

"Here we go again," mutters Chris.

I take a deep breath. Okay. Okay. Okay.

I put the box in my lap. I point at it. Then I point, as though at a crowd: you, and you, and you, and you. Then back at the box. I pick the box up and shake it. Make a circle with my hand. Point at the box again.

"Chocolate for everyone?"

Thumbs up! Big grin. Now it's easy. I rub my fingers across my thumb—money—and point at myself. Another circle.

"You want to buy chocolate for everyone?"

Bingo! Oh my word, what a relief! I want to leap out of my chair. Bang, bang goes the box against my wheelchair while I gurgle and grin, undignified as a goose.

"Chocolates for everyone."

I nod, grinning.

"Because . . .?"

Thumbs up.

"Because you're happy here?"

Oh.

That wasn't really it.

How would I answer that, anyway? Because the aides work hard? Because we poop everywhere and they clean us up? Because of sundowning and wandering and all the other challenges of a normal day here? I look at Chris. This isn't working. I'm not making myself clear.

I'm not getting into a big snit over it. I give up. Shrug my shoulders. What does it matter, as long as I get my chocolates?

"I don't know if I've ever seen you *happy*, per se, Mom. Funny place to start feeling that way."

I would love to retort.

"No point getting fierce, Mom. But sure. I can get you chocolates."

I point to the calendar, and Chris brings it. Flip to December, find the twenty-fifth.

"You know that's a ways off, Mom."

I nod. I know.

"Alright then. Chocolates for everyone for Christmas."

This time, we both grin.

Chris brings a copy of the Degree of Intervention form so that we can go through it together.

"We *did* do this, after your stroke, you know, Mom."

I shake my head. I don't remember.

"It's not surprising that memory is gone. You were in a bad way; we had no idea how much you'd recover. Essentially I did this for you based on what you'd told me about your wishes in the past." Chris looks guilty. "I *did* read it out to you, but you weren't responding much."

Except for the comment I made about preferring death over living in extended care when Chris was in grade school, I don't remember any conversations or even comments on the subject of my health care wishes.

But Chris is moving right along.

". . . so I hope you'll forgive me if any of the choices I made were . . . um . . . *wrong*."

Oh. So that's it. Absolution. For acting like I was gone when it turned out I wasn't. Well, that's understandable. I reach over and pat Chris's hand.

The questions aren't that difficult. I get a little mixed up over the word "intubation," which refers to a breathing tube, not a feeding tube. Good Lord, "No!" to that. I blithely say no to CPR; I only want to die once. I like the expression "comfort care only." There's a pleasing rhythm to those words.

It all seems very distant and academic until we get to the final designation. Do I want to be transferred to the hospital if my needs cannot be met here? That's an easy no, but the inference is that death is expected.

Of course death is expected. But . . . what if it was *now*?

Chris lets me take my time to think. "You are allowed to change your mind at any time, Mom. If you get sick and you decide you want us to do . . . uh . . . everything we can to save your life, you're allowed to change your mind."

I am still, and there is empty quiet in my head.

"Actually, as your health care decision maker, *I* can change my mind to respect what I know to be your wishes."

No! That sharpens my thoughts. *I* want to decide; I need to decide *now*, while I'm well enough to participate.

When it's time to go, I'm going, and that's final.

Ruby has been wheeling herself up and down the halls looking for the exit. From my bed I watch her scooting back and forth to our room. Molly tries to redirect her.

Where are you going, my angel?

Oh, it's my turn to serve lunch at the church. I'm afraid I'm going to be late.

Molly bends down, bringing her face level with Ruby's.

Ruby, you've been exempted from that responsibility because it's too challenging in a wheelchair.

Oh, I'm not in a wheelchair. I always serve on Wednesdays.

Well, darling, it's Friday today.

It is?

Yes. And I think you should come down to the dining room because I've made a cup of tea for you.

Well, that sounds lovely, but I really do have to go.

You have time.

Molly wheels Ruby away, but ten minutes later she's back, searching through her side table for her purse.

"I'm meeting Connie and Gordon for lunch at the hospital," she tells me. "Gordon has been unwell, you know. I don't want to be late. Where *is* my purse!"

Ruby spends another ten minutes looking for her purse, which is tucked next to the rail at the side of her bed. She can't find it, and when she starts to cry, I ring my bell.

Ruby, what's the matter?

I can't find my Bible!

Oh, darling, it's right here. In the top drawer. Here it is, sweetheart. Have a tissue.

I know I'm going to be late.

Darling, you could never be late. You're always just on time. Come with me. The light in the sunroom is lovely right now, and I've got beautiful music playing, and you can read your Bible and settle yourself. I have a special drink for you too.

I won't be late?

I promise I'll come and get you when it's time.

I feel like my friend has disappeared.

Michiko gets her basin ready for Nana and pulls her curtains while Molly prepares for me.

Is it my imagination or is Ruby a little more confused than usual?

A little? She's totally wack. I've been running after her all morning.

I bet she's brewing a little UTI. Has anyone done a spec on her?

I've got a collection hat in the toilet right now. But it's kind of hard to push fluids on her. She's not a good drinker. She thinks she's going to have to pee all the time.

I know, I know. When you're dehydrated like that, the more you drink the less you have to pee, but naturally they just can't wrap their heads around that one; it's counterintuitive.

Unfortunately she's not the type to be tempted to drink more just because I put a straw and a little umbrella in her glass, either.

Michiko laughs.

You know all the tricks, Molly.

Well, none of them are working for me today. Frannie, lift your arm for me, would you?

Michiko calls out from behind Nana's curtain, her voice sharp with alarm.

Moll, come look at this!

Oh dear. How long has this been going on?

I don't know! I don't remember seeing it yesterday, but I didn't specifically check either.

Her hair could have been covering it.

No, wait. I put her hair in a bun yesterday, and it was fine then.

Oh right. With the polka-dot dress.

How the heck are we gonna heal that? I can't keep her on her back; the coccyx is this close to breaking down. And if I put her on the right side, the hip breaks down.

I know. There's nowhere left to put her.

Call the nurse, will you?

Maybe OT can get her a donut.

A donut?

Yeah, you know. A pillow with a hole in the middle, so there's no pressure on that ear.

Oh God. So you've seen this before.

A bedsore on the ear? Well, sure, Michi. Don't beat yourself up. We should ask the hairdresser to trim her hair back a wee bit, though. I'm sure that's why nobody saw this coming.

Poor Nana.

Indeed.

I suspect Ruby has been given an Ativan in addition to getting her urine specimen done because she's relaxed and cheerful now. Molly tasked her with keeping me company, a very important job and her Christian duty. I'm fine with that. We are sitting in the sunroom enjoying a companionable silence when Alice toddles in to join us. She lurches over to the window, trips on nothing and goes down, smacking her head on the foot pedals of Ruby's wheelchair.

Apparently head injuries bleed like crazy.

"Oh dear," says Ruby. Gingerly she backs her wheelchair away, spins it around and heads down the hall calling, "Oh, Michiko. I need your help."

"What is it, dearest?" says Michi as she comes into the sunroom. "Oh no. Not again!"

"Molly," she calls out. "Grab the Maxi lift and call the RN. Alice is on the floor."

Michi abruptly shoves my wheelchair away from the growing pool of blood. Gloves on, she cradles Alice's head until the RN comes to do her assessment: a quick check for broken bones and dilated pupils. Even though Alice is light as the wind and I'm pretty confident Michiko could pick her up with her pinky, the RN and Molly use the portable lift to get her up.

Get her on the bed, says the nurse. *We're going to need some stitches, and I think we need to X-ray that arm.*

So you're going to send her out.

I think we'd better.

I stay put. That's what I do best.

But when Molly and Michiko come to put me back to bed before shift change, they natter freely.

How many times this week?

This one is the worst yet.

She can't remember to use her walker.

It's too bad, though. They come in here because they're falling at home . . .

Then they fall here too. We can't stop them.

Tie them up, like in the bad old days.

Yeah. That's worse. Way worse.
Better here than at home. At least we know how to pick them up.
We do. Nor do we guilt ourselves as much as family do.
Poor Alice.
I know! It sucks.
It really does.

We are all tucked into bed when Alice comes back from the hospital. Stella strides into our room, flicking the lights on without apology and rapidly turning down the bedspread and sheets on Alice's bed. The ambulance attendants are right behind her. They lift Alice from the stretcher to her bed in one smooth movement.

Lady Alice, you're the lightest load we've had in a long time!

And they're gone.

Her arm is in a cast and the hair has been shaved a bit to accommodate her stitches. It looks to me like the eye is purpling too.

The RN comes in to take Alice's vitals. Stella washes her face and hands quickly, and changes her brief.

They must have given her something good; she's pretty sedated.

Yes, and I have orders for more, so if you think she's in pain let me know. It doesn't look like she needs anything right now.

No. I'm going to give her a hot blanket and hope she sleeps right through.

Which she does.

The sun is shining and my tree is glorious with fall leaves, but my stomach hurts. I look out the window and try to ease my belly, almost rocking, pulling myself towards the bar and letting go. When the nurse comes to hook up my tube-feed, I stop her hand, shake my head and thump the table.

"You don't want this? What's wrong? Your stomach? You're

going to vomit? Okay, I guess it won't kill you to miss a meal but I have to give you a little with your pills."

I acquiesce, and the nurse rolls my bed up to forty-five degrees.

Molly gets Ruby up early—she's off to exercises—and right after breakfast Molly brings the bed flat, puts me on my left side, gives me a suppository, and then rolls the bed back up. Hopefully I'll feel better soon.

The occupational therapist comes in with a standard wheelchair for Alice.

This will do for now. I'll come back to see how well the chair fits her once you've got her up.

Okay, thanks.

I listen to Molly washing Alice in bed. When she flips the curtains back, there's Alice, sitting up uncertainly with her pants around her thighs. I know the shirt Alice is wearing doesn't belong to her. It's loose and stretchy and Alice is swimming in it, but it accommodates her cast. Molly slips a sling behind her like a shawl, and runs the straps under her legs. It's the same type of sling I use.

My stomach quivers. Does this mean Alice can't walk anymore? Or is the suppository working? I feel sicker than ever.

Molly uses the lift to put Alice in the wheelchair. Alice is still dopey and passive, and her eye is decidedly purple and yellow.

Michiko sticks her head in the door.

Hey, can you give me a . . . what, you used the lift? She can't transfer?

I'm sure she can but she hasn't been assessed, and I just can't be arsed to have my hand slapped so early in the week.

The nurse pushes past Michiko, who leaves without whatever she came for, and comes over to unhook my tube-feed. Molly wheels Alice over to the bar, and with one hand Alice grips it and pulls herself up while Molly pulls up her pants and removes the sling. I hear Alice sitting down hard.

I've belted her in and I hope she'll stay. I know it's a restraint because I'm pretty sure she doesn't have the capability to get it off. I left the foot rests off. If she does get the belt off and she decides to stand up and make a run for it, I don't want her to trip on her foot pedals. Plus, if her feet are on the ground, maybe she'll be able to paddle herself around in a bit. Like, when the drugs wear off.

We'll have to talk to OT about it.

Yeah, please do. I think we're okay for today because she's still pretty sedated, but as soon as she gets restless again, I'm going to need to know how you want me to handle her.

There's a lady on third with a doctor's order for a seatbelt restraint.

So it can be done.

We'll see, says the nurse on her way out the door.

Crap, what's happening in this room!

Michiko emerges from behind Mary's curtain with the wash basin in her hands.

Alice has a cast, Ruby's got a raging UTI, Nana's got a bedsore and Mary can't eat or shit. There's some evil-ass spirit operating here!

We need some of your Wiccan magic, Michi. We gotta protect Frannie— she's the only one unscathed!

The tube-feed, little as it was, isn't agreeing with me at all. I shift awkwardly and, to my embarrassment, let out a tremendous burp.

Molly and Michiko laugh outrageously.

"Tell it like it is, Frannie!" howls Michiko.

"Oh my goodness, Fran. Don't look so horrified! It's a good thing. Don't you feel lighter? Better out than in."

"Frannie doesn't need my Wiccan magic . . . she ate those bad spirits, and they gave her gas."

"Yeah, Frannie, did you swallow the suffering? Because that was a mighty wind you let out."

"Quick! Chase it away."

Michi grabs a towel and flaps it into a breeze—Molly quickly follows suit. They're flapping and laughing when the housekeeper walks in.

What are you doing?

We need a change of air in here!

The housekeeper marches over to the tower fan tucked away at the head of Alice's bed and turns it on.

It's working. Didn't you try it?

The housekeeper looks at Michi and Molly as though they're a couple of lunatics on a binge. She shrugs.

Michiko is still giggling. Molly says, *We never thought of that.*

She looks at Michiko and they both burst into laughter again.

They're pretty loud. I take the opportunity to fart as quietly as I can.

Chris gets Astro certified as a companion dog so he can bring him in anytime. Anna, it's amazing how much conversation a dog generates. Chris is a proud parent; he shares every detail about Astro's progress at obedience classes. He's a clever pup, you can tell that right away.

Listen to me! Who'd have thought I'd be acting like a grandma to a dog.

I watch Astro, not paying attention to what Chris is saying until a few words draw my attention.

"That's what my counsellor told me."

Chris in counselling? Well, wonders never cease. Every part of me that can flaps wildly, and I have a huge grin on my face.

Chris returns my smile.

"Got your attention, didn't I? Yeah. That's right. Me, Christian Henry Jensen in counselling. Kind of a surprise, isn't it, after refusing so stubbornly when *you* wanted me to go." Chris playfully almost punches my arm; it's just a tap but I'm astounded. Chris, goofing off!

"Yeah, actually I started going long before all this happened." He must be catching my penchant for gesturing, because the swoop of his hand seems to encompass it all.

"A friend at work got me into it. She's got a couple of kids and Theresa and I were, you know . . . hoping that was going to happen for us. I realized I was looking forward to that baby more than I ever imagined I would. So I asked her, 'Do you have any advice for a prospective parent?' She said, 'Yeah, as a matter of fact, I do. Buddy, you should make a point of knowing yourself, so that you can learn to love yourself. You'll never be able to love anyone more than you love yourself, and you're going to find you want to love that baby real good.'

"You know how sometimes something just hits you? I said, 'I don't know what you're talking about.' My friend looked me in the eye and said, 'Bud, you're so numb you don't know your ass from your elbow.' I was so shocked, I just let her keep talking. She said I'd never dealt with what happened to Angelina. Which was true, I'd never talked about her. Then she goes, 'If you ever need the name of a good counsellor, you just let me know.' She acted like she'd been dying for the opportunity to give me her piece for a long time.

"So I thought that over for a couple of days, and then I chased her down and got that name. I was thinking what with Theresa acting so hormonal from the fertility drugs, and Anna dying, never mind work and learning all that stuff about running the diner, I had a lot coming down the pipe. My God, that would have been enough on its own but as it turned out, um . . . with your stroke . . . Well. I had no idea how big a shit show I was in for, did I? I still wonder if it was an act of God that got me hooked up with my counsellor before all this happened. It's been bad enough, but without her help, honestly, Mom, I think I would have drowned."

I shiver before putting my hand on my heart and I close my eyes for a moment.

"I know, Mom. You want me to be okay. I'm okay. That's why I'm telling you."

I want to grab that counsellor by the shoulders and kiss both her cheeks.

Grief is a peppercorn: it flavours the stew, but right to the bottom of the pot, there's always the possibility of biting down on the real thing and then it hurts.

About five years ago, I went to the lab for some blood work that my doctor ordered, and there, looking poised and professional in her scrubs, was Angelina's best friend, Raven.

I felt broken, as if seeing her there reopened a jagged, gaping wound. That girl was every bit as wild and saucy as Angelina was back in the day. I know my feelings were unreasonable, but I begrudged Raven the success she'd made of herself, hated her for showing me what my girl might have been.

Raven recognized me right away; she went pink, and her lips were tight. She didn't say anything about Angelina, though, while she kept her eyes on the vial that was filling with my blood. I can't blame her—I have been rude to her many times, over the years. I recall that I didn't hold back when she and Ang took their fake ID and got matching tattoos done just before Ang moved out. I'd believed that Raven got Ang into trouble, when if I'd been honest with myself, I knew very well that those two were pretty equally to blame.

Thinking about it put me in a temper all over again.

"Do you still have your tattoo?" I asked roughly.

The colour in Raven's cheeks deepened. She capped off the vial, peeled back her gloves, and lifted the sleeve of her scrub top to reveal her upper arm.

There was the butterfly, turquoise, green, sky blue covering the whole left shoulder like a cap sleeve, just like Angelina's. My eyes filled with tears, and I regretted my unkindness.

"You never heard from her?" I said, unevenly.

"Don't you think I would have told you, Mrs. Jensen? Chris asked me many times. I miss her too, you know."

Fall is slipping away into winter.

I haven't been feeling well, Anna. It's hard to take an interest. I've folded into my body, huddled, cocooned, protecting a glowing coal, waiting.

I'm waiting to feel better. Waiting like a sick cat, quiet, hidden. I sleep a lot.

Is this how you felt, Anna? How did you feel?

I wish I could ask you, now that I'm weakened. If this is what you felt like, I wish I had known.

It's hard to imagine until it happens to you.

On the other hand, the antibiotics are working for Ruby. It was unnerving when she was loopy. I missed my thoughtful, loving friend. She seems to be back to normal now, for which I am very grateful.

The sky isn't even grey yet when Molly comes spinning into the room, extra wired, flipping on the lights, announcing, "We're short today, folks! Happy flu season!" She whirls from bed to bed rolling everyone up for breakfast.

Somehow I've managed to slide so far down my bed that I'm almost past the rails. "How'd you get way down there?" Molly asks, without expecting an answer. She raises the foot of the bed and lowers the head and, reaching over the headboard, grabs the slider from below my shoulders with both hands.

"Bend your knees," she orders, "one, two, three," and as I slide up the bed, I see Molly's face contort with surprise and pain.

"Fuck fuck fuck," she mutters under her breath, turning away. That's the last I see of Molly.

Breakfast is late, and when it does come, it's brought by Janika, a casual.

"Thanks for coming in," says the RN, hooking up my tube-feed.

"If I know I will be alone, I do not come! I do overtime today."

"Blaire said she's coming down to give you a hand," the RN is saying, as Blaire walks through the door.

As soon as the RN is gone, the girls start to chatter.

And Molly? She is not sick, is she?

Molly, no. She pulled her shoulder bringing Frannie up the bed.

Did she by herself?

Blaire nods and Janika clucks with disapproval.

She will not be covered. If there is no one to help her, she must be waiting.

But we've all done it, how many times?

No. I will not do it. I saw with Jeet. They do not help her, what you call, workman's comp? They do not help her.

Molly thinks she's invincible.

What is this?

Molly thinks she can do anything.

Hmph! No one can. So who should to be here? It is Lily?

No, Mich has the flu. So you must be Mich, right? When did they call you?

I am called at seven thirty and say they are desperate.

Yeah, so you're Mich. They told us at report that nights hadn't been able to cover that shift and Molly would be short. Now they'll have to find someone to cover Molly.

It is unacceptable! They should do something! I am not liking working alone!

I know.

The carcass of a cold, dead seal is turning over in my stomach. Oh, Molly. Please let her be okay.

Amit comes in for a day, and Michiko is back, sniffling and grumpy.

Are you well enough to be here, Michi?

I'm okay. It's just . . . hard to go from zero to sixty. It's not like we can say, "Oh sorry, folks, I'm feeling a bit off today, so I'm going to take it easy, I'm not going to wash you." We kind of have to be up for the marathon.

But you don't like to call in unless you're dying.

Basically, yeah.

You and Molly. What a team. Two words for you guys. Self. Care.

Oh hush. My head aches.

So your partner nailed herself?

I texted her last night and she says she thinks she just gave the shoulder a little pull. So she's doing the ice and ibuprofen cure.

Same shoulder she injured on Joyce a couple of years ago?

Yeah, that's why she wasn't taking any chances when it happened. She just bailed right out. She was off quite a while with that injury.

She told me she went hardcore with the weights after that happened.

Oh for sure. Molly's a serious gym rat; she's super fit. But she knows she's not twenty, and that shoulder is vulnerable. She also knows she's not supposed to be lifting people up the bed by herself too, and she did it anyway.

I happen to know she has about a million sick hours.

Exactly. I told her she can stop being so freaking dedicated. Or rather, be more dedicated, and take care of herself so she can continue to serve us all like a slave. Either way.

Amit laughs.

D'you think she listened?

Who, Molly? Nah!

Amit laughs again.

That's our girl!

Well, she's off today, and that's good. Then she's got days off, so that's good too. Lily dropped by her place with a couple of magazines and a jar of chicken soup. She told Molly's husband not to let her move.

Oh yeah? What did he say?

He said, "You try and stop her!"

Oh, perfect! Thank God she's not my resident!

Amen!

When Molly comes back after her regular days off, Michiko and Blaire tease her.

You sure you're good to go?

She's too much of a supernurse to be subdued by a minor injury!

Oh sure. Supernurse. That's just another way of saying control freak, says Molly.

Oh yeah. You're that too.

Molly tosses her head.

All nurses are bossy and controlling. It's a prereq for the job.

But you're over the top.

That's Blaire.

A shadow of uncertainty passes over Molly's face.

Indomitable Molly? I didn't know she had an Achilles heel.

Hey! Quit picking on my partner, slacker! chides Michiko cheerfully. *We're just glad you're back.*

She hugs Molly with one arm.

Nobody feeds me when you're gone.

The girls laugh together.

Hey! I'm feeling better again. I've been feeling better for a while and I didn't even notice the change.

Unbelievable that I could take feeling well for granted again so quickly.

The next time Molly reaches to bring me up the bed by herself, I slap at her wildly and shake my finger.

"You're right," she says. "I'm sorry. Thank you."

Lily helps her slide me up the bed.

You should have been here in the bad old days, before we had electric beds and ceiling lifts.

I can't imagine.

It was a self-perpetuating job . . . We screwed up our backs and got ready to be the next residents!

Things have really changed.

Mostly for the better. Remember when they used to feed people with syringes even if they didn't want to eat?

Oh my God! Did you do that?

No, that was before my time, but the old nurses used to talk about it.

Those head nurses, man, were they strict!

Remember Mrs. Smith?

Oh, I do! Wasn't she *a stickler for the army-style bed. She wanted us to be able to bounce a penny off it.*

I do like a tidy bed, me.

Sure enough, when they're empty, but Mrs. Smith wanted the beds like that even when the patients were in them. A body likes to be able to wiggle the toes.

Mrs. Smith's beds were like a straitjacket.

Painful.

And a wash from her was as good as electroshock.

The RNs actually washed patients in extended care in those days. That would never happen now.

What happened to her, anyway?

Mrs. Smith? She died of cancer. Ages ago.

Well, at least she didn't end up in extended care.

Ha ha, good point.

Oh my goodness.

Not only am I glad I didn't know the unbending Mrs. Smith, I'm also very grateful that I didn't go into nursing.

Maybe I wasn't an especially nice person, but at least I never held anyone down and syringed their breakfast into them.

On the way down to the dining room, Molly and I hear crying coming from room 112.

Dolores. She is aptly named.

Darn it.

Molly parks me just by her door and puts my brakes on. "Give me a sec, Frannie," she says, sliding into Dolores's room.

Oh, sweetie. What's wrong?

Why am I here?

Your body is breaking down and you need help to take care of yourself.

But what is it all for?

You mean in the existential sense? It's a tale, told by an idiot, full of sound and fury, signifying nothing.

Dolores sobs. Molly sighs.

Look, honey. Like everyone else, you have to live until you die.

So I'm waiting to die? Is everyone just waiting for me to die?

No, Dolores! Of course not. I simply meant we are all going to die. That is life in a nutshell.

I'm used to being busy.

Of course! You had all the responsibility and work of six kids, to say nothing of their friends and later your grandchildren, and you were crazy busy all your life. Now that it's your role to be cared for instead of being the caregiver, you don't know how to take it.

Dolores wails: *Yes!*

But you have to trust that both sides of the coin are equally important, caretaker and care receiver. That's really crucial. You don't know how you're going to affect another person, even now. You just don't know. Something you say, some part you play may completely change someone's life, maybe my life. Maybe your own life. You just have to trust that your life is still significant. You will get through this the same way you got through everything else—one day at a time.

Snuffling. Dolores sounds like a dog nosing about its dish.

Besides. I love you.

Yes. You do, don't you?

I do. Now let's go have lunch.

Molly wheels Dolores past me.

She'll be back in a second. I can wait. I know how.

A bout of insomnia got me hooked on the Travel Channel.

"If you could go anywhere in the world, where would you go?" I asked you idly one day over coffee. Theresa and Chris were married in Aruba. Other than that, we didn't travel, either of us. We didn't make it a priority. In fact, except for your yearly ski week, neither of us ever seemed to take holidays. I was so out of practice with the idea of vacationing that travel had become frightening. Having recognized that, I wanted to confront it. Dragons are for slaying.

The idea that we might travel together was gestating in my mind.

Looking up, I noticed that you were looking very tired, and I remembered that you'd been looking tired the last time I saw you too.

"Hawaii is supposed to be beautiful," I said.

"I found a lump," you said.

BUTTERFLY

Christmas is coming. All the day aides from both wings help the activity aides put up the big tree in the dining room and the glittering garlands in the sunroom. The skies outside are stubbornly grey, and only the tinsel and fairy lights brighten the room. No wonder the ancients devised this holiday, Anna, to distract us from winter's gloomy prospect.

Remember the wonderful breads you used to make? The stollen, the braided bread stuffed with marzipan and chocolate, the poppy-seed rolls? The diner was fragrant as a bakery with the smell of fresh bread and coffee. Oh my God, I can feel my bones relaxing.

We made some good memories, didn't we, Anna? Angelina's glee at receiving the very skateboard she'd wanted. The year Chris invested hours making a science fiction gingerbread starship. The expensive robes the kids bought for both of us the year that Chris and Angelina took a paper route together. I remember good food too, and afternoons playing Monopoly. Normal family stuff.

When I think of actual Christmas Day, though, I always have an aftertaste of disappointment. Everyone decries the materialism, but it was more than that: it was the bloody unreasonable expectation that somehow for a day we would be better than we were. Angelina didn't magically become compliant, I certainly didn't suddenly have more patience, and Chris didn't stop disappearing at the first sign of tension just because it was December 25. I couldn't make Christmas perfect for the kids . . . or make them perfect for it, not even for a day. I see that now.

So why does my heart rise at the sight of a few glass balls set in a bowl of holly? Why should my eyes mist up when Lily comes dancing into the room wearing a Santa hat, in a red and white candy-cane-striped scrub?

Then I think, who cares about the "why"? I'll take the gift . . . the light and the glitter, and Lily like a little Christmas pixie. For now I feel good. That's all that matters.

Lily and Michiko are my nurses for all of December; I have that to look forward to.

Lily has been glowing lately and it's lovely, but . . . has she found a man? Is that the reason for her shine? Is she headed for another fall? Frankly I'm a little worried.

"Would you like to know a secret?" she whispers, while doing my care.

Of course I do!

"I'm seeing someone."

Here we go. I sigh a little.

"You guessed, didn't you, and I can see that you're worried, aren't you? You're justified in being skeptical, but this time is different."

Like a sweater is different from a pullover. I can't even pretend.

Lily smiles.

"I think you'll like this. Do you remember when I told you all I wanted was a decent man? I think I finally heard myself. Listen.

"I've been friends with Nathan since high school and he's been Sierra's chum ever since she was born. He went into nursing, and got his RN, then spent a couple of years up north, and then he did some volunteer work in Ghana. We stayed in touch on Facebook, of course.

This fall he came home and started working in the hospital, so we've been spending a lot of time together, Sierra, Nate and I, just as friends, as we've always done in the past. About a month ago, he said, 'I want you to think about something.'"

Lily swipes at my armpit ineffectually with the washcloth.

"I said, 'Of course,' and he said, 'I know you don't feel this way about me, but I've always loved you, and I love Sierra, and I think we'd make a good couple.' My heart just sank, Francesca." Washcloth still in hand, Lily put her hand to her chest, as if to protect a sore spot.

"I thought, *Here we go, this is where I lose my friend*, and I tried to brush him off gently. I said, 'Nate, that's very sweet. . .' He just stopped me right there. He said, 'Don't say anything. You can do the same old thing that you've been doing over and over, because God knows that works so well for you, or you can try something different. You think it over. Think about what it might be like to choose a man who really loves you, even if you don't start out feeling the same way. If you think it might be worth trying something new, call me, and we'll go on a date.'

"Then he got up and left, just like that."

I'm getting cold, because Lily has stopped washing me entirely, but I don't care. I want the rest of the story.

"I truly didn't know what to do, Francesca. On the one hand, I didn't feel any chemistry at all, because Nate's always been just my good friend Nate. However, when I spoke to some of the older married ladies that work here, especially the ones who've had arranged marriages, they said the chemistry only lasts the first ten minutes anyway. Of course my younger friends said, 'How can you have a relationship if there's no spark?'

"Then, I met this other guy, who shall remain nameless, because he's not important, and he was just as good-looking and suave and sexy as River or any of those guys ever were, and I thought, *He's the one. I'm just going to have to tell Nathan my heart is elsewhere*. I made up my mind to do that, and I felt the relief one feels when one makes up one's mind, but I hadn't done the deed. One night, I was texting back and forth with this new guy just before bed, and I fell asleep with my phone in my hand, and I had a terrible dream. I dreamt I was chasing butterflies, getting very tired, because whenever I caught one, it would turn into the Cheshire Cat from *Alice in Wonderland*, except that it had River's face. The thing would laugh at me and say, 'It doesn't matter, does it?' and disappear and then I'd have to start running again. I woke up sobbing . . . do you know *Alice in Wonderland*?"

I nod. I was very small when Papa read it to me.

"Oh, I loved that book as a child. I read it about a million times. Do you remember when Alice asks the Cheshire Cat which road to take, the cat asks where Alice wants to go, and Alice says she doesn't know, so the cat says, 'Then it really doesn't matter, does it?'

"I got up, right there, still crying, and I made myself a gin and tonic . . . a really nice one, Francesca, with the good gin and a real lime, and I sat there thinking about River, and that guy I fell for last spring, and the hot new guy and all the other hot new guys out there, and how they've all been alike, and how I just have to get their attention and how they never once cared for me, and I had a really good blubbering cry. Then I called up Nate, oh, it must have been about three in the morning, and I said, 'Okay. Let's give this a try.' He said, 'Great. I'll see you tomorrow.' We've been together ever since."

Lily starts working again. She slips my left arm into my valentine-red shirt from Carlotta's Boutique, and shimmies the shoulder into place.

"And you know what?" she asks as my head pops through the neckband. "You won't believe this." She brings my right arm through.

"I think I'm falling for him!"

Lily gives me a soppy look. I give her a motherly smile and pat her hand. She hugs me and I can feel all the love she has to give; she burns with it, under her tidy scrub and under the skin of her baby-soft cheeks. Lily, my Lily, was made to be loved.

He'd better not change his mind, I'm thinking. If he changes his mind, I'm going to hex him. That's what I'm going to do.

I didn't really stop secretly obsessing about Angelina (nursing my sorrow like an alcoholic drinking quietly in private, hiding her empty bottles) until your diagnosis. Then I was incredibly angry at myself. Why did I waste the time I had with you, steeping in a misery that couldn't be changed? I didn't want to lose another precious minute and I threw myself into your life with desperation, to the point where you finally said, "Look, *liefje*, I am not so sick yet, but I will be if you don't let me breathe."

"I'm just trying to help you!"

"You're smothering me," you said.

I learned. Then I learned flexibility as your prognosis changed from serious to critical, and you needed more help.

It was terrible to see your life taken from you by inches; your suffering was profound. I don't need to tell you that—you lived it. But I hope you also know that it was wonderful.

I didn't have companionship looking after my children—they were not my equals; they were my children. We were three in a tippy boat. I was trying to stay afloat, aiming for shore, pulling hard. What happened with you was a completely different kind of caretaking. A different kind of love.

The pain, the time-eating day-to-day challenges, the treatments, the fear, the doctors' waiting rooms, the vomit, the misery of it all. I wouldn't wish it on anyone. But I had my silver lining; I got to show you how much I loved you before I lost you, and that was a gift. I wrapped it about me like a cloak.

Lily stops in on her coffee break, phone in hand, to talk to Michiko.

Molly just texted me. She's at the dollar store. Do we need anything?

Tell her to get some of those barrettes for Nana, I can't think where the last ones got to, and some socks for Dolores.

Can't we ask the family for socks for her?

We did, and they got us a big bag of those men's cotton crew socks that don't have any give, they're totally useless. Even if I could get them on, which I can't, they're too thick to fit in her shoes. Look, it's easier to buy the damn socks than it is to talk to that family, and we're making our own lives easier. Molly will know what to get, she was bitching at me about those stupid socks yesterday. Tell her I'll chip in.

I see Melissa's got a couple of really nice new sweaters, where did those come from?

Gurinder brought them in.

Gurinder from the third floor?

No, Gurinder from the kitchen. She says her mom lost a ton of weight.

Well, bless her, because Melissa's gaining weight, and it's getting to be a nightmare to dress her. Everything she owns is too tight except for those sweaters; they fit her perfectly . . . Oh my goodness, look at this: Molly found Christmas earrings that light up!

Let's tell her to get a pair for Frannie!

Tacky! I make a face, and Michi and Lily laugh.

It's been a lazy kind of a day. Even the aides are relaxed. I am sitting in the sunroom, which actually *is* a sunny room today, and Michiko and Molly are pretending to fill in their bowel books and shift reports, but really they finished long ago. They have surrendered to the warmth and light—so unusual for December on the west coast. I'm not sure I've ever seen Molly with her feet up before. Lily is working in the East Wing today, but she's come down to tell Molly that she's finished the mending Molly asked her to do, and now she's sitting on the side of Michiko's chair, leaning over to rub her shoulders. It's an old-fashioned feeling. There is warmth and companionship and ease . . . it's lovely.

To make my happiness complete, Chris comes in and leans against the window chatting with the girls, who make a fuss over Astro.

Astro makes Chris relax. He's friendlier because Astro is so friendly.

"You're looking good since you started swimming again," says Michiko.

How does *she* know? Chris smiles at me.

"You probably don't remember, but Michiko was in some of my classes in grade twelve."

"But you went to class, I didn't."

"You rebel," chides Chris.

"You nerd," she counters, grinning.

Lily is scratching Astro behind the ears.

"It feels so good to move. Since my mom had her stroke . . . it was a terrible blow. I don't take mobility for granted anymore."

"It's a gift, that's for sure."

"We all say . . . well, people say, 'Oh, I wouldn't want to live like that. If that happens to me, let me die.' Mom used to say that. But she's adjusted. Haven't you, Mom?"

I nod. That's the short answer. I don't have the energy for the long answer. I snap my fingers and Astro jumps onto my lap. His claws hurt me, but I don't mind.

Chris is still talking. "Do your people here ever say they wish they could die?"

I lose track of the voices when everyone talks at once.

Sure they do.

We get that a lot.

But people don't always mean it.

Sometimes they mean it.

Sometimes they're just bitching. They get a little ache and they're all, "Call the doctor!" and "Why don't you do *something?"*

And people don't get that there comes a time when we can't do anything for them . . .

Or the cure is way worse than the disease.

They want death to be easy, but it's not, it's hard.

They want death to be simple, but it's complicated. You get sick, you rally, you go down again . . . it can be a real roller coaster.

Yeah, lots of times we just don't know when someone is going to die for sure. They bounce back.

And it's really hard on families.

Why is that? The roller-coaster effect, I mean. That's Chris.

Well, modern medicine, right? So we take good care of them, and they rally, and they swoop down again, and we take good care of them, and they rally and on it goes.

So when they finally die, it's a shock, because they've come back so many times, it doesn't seem possible that death will actually come.

I shudder. When I take a run at that buffalo jump, I hope to God I'm going over. On the other hand, that's what I always said before, and I changed my mind when I came here. When my time comes, will I just want to live?

Astro jumps off of my knee.

The worst is when they can't swallow, so we have to stop feeding them.

Suddenly we are all very serious, because we're thinking about Mary.

Yeah, that's bad.

Well, what happens then? asks Chris. *They just . . . starve to death?*

All the girls talk at once again.

It's not quite like that.

It's just like that!

Because what are you going to do? You can't feed them if they're choking . . .

Chris says, *Can't you adjust the texture of the food? I know some of your people are eating a purée diet.*

We're talking about someone who can't even swallow thickened or purée. Like your mom, but there's no point in putting a tube in this person because they've requested that not be done or because physically it's not an option.

But it's a long, slow death and I hate it.

Now it's Chris's turn to shudder. *Isn't there anything you can do?*

Oh, we give them buckets of drugs.

But there's a legal limit. And we'd be lying if we said it isn't a horrible death because it is.

Can we not talk about this? says Lily. *I think we're upsetting Francesca.*

All eyes on me, I try to smile.

"Come on, Mom. Let's take a turn outside."

"I'm sorry, Frannie," says Molly. "We got a little carried away."

Michiko looks a little shame-faced. "Sorry, Fran. Didn't mean to bring you down."

I wave like the queen. All very informative, I'm sure. I'm just grateful I didn't throw up. On impulse, I mime sticking my fingers down my throat, and everyone laughs out of proportion to the joke.

We needed to. Laugh, that is.

But I feel differently, now, about what you did, Anna. I was so angry when you stopped treatment, I wanted to kill you myself.

"You're giving up!" I said.

You said, "You think love is trying to fix someone."

"You still have a chance. Thirty percent, the doctor said. Why won't you fight?"

"Thirty percent!" You coughed, bringing up blood, which you deposited in a tissue. You were so thin then, all your golden hair gone.

"Thirty percent is just the doctor's way of saying 'I'm covering the tush now.'"

"You don't know that."

"The cure is worse than the disease."

How could I argue that, my poor friend?

"I'm not giving up," you said. "I'm choosing what I want."

It was a bitter cup. I had no choice but to drink it.

How can I blame you now, when I look at Mary, her health failing a little more every day? Who would want that?

Mary is on our minds because she's barely eating now. She can still swallow, but only thickened juice.

"You can live a long, long time on just fluids," Molly tells me, her eyes kind.

When Mary has a bed day, which is more often than not now, Ruby stops beside her and rests her hand on her tucked-in shoulder and says a little prayer. I think it's "The Lord is my shepherd, I shall not want," but I'm not sure. Ruby keeps her voice low.

It's odd to think how little I know, or Ruby either, for that matter, about the person who has stopped eating in the bed across from mine. Did she love her husband? How many children did she have? Did she prefer Dickens or did she read romances in the afternoon? When she had a bad day, did she put a dram of whiskey in her tea? We don't know any of these things, and yet Mary belongs to us. This is Mary now, and she is ours.

I know the girls worried about Alice walking again (or rather, falling again), but somehow her latest tumble seems to have changed her permanently. She sits in the wheelchair, picking at threads in her sweater. Twice a week, the activity aides belt her into the upright walker and take her for a turn, one person at her side and another following with the empty wheelchair right behind her, as they used to do for Mary. Hearty Josie comes and takes her mother out, wrapping her in a huge cape, swaddling her with scarves and jamming a thick woollen hat with knitted posies on the brim securely over her ears. Tucked in with lap blankets, Alice looks like a pile of bedding bound for the laundromat. Hello, Lady Oak Bay, I think unkindly, with a grin. Sometimes Josie brings ice cream and spoons it into Alice's mouth while Alice smacks her lips.

"It's a far cry from gin and tonic and appies, isn't it, Mom?" says Josie. "But it will have to do."

Chris and I have a serious conference about the Christmas chocolates.

"I know Michiko is going away just before Christmas, and you like her, don't you?"

I nod, dying to ask how he knows Mich is going on vacation and what she plans to do, but we're moving right along.

"So I'm thinking we should do this pretty soon, okay?"

It makes sense, so I nod.

"I've been thinking about the chocolate thing too, Mom. How attached to the idea of chocolate are you? Because we get a lot of Christmas chocolates at the office too, and it gets a little sickening. It makes us all jonesy."

It's true. All that sugar gets to be a bit much. But what is "jonesy"? I wish I could ask.

"What do you think about one of those baskets for the whole team? Something with boxes of tea and lots of fresh fruit and that kind of thing? With a really nice card expressing your appreciation."

I nod, but I'm not jumping up and down. What I really wanted was to be able to give something to my girls personally.

Then Chris pulls out a tiny, shiny box. There are two exquisite chocolates in the box and they smell heavenly.

"I've brought this for you to try, Mom. I can't be bothered with cheap crap chocolate, but these are really delicious. I think if I put a little on your tongue, it will melt there and you shouldn't choke. Are you willing to risk it?"

Oh God, yes I am! Chris bites one of the chocolates, leaving a sliver in his fingertips. I open my mouth and he places it on my tongue. It melts there, tasting like heaven. I close my eyes. Bliss!

"Pretty nice, huh? Okay, this is my plan. I'm going to buy you a bunch of these. The little boxes will keep the chocolates from being squished, and you can keep them in a bag and hand them out. You'd like that, wouldn't you?"

I put my hand on my heart, pat it, and then give a thumbs-up, grinning.

"Not bad, eh? Last year was a bit of a nightmare, but I think this year is going to be better!"

I take my fist and swing it across my body, as I've seen Michiko do: go get 'em, cowboy!

"We can do this, right? No more crying!"

I grin and Chris grins back.

"Is there anything else you can think of? Have I got you covered?"

Suddenly I remember the most important thing of all. My breathing comes quicker and I jab at Chris. Tears start to come. Who is going to buy a present for him?

"Hey! What's this?" Chris reaches for a tissue and swipes at my cheek. "What's wrong, Mom?"

I try to mime a box for Chris. It's pretty poor acting, but by some miracle, he gets it.

"You want a present for me?"

I nod and gasp for air.

Chris sits back down. "Easy does it. I'll tell you what, Mom. You know I have control of your money, don't you?"

Actually, I'd temporarily forgotten, but never mind that.

"I don't need any more stuff, but I'm planning to take Astro up island for a little getaway between Christmas and New Year's. How about you take me out to dinner somewhere really nice? That's something I wouldn't do for myself. Would you like that?"

I nod and snuffle into my tissues, point to myself, and rub my fingers against my thumb: I'll pay!

"Okay, then. That's a nice present that I won't have to dust. I'll really enjoy that. Thank you, Mom. I'll take pictures."

Maybe it will be a good Christmas after all.

Then I have another spell of not feeling well. It fogs up my brain, leaves me apathetic. I'm shocked when Lily tells me it's been a week since I got up. How did that happen? Out of the blue, I think, "Will this be the last time I sit in my chair? Should I treasure this moment?" It's a morbid thought.

I remember how you used to have good days and bad ones, Anna, even before you decided you'd had enough "treatment" and switched to palliative care. Once that happened, I bought that hospital bed and put it in the living room, so that you could look out the bay windows into the garden. I was glad that I'd planted extra tulip bulbs the previous fall. The garden was a riot of colour that spring. It does me good to remember you reclining there, rolled up in your bed, enjoying the flowers with all your being.

There was no pleasure in food by then. You said you missed your appetite, but the sight, the smell, the very thought of food made your stomach heave. I didn't make coffee; I bought it in takeout cups and drank it in the car, brushed my teeth before coming near you. When you died, the smell of coffee made me sad for months and months.

I don't remember my last meal. The last time I danced. The last time Chris held my hand on the way to school. The last time I blew raspberry kisses on Angelina's belly to make her laugh.

I don't remember when I learned what I now know: Angelina was her own person. She had her own path and it wasn't wrong of me to let her go. I can't remember when I learned that, or how. I wish I'd had more time, and more acceptance. That knowledge didn't come soon enough to help her. But it's here soon enough for me to forgive myself, I realize now. I still have time for that.

Lily is bent over Ruby, combing her hair, and I watch them both fondly.

Sometimes you get lucky: you get a roommate like Ruby, a nurse like Lily. You have the insight you need when you need it. You choose the right path.

Sometimes you don't. You stumble in the dark, hands outstretched, hoping to get your bearings, never realizing that all you have to do is open your eyes.

One day in the week before Christmas, Lily keeps me up after lunch. We are all up, even Mary, who is looking very frail, and we're herded into the dining room, where we sit in a circle like scouts around the campfire. We wait and wait until our bums ache and burn, when, accompanied by a small choir of amateurs stumbling over the words to "Joy to the World," Santa bursts into the room, complete with the red suit and the black belt and the white beard.

"Have you been a good girl, Francesca?" he roars, close enough for me to see the perspiration on his forehead before he flings himself in my lap, carefully letting the arm of my wheelchair support his weight.

It's Amit!

"Let's see: I'd like new skis, and some chocolate, and"—flinging off his Santa Claus hat—"some new hair to cover the spot that's bare!"

Everyone is laughing and I push at his back until he pretends to fall off my lap with a jingle of bells, more like a hefty jester than Santa Claus.

A couple of tiny elves in green suits take beautifully wrapped presents from a trolley and deliver them, one for each of us. Lily is helping an exquisite wee elf who looks just like her . . . oh, Sierra! They bring me a flat silvery package with a sparkly ice-blue bow. Sierra helps me open it: an empty photo album and a calendar.

"For your snapshots, Frannie. So they don't get lost."

I am delighted.

Ruby gets chocolates and a soft velour blanket in a rich peacock blue that matches her eyes. Mary gets bed socks (pink) and Santa puts a string of cranberry-red beads around Alice's neck. She tangles her hand in it, pulling hard. Molly bounds for it just as it breaks and the tiny balls go skittering across the floor.

"Oh dear! I guess those weren't appropriate for you!" she says, handing Alice a cookie as she deftly wheedles what remains of the necklace out of her hands.

Nana gets lavender-scented lotion and Lily opens it and gently massages a little into Nana's hands. Michiko bends down and, laughing, allows Sierra to position a large red and green bow in her hair. Amit kneels and kisses Ruby's hand. Two of the singers are doing a wonderful job with "Baby, It's Cold Outside." One of the elves throws a shower of confetti snow, then takes a run at it, sliding across the floor almost into Alice's lap.

Just like life, the whole thing is over in a matter of minutes.

"Merrry Christmas!" calls Amit, while Sierra, taking her responsibility seriously, shakes a heavy red ribbon mounted with bells.

"If I don't see you, have a great time in Montreal, Amit!" calls Molly.

"On Dasher, on Dancer, on Prancer, on Vixen, we're off to the East Wing, my bald spot needs fixin'!"

When Chris brings in the Christmas basket and the little boxes of chocolate, he has a package for me too.

"Do you want to wait for Christmas or do you want to open it now?"

Now! Always now!

With only one functioning hand, I make a mess of the beautiful paper, which is a pity, but I can't wait: my inner child is fully alive and well and I claw at the wrapping like a hungry bear. It must be clothes. What else would it be? Does Chris know how to buy clothes? That's what I'm eager to discover.

The shirt I finally extract from the tissue paper in the box is gorgeous, the deep ocean shade of blue that was your favourite colour, in a stretchy knit fabric that will make it easy for the aides to dress me.

"Do you like it, Mom?"

I know he can see how much I love it. My smile is reaching right up to my eyes.

There's more.

Chris puts a smaller box on top of my new shirt, now spread across my lap. I shake the box. Jewellery.

Chris helps me with the tape on this one. He holds the bottom of the box while I pry off the lid.

It is a silver pendant, a concave circle and on the top, off centre, there is a round piece of amber held in place by a smooth silver lip, so that the golden yellow jewel appears to be floating like a full moon in the sky.

Lying on my new blue top, it's absolutely exquisite.

"I have a little apology to make about this one, Mom. Anna bought this for you."

I'm shaken. Anna? I stroke the beautiful silver with the tip of my finger.

Chris babbles on.

"I haven't really got an excuse. She asked me to hang onto it and give it to you for Christmas after she died. But then Theresa had another miscarriage, remember? I had a lot on my mind and I guess I just forgot all about it. I found it when I was getting all my stuff out of Theresa's house. Anna said to tell you, 'Thank you.' She said you'd understand. I'm sorry, Mom, I really am."

I bring my finger to my lips . . . shhh. I reach for Christian's hand and kiss his knuckles.

The little boxes of chocolate are a huge success. Chris brought them in one of those reusable grocery bags so that I can keep them accessible on my table to hand out personally whenever I want. Most of the boxes are shiny gold, but others are sparkling blue. "Those are for anyone who is vegan or lactose intolerant or allergic to nuts," Chris says. So I gather he's figured out that Michiko is vegan and I wonder what else he knows.

Chris has put little handmade stickers on the bottoms of the blue boxes that say, "Nut and dairy free" so, he tells me, that I don't get myself in a frustrating tizzy trying to explain. I'm grateful for that.

"You know these are the best chocolates money can buy, don't you?" Lily says, opening her box and placing one on her tongue as though she was receiving holy sacrament.

"Frannie, you're spoiling us!" says Molly, hugging me.

Fabby takes hers to eat on her supper break and comes back to tell me that my chocolates went straight to the baby and he's been doing a happy dance all evening. She puts my hand on her belly so that I can feel the little guy kicking. Stella says she's going to eat hers when she has her tot of Scotch before bed. It turns out the night nurses, Heather and Julie, are both allergic to nuts and they receive the sparkly blue boxes.

When Michiko is working with Blaire, I give them their chocolates.

Oh my God, this is heavenly, swoons Michi after thanking me.

Now you can get fat with the rest of us, says Blaire.

Aren't you going to eat yours?

Blaire flushes. *It's such a pretty box. I thought I'd save it for Nadine's stocking. There's lots of chocolate at the team centre.*

Not like this, there isn't.

When Michi leaves the room, I bang my box of tissues to get Blaire's attention. It's not easy because when Blaire is not my nurse, she pretends that I don't exist. It's not personal. She treats all of us that way. "Not my group," she says. But I persist, and when Blaire saunters over, I slip a second box into her hand. It's for Stephen, and I try to make her understand by signing that I'm patting a small boy's head. I don't know if she gets it. Her eyes are both sad and angry as she thanks me. But that's okay. That's just Blaire.

On Christmas Day, volunteers come in and there is chamber music: two flutes and a harp.

Ruby loves this. Janika, who is covering for Michi, got Ruby up early so that Milton could take her to the morning service. They were back in time for lunch and now Milton is sitting next to her, holding her fingers like a courtier escorting a duchess.

Anna, I finger your necklace, thinking irrationally how beautifully the silver complements the tinkling flowing music.

When the music is over, we applaud as best we can. Tea is served and treats doled out on red napkins printed with holly and berries. They have shortbread decorated with maraschino cherries, fruitcake and mince tarts. The sweets don't tempt me. But if someone offered me a bowl of Mama's good Italian Christmas soup and a handful of your speculaas, I'd think I'd died and gone to heaven.

On Boxing Day, I am sick again. I have a lot of pain in my stomach.

"Something is going on here," says Lily, "this isn't normal." She gets the nurse. Apparently I'm running a low-grade temperature.

"Do you want us to hold the tube-feed again?" asks the nurse, and I nod, grateful.

I'm given Tylenol and Gravol suppositories, but they do nothing for the pain.

You never got to the stage where you needed twenty-four-hour care, Anna. You chose not to get there. You had lots of medications, more than enough, and when you decided to take them all at once, you knew that you needed to take Gravol first to keep from throwing up. When you chose to stop active treatment, you told your doctor in a general way that you wouldn't be waiting around for the bitter end. You made sure that she only half believed you. You didn't want any social workers poking around, fussing about whether you were a suicide risk.

You never told me the day you were going to die. You left notes. You did your best to protect me from any shadow of accusation. I got a visit from the police. Even at the time, I felt that was fair enough.

I don't believe in suicide, as a rule. But I know why you did it and I respect that.

I really don't feel good.

It's too late for me to plan the way you did, Anna. The best I could do was to fill in the Degree of Intervention form. I ask myself, do I regret that I don't have the option to make the choice you did? I search my heart as truthfully as I can; the answer is no, and I am pleased.

When the nurse comes back to see if the Tylenol has had any effect, I shake my head.

"I'm going to phone the doctor and see if I can get you some better drugs," she says.

Good. I'm not in excruciating agony, but I certainly don't want it to get any worse. The pain is taking up a lot of space in my brain.

Guess who I saw the other day, Michi?

Can't.

Muriel.

Muriel, Muriel.

Oh, you know. Muriel Tan.

Oooh. I loved her! How is she doing?

She's doing great. Says she's seeing a really nice guy.

Was she glad to see you?

Well, you know, kinda.

Oh, Molly. She didn't want to be reminded, did she?

That's it. I mean, the last few months of Frank's life were pretty horrific. ALS is such a bitch-awful disease.

Remember, she promised she was going to drop in and keep in touch, but she never did, and I totally get it.

Me too. Family doesn't want to come back here after their loved one dies.

Muriel did a stand-up job of supporting Frank as he was all through the progression of his disease, but when he died, she got to have the guy she married back, y'know? Happy as she was with the care he got here, to say nothing of the support she got, she really doesn't want to be thinking about the guy Frank became.

But it's tough for us, right? We not only lost Frank when he died, we lost Muriel too. And the kids. Damn, those were nice kids.

The whole family was awesome. Yeah, I remember . . . this was before your time, Michi, just after I started working here. There was this younger couple, probably early seventies. They'd only been together a couple of years; they were in love, really adorable. He had a massive stroke on the ski hill. She came to see her guy every day, like, she was dedicated. *I really admired her, we chatted all the time. When the dude died about six months later, she was in packing up his stuff, and she thanked me for everything we'd done for him, and I said, "But we'll see you around." See, I was green, I didn't know any better. She said, "Hell no, I won't be back." She said, "I was afraid I'd grow old here, waiting for him to die. I'm off to Catalina Island; I've got a job there. Toodle-oo. You've been a peach." She gave me a big hug and I never saw her again.*

Sounds like my kinda girl!

You know, I wasn't thinking that way, but now that you mention it, yeah!

Happy New Year.

My new drugs are amazing but I'm very tired and quite groggy. I am not sure why but it seems that both Ruby and I are more and more content just lying on our beds, resting.

Those two are going down together, says Molly.

My eyes are closed; I'm breathing deeply and the girls' voices are low. My Molly. My Lily.

Yes, I wonder if it's coincidence or . . .

Grace?

Or maybe will.

You think so? I know Ruby's ready, but Frannie? She's still so young.

Comparatively young.

Yeah, but . . . I've always thought of Frannie as such a fighter.

Absolutely, but I definitely see a mellowing in her. And a letting go.

Molly speaks with affection: *Well, you're the psychic.*

Oh nooo. I just meant . . .

I'm teasing you, sweetie. Hey, I value your opinion, Lily. Besides. What we think isn't gonna change a thing. We're just here to support the journey.

That's a strange conversation to overhear. Now that the girls are gone I open my eyes and look over at Ruby. She's deafer than I am, and she appears to be deeply asleep, but who knows. Maybe she's a plausible faker, like me.

So I'm "going down," am I? Is that what this is? I feel a flash of anger and a twitch in my bum right arm as if I had narrowly resisted the urge to slap someone. I experience a sensation of falling, and then, almost like a hallucination, dozens of images from my life speed through my mind: a pearl earring lost in my twenties, Ang laughing as she chased after Chris on the beach, the smooth length of my thigh as I put on nylons, the taste of real maple syrup, the crippling grasp of my favourite client's handshake, the smell of paint when we put a fresh coat on the living room, a tulip broken in the rain lying on the ground in my garden. The sensations form a giddy montage. I feel a bit nauseous and I'm glad when the swirling stops as abruptly as it started.

I recall a conversation that I overheard shortly after I came here; I feel it nudging at my consciousness. I was sitting quietly in the sunroom, listening to Molly, Michi, Blaire, and maybe a couple of others I couldn't name. They were talking about someone I didn't know.

What is she hanging on for?

We want to believe that when someone's ready to go, they'll go, but when we get one who's lying there day after day, saying "Why can't I die?" it kind of shakes that belief.

There must be a reason.

No reason!

Death is like labour. It's hard work!

People don't realize that.

Yeah, they think there's a drug for that.

We do the best we can and sometimes it's still not enough.

I've seen some hard deaths.

We all have.

Like this one we've got going on right now.

There was a kind of universal shudder.

The morphine isn't touching her.
Have they tried a fentanyl patch?
Every night I pray she gets to go.
Oh God, me too.

Odd to think that the woman they were talking about is long gone now, and although I never met her, she has this place in my brain.

This "going down," if that's what it is, is beyond my control.

I am here and now. Ruby is over there. Lily and Molly are close. This is the quilt you gave me, Anna, soft, like the fuzzy warmth of a baby's head.

My eyes are closing again and I let them.

The pain of losing Angelina was so terrible, there were times I thought it would have been better if she had never been born.

But then again, if I hadn't been pregnant with Angelina, if I hadn't had Chris in tow, I would never have gone to your diner that day. We would never have become friends. Chris would have never been an older brother, and he was a *good* older brother, patient, loving and kind. I remember him playing pony with Angelina laughing on his back. Reading her stories. Helping her learn to skateboard. Even as she got older and wilder, and they had no interests in common, he still cared for his sister.

I'm so grateful that I had my wild child, my darling Angelina, even if it was only for a little while. She was so beautiful, especially when she was in motion: jumping on the trampoline in Raven's backyard, her hair flying; running arms outstretched after the ducks at the park; throwing herself at me, fiercely physical, so rough always.

After all these years, it still hurts. But it's a dull ache now.

So you know that little one that's dying on the third floor?

Yeah, yeah, skin and bones, right?

Right. So the daughter came in with a bunch of ice cream. She told the staff, don't bother with the Ensure and the yucky protein shakes, give her ice cream three times a day if she wants it, cuz this time next year she won't be here.

Aw damn, I love that!

Yup. She said her mom's been on a diet her whole life and they used to laugh and joke together about this day and how she's gonna eat all the ice cream she wants. She brought strawberry ripple and butter pecan and triple chocolate threat and the kitchen put it in the freezer with her name on it.

Oh my God, I'm tearing up.

I know, right? It pays to talk things out with your family, there could be ice cream in it for you when it really matters!

Good call.

Ruby bounces back. After a couple of days she is up and about again, going to exercises and chapel as she did before.

I'm happy to have my eyes open, but I just want to lie here. That's all I want to do.

I'm glad I had Chris and the nurse help me with the Degree of Intervention form. I don't think I'd be up to doing it now. I don't think I could concentrate. I haven't touched the things on my table for days. My new calendar is still in its cellophane wrapping.

I'm getting my meds by injection now. It's my turn to have a "butterfly" needle attached to my arm. What an image! Butterfly. Beautiful. Fragile. Capable of flight, like an angel.

My thoughts are capricious; they amuse me. The pain is still there, but I don't care. The morphine is effective.

I drift away again.

"I don't know how to say this, but I've got to try. It's not that I don't want you around. You're still important to me. But I don't *need* you. I'll be okay. I don't want to see you suffer. So if you want to go, go. I know you love me. And I love you."

I can't get my eyes open. I should show up for this—look! Chris is making an effort to express his feelings. I never thought I'd see the day. Lord, I never even knew that I *wanted* to see the day—didn't even know that I was craving and needing that until the words came out of his mouth. Inside I smile, but I can't drag up the energy to make my muscles move.

If only I could open my eyes.

Now Chris is taking my hand. "Are you ready?" he asks me.

It is for his comfort and peace of mind that I am able to will everything I have left into squeezing once, and letting go.

There. I've done my best. Dearest son, I hope you understand.

It is afternoon. Almost shift change. Molly and Lily are doing their final room checks, and I know they're talking about me. My eyes are closed, but in my mind, I see the three of us. It all feels very distant, very remote.

It looks like she's going to beat Mary out the door.

That's Molly.

Yes. We weren't expecting that. But her directive says "comfort measures only." She went through it with Chris only just a little while back.

Where is Chris?

I think he said goodbye. I don't think Francesca would feel free to go if he was here. She was pretty protective.

She'd spare him. Oh my God. I don't know who I feel worse for.

Francesca or Chris?

No! Frannie or Mary.

Molly, don't feel bad for Francesca.

I do!

Oh my gosh. Mama Molly is crying.

Oh, sweetie. You're sad for yourself.

I am! I love her so much. And I have the feeling she got ripped off. Her life was hard and short. It isn't fair.

She's choosing the happy ending, Molly.

What do you mean? This doesn't look like a happy ending to me!

But it kind of is. An ending is when you close the book. Think of where Fran is now compared to where she was when she came to us. We all love her to pieces. She has this adorable friendship with Ruby. Chris is doing so much better. Remember how he was when Francesca first came in? Or even a couple of months ago? His whole body language has changed. He's so obviously in a much better place. I don't know if he's told her about Michiko, but Michi is going to be really good for him. That means everything to Francesca. This is a great ending. But life goes on; there'll be another story with new tensions and trials. A happy ending has everything to do with timing.

But why can't she have some time to enjoy all that, Lill?

She's not the type. She's not the kind of person who's still hanging on at the end of the party having one last highball and a cigarette while the hosts are yawning their heads off and trying to put away the beer bottles and air the place out. She's the kind that would stand up and say, "Well! That's been fabulous," and kiss you twice and be gone before you had a chance to say "More wine?" She's a take-control kind of a woman.

Oh, Lily. When my turn comes, I can't think of anyone I'd rather have tuck me into bed.

Thank you, dear. Coming from you, that's a real compliment.

Molly blows her nose.

Well. God knows, long and slow is no way to go.

It absolutely isn't.

Lily comes closer, places a hand on my cheek. It's cool and comforting.

She can hear us, you know. She hears every word.

Molly bursts into tears again. Lily turns to her, and holds her.

Don't worry, Molly. Everything is going to be fine. Look! I get to give you tissues for a change.

Molly gives that shaky kind of laugh that means it's time to pull yourself together. Then they both kiss me, and tell me that they love me, and wish me safe journey.

My eyes stay closed, my body inert, but I am surprised to find my heart is full of contentment.

Sepsis.

I am hot and every part of my body aches. My right arm is weighing me down—I cannot toss but I writhe, skewered, without comfort. Finally the crazy night nurse makes her rounds, and calls the RN to give me something to lower my temperature and something else for pain. I start to float, and then I'm dreaming.

I'm in the pool with Chris, who is a toddler, and I'm teaching him to swim. My black bathing suit hugs me, my body is strong and mobile, and Chris is an extension of me as I balance him lightly on my palm while he floats on his back. I show him how the water will support him when he flutters his feet with the gentlest of kicks. His eyes are wide with possibility, blue as the water; his face registers fear and then amazement. A current of pride races through my body, a lightning bolt of joy.

Then a whistle blows, sharp and piercing, and it's time to get out of the pool, and there is Angelina, reaching to help me, one lovely arm extended. Her body is my mother's body, and my own: long, muscular brown legs, a slim waist, firm breasts, and such a proud neck, long as a queen's. Angelina, my beauty, my darling. I reach for her . . .

But Chris—I've forgotten him—I turn back and there he is, full-grown. He is swimming away from me, doing the butterfly, the most difficult of strokes, his powerful shoulders cresting and sinking, spray shooting like fireworks gracing the sky. Like a whale breaching for the sheer delight of wind and water, Chris rises and falls with pounding effort, making his purposeful way across the pool.

AUTHOR'S NOTE

I have been working as a care aide for over twenty years now. I still feel passionate enough about my work to ramble on at length about it to anyone who will listen.

All of the characters in this book are fictional; the things that my characters say have been said many times, in many different ways, by many different people, but no one person ever said these things.

I want to mention that the care aides in this book are appallingly bad about talking shop in front of the residents, which is a professional no-no. I let them talk that way, even though they're supposedly good aides (at least, I think they're good aides) and should know better, because I wanted to write about what actually happens, rather than what ought to happen.

I have tried to write as realistically as possible to the best of my ability, with one glaring exception: the dynamics in Francesca's five-bed ward work out pretty well for the most part in this novel. That is rarely the case in real life. In our culture, we value privacy highly and consider having our own room to be the bare minimum; even double rooms are usually nothing but trouble.

ACKNOWLEDGEMENTS

Many people deserve my thanks for the making of this book. I am very fortunate to work in a facility that prioritizes high standards of resident care and safety. I want to thank everyone at Mount Saint Mary's and especially the Sisters of Saint Ann for creating a very special place; my life is richer because of you. I have fed my family and my soul. To my residents: it has been an honour to care for you. To my amazing, diverse and talented co-workers: I have learned so much from you.

Thanks also to Bente Birchall and Susan Link, who answered my questions about what it was like to be a woman in the accounting business on the west coast in the seventies, eighties and nineties.

Thank you to my many first readers, especially Joy, and also Eva and the Judes, for the reading the half-baked, semi-raw versions of my book and encouraging me. I am very lucky to have you guys in my life.

Thank you to Honora and Ann-Marie, for championing my book; without you, I would never have had this incredible experience and I am so grateful.

Thank you to Anne Collins at Penguin Random House for taking a chance on *A Funny Kind of Paradise* and to my wonderful editor, Amanda Betts, who helped my book step out of its stinky sneakers and put on some classy, hard-wearing Blundstones. Thank you to the whole team that helped in the production of my book: my copy editor, Tilman Lewis; my cover designer, Kelly Hill; and my publicist, Danielle LeSage. Just the fact that I get to say these words is a huge thrill.

Thank you to Don Craig for the skookum author photo. I look great!

Finally, I'd like to thank the usual suspects on Team Jo: the friends, family and professionals that keep me safe, sane and functional. Thanks to Susan Farling. To Veronique, Avery and the good folks at Westcore Fitness. To Kim and Murray, who always have my back, and my present partners, Ross and Regina, who teach me something new every day. Thanks to Shirley, Shiela, Valerie and Saskia, who bring me rainbow colours in a million shapes. To my extended family, both my side and Clayton's, whom I count as my own: Kay, my brother, my brothers-in-law and sisters-in-law, my cousins, my aunts and uncles, and my awesome collection of nieces and nephews—I've been blessed. Special thanks to Allan—when the sky started falling down, you were right there for us—and my sister Shelley, my biggest cheerleader. Most of all, thank you to my mom, who always had faith in me. Safe journey, Mama.

And at the very core of my heart, my husband and kids: you mean everything to me.

When the author of an enjoyable book provides a soundtrack of music that complements their text or inspired them, I am always utterly delighted, so I've decided to include the music list that I compiled while writing this book:

"Bless the Kind Heart," Pied Pumkin:
a dedication to health care professionals everywhere.

"I Will Survive," Gloria Gaynor:
this song is for Fran, because she's a survivor.

"Danny's Song," Loggins and Messina:
Anna, falling in love with Chris.

"Smells Like Teen Spirit," Nirvana:
this is the song that kept playing in my head when I was writing about Angie.
As well as: "Think I'm in Love," Beck.

"I've Got You under My Wheels," Alice Cooper:
Angelina and Alice Cooper both like to stir the pot.

"Sweet Disposition," The Temper Trap:
this song makes me think of Lily.

"Matches to Paper Dolls," Dessa:
a brilliant song about making the same stupid mistake over and over again,
even though you know better. Also for Lily.

"Break Don't Bend," Quote:
this song is for Chris, just trying to get through another day.

"Burdensome," Quote:
there are times when Fran feels like a bug pinned to a felt board and she'd do
anything to squirm away.

"I've Got You under My Skin," Cole Porter and Lou Rawls:
Michiko sings this to Mary.
I particularly love the Lou Rawls version because it adds
a little touch of lightness to a song that almost borders on obsession,
and I like to think of Michiko as a leavening element in Fran's life.

"No, Not Much," The Four Lads:
another one of Michi the Tattooed Vegan Warrior's favourite oldies.

"Bitter Sweet Symphony," The Verve:
no matter how long I work in extended care, death is still hard,
still bittersweet. It's never easy. Besides, I just plain like this song.

"Catabolysis," Ueda Kurou (Quote):
"I hope you can't tell how much I want you to like me."
I played this for Lily, hoping she'd find her love.

"Our House," Crosby, Stills, Nash & Young:
any house that has Ruby in it is going to be a very fine house.

"Help Yourself," Amy Winehouse:
Chris choosing counselling. Good work, Chris! So proud of you.

"This Flight Tonight," Nazareth:
the beat in this song is the beat in Fran's head
whenever she can't make herself understood.

"As Good a Time as Any," Ueda Kurou (Quote):
this song is for Fran because she's making a really difficult
and conflicted journey, as is the person in this song.

"Hooked on a Feeling," Blue Swede:
a schmaltzy love song for the couples at the end of this book.

JO OWENS lives in Victoria, B.C. She has worked as a health care aide for twenty years. *A Funny Kind of Paradise* is her first novel.